Praise for

JOHN D. MACDONALD

"The Dickens of mid-century America—popular, prolific and conscience-ridden about his environment...A thoroughly American author."
The Boston Globe

"It will be for his crisply written, smoothly plotted mysteries that MacDonald will be remembered."
USA Today

"In McGee mysteries and other novels as well, MacDonald's voice was one of a social historian."
Los Angeles Times

"MacDonald had the marvelous ability to create attention-getting characters who doubled as social critics. In MacDonald novels, it is the rule rather than the exception to find, in the midst of violence and mayhem, a sentence, a paragraph, or several pages of rumination on love, morality, religion, architecture, politics, business, the general state of the world or of Florida."
Sarasota Herald-Tribune

Fawcett Books
by John D. MacDonald

JOHN D. MacDONALD

Cancel All Our Vows

FAWCETT GOLD MEDAL • NEW YORK

A Fawcett Gold Medal Book
Published by Ballantine Books
Copyright © 1953 by John D. MacDonald Publishing, Inc.

ISBN 0-449-12886-5

Manufactured in the United States of America

First Fawcett Gold Medal Edition: July 1972
First Ballantine Books Edition: June 1985
Eleventh Printing: January 1989

To Dorothy

Since there's no help, come let us kiss and part;
Nay, I have done, you get no more of me,
And I am glad, yea glad with all my heart
That thus so cleanly I myself can free;
Shake hands forever, cancel all our vows,
And when we meet at any time again,
Be it not seen in either of our brows
That we one jot of former love retain.
Now at the last gasp of love's latest breath,
When, his pulse failing, passion speechless lies,
When faith is kneeling by his bed of death,
And innocence is closing up his eyes,
   Now if thou wouldst, when all have given him over,
   From death to life thou mightst him yet recover.

—Michael Drayton, *Poems,* 1619

*Cancel
All Our
Vows*

Chapter One

The early afternoon edition of the Minidoka Herald had a red-bordered box on page one titled WHEW! It stated to the suffering citizenry that this Friday was the hottest June twenty-seventh on record. An exceptionally dry spring had shrunk the Glass River. It curved meagerly under the new Jefferson Boulevard bridge, under the old Town Street span, under the railroad bridge and, four miles south of the city, under futuristic concrete of the new Throughway bypass bridge. It was dwindled in its channel, and on the steep mud-cracked banks bottles glinted, half buried.

The city spread from the riverbanks up the slight slope of two hills, one on either side of the river. The city sizzled in the gentle valley. North of the city the hills steepened. South of the city they finally flattened into a plain. The paper said that the temperature at the airport, five miles to the south, was a hundred and three. The unofficial temperature in the city was a hundred and four, but it felt hotter. The hills seemed to constrict the heat, and prevent any vagrant breeze from reaching the city. With school out, both municipal swimming pools were jammed with children. Their elders—those not tied to a job—sought the air-conditioned theaters and bars.

All talk seemed to be about the weather. The sky was a white misty blaze. All asphalt streets extended into a wet shimmering mirage. The siren sounds of the ambulances were smothered by the humid blanket of heat as they took the heat prostration cases to Municipal Hospital, and to St. Joseph's on the other side of the river.

At precisely twelve minutes of three the big air-conditioning plant which kept the office building of the Forman Furnace Corporation cool, burned out. For a time the low,

9

flat-roofed, modern building retained its electrical chill. Outside sprinklers turned slowly, keeping the surrounding landscaping green. By three o'clock, however, when the factory let out, the dainty blouses of the office girls had begun to stick to them.

Marcia Trevin, secretary to Mr. Fletcher Wyant, the treasurer of the Forman Furnace Corporation, sighed and patted her forehead with a damp Kleenex. The door to Mr. Wyant's office was open. By leaning forward a bit she could look in and see him at his desk. He had taken his coat off and he was working in his shirt sleeves, making out one of his interminable comparative balance sheets, making those tiny and scrupulously neat figures which always seemed to Marcia so very strange when you thought of the bulk of the man who wrote them.

She watched him for a moment or two, watched the expressionless remoteness on his big, strong-featured face, the heavy wrist and hand moving the hard pencil. One lock of the hair, so rank and black that it always made her think of Indians and horses, had fallen across his forehead She would have given her soul for the courage to walk in and smooth it back in place. She was silently convulsed as she imagined the look of pure horror that would spread across the big face. Or maybe it wouldn't be that way at all. Maybe he would . . .

She leaned back for a moment and indulged herself in a daydream of six years' standing. He would take her hands and look right into her eyes with those funny pale grey eyes of his. He would say, "Marcia, my darling, forgive me for being so stupid. Forgive me for not seeing, until now, what has been right in front of my nose for six long years." And then he would kiss her, of course. That was the way it always happened in the stories. I know I'm too heavy, but my ankles are good, and I know my eyes are pretty.

A drop of perspiration trickled down between her breasts and brought her out of her daydream. The top edge of her girdle was soaked. She was suddenly irritable. It was all right for him to sit in there and play around with the figures, figures that she would eventually have to type in quadruplicate and then cut stencils of. She got up with

10

determination, plucking her shirt away from herself, and walked into Mr. Wyant's office. With each step her resolve grew more dim and indeterminate, and finally she stood looking across the desk at him, wondering how in the world she was going to state it.

Fletcher Wyant slowly became aware of someone standing silently on the other side of the desk. He finished his problem in simple subtraction and wrote the new figure on his work sheet before he glanced up.

Miss Trevin stood there, her wide face flushed, her pocked cheeks damp with perspiration. Poor gal. The heat was rough on her. And the flush meant she had something personal to communicate. Seeing the steamy condition of Miss Trevin made Fletcher Wyant conscious again of his own discomfort. He tossed the pencil on top of the half-finished work sheet, and leaned back, stretching, then pulled the shirt sleeves free where they had stuck to his arms.

"They going to get that thing fixed, Miss Trevin?"

"No sir. I got through to Maintenance a little while ago. Everybody has been calling. They have to get a new part or something."

He got up and went over to the window, opened it and stuck his hands out. "Now it's about the same inside as out. Might as well leave it open. A breeze *might* come along."

"Mr. Wyant, sir, I was wondering . . . I mean the heat being so brutal and all. And Miss Coward is letting the girls go from the stenographic pool . . . if . . ."

"You mean you want to go home? God, there's no objection to that. I just didn't think of it. And it must be hotter out in that little box of yours than it is in here, even. What's lined up?"

She couldn't help a sigh of relief. "Well, the only thing is that call you placed, about the tax refund case, and Mr. Corban dropped in while you were out and said he'd come back later."

"Cancel that call, then. I want you taking notes when it does come in. Get Mr. Corban on the line for me, and then you can take off."

"Thanks loads, Mr. Wyant. All I want to do is get home

and get these clothes off before I . . ." She flushed violently and fled, saying good night in a muted voice as she went through the door.

Fletcher grinned at the empty doorway. Marcia Trevin was good luck in the secretarial department. Quick and smart and loyal. And the greatest of these is loyal. She always let him know who had their knife out. Little spinster, built on the same general lines as a fireplug, and almost embarrassingly adoring. Due for another bump, if Personnel will stand still for it.

The communication box on his desk said, "Mr. Corban on the line, sir. Good night."

"Thanks. Good night, Miss Trevin. Hello, Ellis?"

"Hi, Fletch. Dropped in about an hour ago but your girl said you were visiting."

"Fighting, she meant. I was out in the shop. God, what a day!"

"A brute indeed. I suppose Laura called Jane to remind her, but I thought I'd remind you too. You are our guests at the club tonight."

Fletcher winced, but his voice was affable. "I hadn't forgotten, Ellis. It's going to cost you, though. I'm going to drink rum Collins until they come out my ears."

"Good deal. I've got the same general idea. Little anaesthetic against the heat. About six then. We could pick you up."

"No. That's too far out of your way, Ellis."

"No trouble, really."

"We'll meet you out there, maybe a little after six."

"Look for us on the terrace."

When Fletcher hung up, he leaned back and frowned. Hell of a night to try to be festive in. And Ellis Corban would be a little wearing, even on a comfortable night. But that wasn't the proper attitude toward a protégé. When the opening had come, in mid-April, Fletcher had brought up Ellis Corban's name. Stanley Forman had preferred, as usual, that the slot be filled by promoting one of the men already working for Forman Furnace. So Fletcher had to prove that they didn't have anyone available who could carry the load. He had met Ellis Corban at several meetings at the tax division at the state capitol. Over a couple of drinks afterward, he had discovered that Ellis wasn't happy with the firm he was working for. And he had learned, in the meetings, that Ellis Corban had one of the finest financial minds he had ever come across in a man of thirty. Stanley Forman had reluctantly permitted himself to be convinced, and during the month Corban had been with Forman Furnace he had already justified Fletcher's evaluation of him. Stanley Forman was pleased.

But that doesn't mean, Fletcher thought, that I have to like the guy personally. He's got that damned pontifical way of speaking, and that jolly-boy approach. Some day when he gets his feet under him, the bastard may try to knife my job out from under me. But until he gets around to trying it, he's taking a real load off my shoulders. He's the type to try all the angles.

Jane had helped Laura Corban find a house to rent, and it was hard to find one the right size because of the two small Corbans. In addition to that Jane had taken a firm dislike to Laura Corban. He couldn't understand that. The two or three times he had seen Laura Corban she had seemed nice enough. On the quiet side. Little anemic-looking, but certainly pretty, and knew how to dress and walk. Sort of a sly sense of humor, too. Crept up on you when you were least expecting it.

Jane had suggested they put the Corbans up for membership in the Randalora Club, and so Fletch had done it, and the membership committee had passed on it quickly. This was the traditional evening—the one where the Corbans entertained the Wyants at the Randalora Club for cocktails and dinner and the June dance, in return for the favor of having been put up for membership. It wasn't the sort of thing you could duck out on. But he wished he could. He wanted to spend the twilight on his own terrace, clad in shorts, drinking beer, slapping mosquitoes, and watching the lights of the city below.

He was just turning back to the report when Stanley Forman came and leaned against the doorframe and said, "Such devotion to duty, my friend."

Stanley was thirty-seven, only a year older than Fletcher, but Fletcher thought, and Jane agreed with him, that Stanley looked at least fifty. He had come into the

13

company very young and five years later, when his father died, Stanley had been made president. He seemed almost to have forced his appearance to correspond with his responsibilities. He was prematurely bald, tall, heavy, slightly florid. He had a lazy casual manner, but his mind was quick and shrewd. By taking gambles both in design and in the functioning parts of the Forman Furnaces, and in insisting on an aggressive sales and promotion approach, he had moved Forman up from a negligible factor in the industry to a husky and respected competitor.

Though his manner was uniformly casual, Stanley Forman managed always, in some subtle way, to continually underline the employer-employee relationship when dealing with his executives. Fletcher was conscious of this attitude, and frequently resented it, but there didn't seem to be anything which could be done about it. The attitude itself was fallacious. In forty-nine when the income tax burden on executive salaries had become excessive, all major executives of the company had been put on a stock deal, whereby they were permitted to buy Forman stock at less than market.

Fletcher had accumulated a good holding, and he knew that Stanley Forman, except for the difference in size of the holdings, was no more owner of the company than he was. But Stanley seemed to fancy himself as the wise and tolerant commander of troops—one who wanted to get along with the boys, but could break anybody any time he wished, right from the executive officer on down.

Most of all Fletcher despised his own response to this attitude of Stanley's. It seemed to make him overly affable. Like a damn Airedale. Never could seem to treat the man in a normal way.

"Devotion, Stanley? I'm about to take off and get a beer."

Stanley looked at his gold pocket watch. "If you don't manage it in about five minutes, you'll be the only one left in the place. I'm going around shooing everybody out."

Fletcher stood up and stretched, scratched his ribs. In front of Stanley even the stretch seemed forced. "In that case, I'm off."

"Don't try to play golf. You'll drop dead out there."

"I'm just a little foolish, Stanley. Not completely crazy."

Stanley plodded heavily off toward the next office down the corridor. Fletcher slid the work sheets into his top drawer, closed the window, hung his coat over his shoulder, perched his hat on the back of his head, and went down the corridor toward the entrance, shutting his office door behind him. Stanley was in with Hatton, the sales manager, and Hatton, in his raspy voice, was telling one of his brutally bawdy stories. Of all the executives, Hatton seemed to be the only one completely unaware of Stanley's air of austerity and command.

He heard Hatton say, "So this girl, she looks at the guy again, and she says, 'Look, I don't mind you bringing along your Canasta deck, but when I . . .' "

The words were lost as he walked out of earshot, but just as he was walking by the reception desk he heard Hatton's hard burst of laughter which followed the punch line.

The sun leaned hard on the back of his neck as he crossed to the parking lot. The maroon Pontiac sedan was like a furnace. He rolled down the windows and opened both doors and stood outside the car for a few minutes in hopes it would cool off a bit. The car was pretty dusty. He decided he'd wash it tomorrow if it turned out a little cooler. The car would be two years old in October. Only thirty-one thousand miles on it. Wouldn't be that much if he and Jane hadn't decided, last summer, that the kids ought to see Yellowstone. Trade it again this fall, he thought, if I can get a good deal. If not, it will go through the winter all right. Replace these bald-headed tires, have new shocks put in, and a complete motor job. New battery too, maybe. Might be simpler just to get a new one. The damn house ate money though.

He got in. It hadn't cooled off much. He started out as quickly as he could, turning the window flaps inward so that the heated air blew hard against his face. One thing about leaving early. Traffic wouldn't be as wicked. Minidoka was going to have to do something about the damn traffic. Do it soon.

He drove down to Town Street, turned left and crossed the bridge, hitting the light side on the far side of the bridge. On the other shore of the Glass River he turned north on Dillon Drive. The wide drive climbed steadily toward the newest residential area on the north of the city, high on the hills overlooking the city.

His street turned left off Dillon. The street sign was rather disturbingly rustic. It said Coffeepot Road. When they had looked at the lot he had told Jane that the name of the road "is just too goddamn quaint." But Jane loved the hill, the name of the street, the lot, and, after far too much money had been spent, the completed ranch-type house.

Fletcher didn't know whether the name of the street had marked him, or whether it had been the very impressive sketch the architect had made, or whether it had been the final contractor's bills, but in the year since they had taken occupancy, he hadn't quite been able to accept the house as home. It was still all house, and very little home. What the architect and the contractor hadn't done to make it on the austere side, the decorator had added. Fletcher found himself living with a great deal of glass and wrought iron and ceramic tile. He could take a great deal of pride and pleasure in looking at the house, or in looking down the really impressive expanse of the thirty-five-foot living room. But when he came to sit down, either inside or outside, he had the odd and uncomfortable feeling that he was taking his place in a picture that was just about to be snapped for an article in *House Beautiful* or *House and Garden*. His standard gesture of protest was to take off his shoes and tie at every opportunity—though always with a slight feeling of guilt. As though he were spoiling the picture.

He parked in the drive and got out and looked at the lawn and the plantings. The grass had a parched look, and the plantings weren't living up to the landscape gardener's promises. He shrugged and went into the house.

Jane came through into the big living room, moving fast. She slowed down when she saw him. "Hey, I wondered who was barging in. Plant burn down?"

He tossed his coat on a chair. "Air conditioner stopped. Stanley shooed everybody out."

"Big of him. Oh, Jesus, what a day I've had!" She wore a wilted halter and shorts. She was a big smooth-limbed

16

blonde woman with a round face, pretty blue eyes, a generous mouth. She moved, always, with the beautiful economy of a natural athlete. She played a man's game of golf, was a sought-after mixed doubles partner, and was more seal than woman in the water.

"Troubles?"

"That wretch, Anise. She's supposed to get here at nine on Fridays. So at ten she calls and says she's got the "arthuritis something miserable." It's only two days a week that she's supposed to come here, and this is the fourth day she's missed since the first of the year. Every darn time I want to entertain on the weekend she has to miss Friday. Now she won't come until next Tuesday, and with the kids home from school you have no idea what a shambles this house turns into in nothing flat."

"Where are the kids?"

"They went off on their bikes to the pool. They took a lunch."

Fletcher frowned at her. "Damn it, I thought we agreed they wouldn't go in the public pool. Polio season is starting. It seems to me that you could at least . . ."

"Honey, it's just too damn hot and I'm too tired to squabble about this. They teased and teased. I would have taken them out to the pool at the club, but you had the car. They promised to be careful. Besides, that article said that you shouldn't let them get overtired and chilled. Who is going to get chilled on a day like this? And they promised faithfully to be back here by five."

"And spend half the night while we're out looking bug-eyed at that television screen."

"That was part of the promise too. Bed at nine thirty for both of them."

He looked at her hard. "I suppose it's okay. But backtrack a little. You said something about entertaining this weekend. It sort of got lost in the rush. What about that? Are we, for God's sake?"

"I thought it would be nice if tonight we ask just a few people to come around Sunday for drinks. There'd have to be the Corbans of course. And then Midge and Harry, and Sue and Dick, and maybe Martha and Hud."

"Lord help us," he said softly.

"Now, you know you always have a good time once it gets going, Fletcher."

He decided that was one statement he was remarkably weary of. He picked up his coat. "Guess I'll take my shower first. Okay?"

"Of course, darling. I'm not quite ready yet."

He went down the hallway. The house was built in the shape of a T, with the crossbar toward the road. On the breezeway end of the crossbar were the children's rooms. On the other end was the master bedroom, and Fletcher's "study," designed so that it was readily convertible into a guest bedroom. The living room took up most of the upright of the T, with the kitchen, dining area, and utility room furthest from the road. This design permitted one portion of the bisected back yard to be used as a terrace, and the other half as a utility yard invisible from the terrace. Fletcher knew, by painful count, that there were nine view windows in the house, each, oddly enough, with a view to go with it. And he also knew that it had been a mistake, at the last minute, to change from duotherm glass to plain plate glass. In winter each view window radiated a vast patch of chill into the house, and it was this tiny change which made the heating system inadequate.

As he went down the hall Jane called, "Your good tropical came back. It's in your closet."

"Good," he said without spirit.

But his spirits came back after he stripped and went into the pristine bathroom. Whenever they had to go out for cocktails, Jane always seemed to be showering when he arrived home. Though he had never mentioned it to her, it always annoyed him to have to shower after her. She was a fervent shower taker. She liked her showers long, hot, steamy and soapy. She left the bathroom as dripping and sodden as the headwaters of the Amazon.

The needle spray was delicious. He stepped out and toweled himself briskly, noting smugly that he had made only small patches of steam on the mirrors of the two medicine cabinets. He plugged in his razor and shaved quickly. Just as he was finishing, Jane banged on the door and said, "Hey, next!"

"Comee ri' ou'," he said, his voice distorted by the delicate procedure of finishing the upper lip. He racked the razor, promising himself to clean it later, pulled on fresh shorts, snapped the two buttons and went into the bedroom. Jane smiled at him and patted his bare shoulder as she went by.

The shower had left him a little sweaty and he decided he'd better wait until he dried off before dressing. He scuffed into his slippers and went to the kitchen. He found the Collins mix and the gin and made himself a drink that was mostly gin and ice. He looked cautiously out the front door, and saw that the paper was within reach. He snatched it and went back to the bedroom and stretched out on his bed with the paper, and with his drink on the night stand at his elbow.

He could see through the bedroom view window, see across the terrace and out toward the summer hills, see a dull red barn that he was fond of.

And, as he was looking, it happened again to him. It was something that had started with the first warm days of spring. All colors seemed suddenly brighter, and with his heightened perception, there came also a deep, almost frightening sadness. It was a sadness that made him conscious of the slow beat of his heart, of the roar of blood in his ears. And it was a sadness that made him search for identity, made him try to re-establish himself in his frame of reference in time and in space. Fletcher Wyant. He of the blonde wife and the kids and the house and the good job. It was like an incantation, or the saying of beads. But the sadness seemed to come from a feeling of being lost. Of having lost out, somehow. He could not translate it into the triteness of saying that his existence was without satisfaction. He was engrossed in his work and loved it. He could not visualize any existence without Jane and the kids. Yet, during these moments that seemed to be coming more frequently these last few weeks, he had the dull feeling that somehow time was eluding him, that there was not enough of life packed into the time he had. The red barn and the hill had something to do with it. As though the window showed him a place where he had never been, and a place he could never reach.

It almost seemed that if he could tell Jane, if he could

19

find the words to describe just how it was, maybe she would understand, and maybe she was feeling the same way this year. Maybe this was the year for feeling this way. Thirty-six. And twice thirty-six is seventy-two. Perhaps, at mid-point, there is a nostalgia for things that never were. Or a greed for more lives than one.

But there were no words to tell Jane. And if he tried to fumble it through, she would have a pat remedy. You need a vacation, darling. You don't get enough exercise, dear. Don't you think you ought to get another checkup? Nothing against her, of course. Rather, the fault would lie with him for not being able to express it.

He took two large swallows of his drink, turned resolutely to Pogo, and then to the financial news.

He glanced at his watch. Five twenty. The kids were overdue. The sadness was lost and annoyance took its place.

Chapter Two

By the time Jane came out of the bathroom, Fletcher's drink was gone and he was into the baseball results.

She came hurrying out of the bathroom, stopped dead and said, "You aren't dressed!"

The look of her pleased him. Ever since the weather had turned warm, she had been taking sun baths on the terrace. She had a pleasant, honey-toned tan, overlaid by the rosy flush of her shower. The ends of her hair were damp. She wore a pair of panties of filmy blue nylon and that was all.

She pleased him, so he looked down at himself with a look of mock astonishment and said, "Why so I'm not!"

"Oaf!" she said, and hurried to the built-in drawers under the windows and dug into the top drawer looking for the proper bra.

He was braced on his elbows, and he looked at her approvingly. If you wanted to be a hair-splitter, you could detect the slightest thickening of her waist, a faint sag of breast, just the merest puckered areas of flesh on the insides of her thighs, but all in all, she was a very exciting-looking woman to be married to, tautly and warmly constructed. He always felt proud of her when, at a party, he saw her on the other side of the room. As she dug in the drawer the smooth muscles moved under the honey skin of her shoulders. He felt the arch and tremor of desire, the suddenly dry mouth. The sex they made together had always been good. They were mated perfectly. He thought that so long as that aspect is under control, nothing can go really wrong. And, as he reached for her, he wondered why in the world he should suddenly be thinking in terms of things going wrong. He thrust the thought aside.

"Hey, you!" she said, immediately aware of intention.

"So we're a shade late," he said huskily.

"No, Fletch honey. Please! We'll be too late. And the kids will be coming any minute. Let's not start anything we can't finish. I don't want to be a spoil-sport."

"The lady is filled with indifference."

"You *know* better than that, darling. But honestly. There isn't time. And besides, I don't want to wear that darn thing around all evening."

"Do you think I want to wear this around all evening?"

She gave him the grin he loved. Lopsided, lewd and urchin. "Go ahead, my pet. Maybe they'll give you a door prize."

But he saw that her eyes were beginning to get heavy in a familiar way. He pulled her toward him. Just then the bicycles were racked against the house. Dink was yammering at Judge about going too fast. The screen door hissed. Jane bounded off the bed.

"Just one big happy family," Fletcher said wearily.

She turned from where she was putting the bra on, her arms craned awkwardly up behind her. "We might just possibly come home just a little bit early."

"It's a thought," he said. He went to the closet and got his suit out, stripping the brown paper off it. He looked for the spot. They'd gotten it out all right.

Jane's voice was muffled as she slid the dinner dress down over her head. "That Mobren woman called me up again today. Oh, darling, that's a dingy shirt. Take one of those with the French cuffs. Those collars look so well on you. And a dark knit tie will look good with that suit."

"Uh huh," he said, refolding the shirt he had taken out.

"Anyway, she keeps after me to be on the committee to pick out the prizes for the women's matches. They decided not to give cups, you know. Useful things this year. Well, I know just how it will be. Nobody has the same taste. If I pick out things, you can be darn well sure that the women that win them won't like them. And that Mobren woman is just trying to pass the buck to me. That shirt is better, dear. Why don't you stand on that paper to put the trousers on. That color soils so easily."

"Okay," he said.

She sat at the dressing table, taking great care with her lips. Fletcher could hear the kids whispering in the living room.

"I couldn't be rude to the woman, but really, she's so persistent. And she goes on and on and on. I keep telling her that I'm spending too much time on the Red Cross Drive and the League of Women Voters. And I haven't been to a League meeting since we had that dreadful fight with those garbage collection people. I've never had anybody call me that word to my face before in my life. Have you thought about Mexico, dear?"

"What!" he said. He was sitting on his bed lacing his shoes. He stopped. "What?"

She turned and gave him a patient look. "About Mexico, dear. About the vacation. Remember? The first two weeks in August while the kids are in camp. We decided it was time we had a vacation by ourselves. Good Lord, thirteen. Fourteen if you count the summer I was too pregnant to enjoy our measly little two weeks."

"You lost me back there in the League of Women Voters."

"Oh, I said no to Mrs. Mobren. I was all done with that. Are you trying to change the subject?"

"I better go over the budget again, honey, on the Mexican thing. Charley hasn't given me the dope on the airline fares yet, anyway."

"You better decide quick. It's nearly July, dear."

He stood up and picked up his suit coat. She stood up. "Do I look okay, darling?"

"Lush and provocative."

"So are you, dear. Please say something to the kids, but don't make it too rough. I don't like to leave them alone after you yell at them."

"I don't yell. I speak firmly."

"Well, what I say doesn't mean much. I'm around here all the time. They get used to me."

Judson "Judge" Wyant was thirteen. He spoke in a spasmodic treble-bass. His original nickname had been Jud. Then, when he was eleven, a note from his teacher led to an eye man who put glasses on him. The kids had started calling him Judge. The family had gradually swung over. Judge had adopted a faintly professorial manner to go with his new designation.

"Half an hour late, people," Fletch said seriously. "A thing which I do not favor. What about it?"

"It sounds pretty silly," Dink said soberly. She was a thin wiry girl of eleven, addicted of late to wearing black jeans and a red scarf around her throat. She had inherited Fletcher's coloring, and her mother's co-ordination. Her athletic skills frequently frustrated Judge, the blond one, who seemed, like his father, to be able to get his feet or his hands or his head in the way of any intricate maneuver.

"Let's hear how silly it sounds," Fletcher said.

"Well, Dad," Judge said in his best judicial manner, "you will recall that Dink lost her watch this winter. It wasn't a good one anyway."

"You have a watch, a good one, and what is this 'you will recall' routine?"

"Just a way of talking, I guess. Anyway, you will recall that my Christmas watch is a good one."

"I just said that."

"So I didn't want to take it down there because I was afraid somebody might steal it. There was this boy we were playing with. He had a watch in the locker room. We told him we had to leave at twenty minutes to five. We made him go in and look at the watch a lot of times. Then he said he had to go and he laughed at us and said it was after five."

"He was a big stinker!" Dink said hotly.

"Curious choice of words, dear," Jane said with ice in her blue eyes.

"Well, he was. He told us he lied to us because he didn't want us to go and leave him with nobody to play with until he had to go. We really, honestly, truly meant to be back right on time. Before time, even," Dink said, close to tears.

"Okay, okay," Fletcher said. "Silly story accepted. What do you do next time?"

"Ask a grownup, I guess," Judge said. "I wouldn't care to take *my* watch down there. There's a lot of rough kids."

"Two boys threw me in," Dink said proudly.

"Don't they have a guard down there to keep order?" Fletcher asked.

"Oh sure," Dink said. "But we didn't bother him. We just waited and got them one at a time and threw *them* in. The big one hit his head and cried."

"I can see that they have a rugged clientele," Fletcher said solemnly. "Now is there more to this pact you made with your mother?"

"Bed at nine thirty," Judge said.

"Correction, please. Bed at nine. Half hour penalty for trusting strangers. Okay?"

Judge looked at Dink. She sighed heavily. Judge said, "I guess that's fair, Dad."

"Your father and I have to go now. Remember the rules. No guests. Lights out at nine. Call us at the club if you need us. Your dinner is in the oven. It's turned as low as it will go. Dink, don't let Judge talk you into doing all the cleaning up afterward, like last time."

"It was a bet and she lost," Judge said.

"Then don't bet this time. Judge, it might rain in the night. So get the bikes under cover, and there's a ball glove in the back. Near the fireplace."

They said good night to the children and went out to the car. The sun was low enough so the car wasn't like a furnace. He backed down out of the driveway as Jane lit two cigarettes.

"This is one of those evenings I could skip," he said.

"You'll be all right once you get there. I bet you'll have a good time."

"You keep saying that to me."

"Don't growl. It just happens to be true. You always do. You know, Fletch darling, I have the strangest feeling about the Corbans."

"So do I. I wish they both broke a hind leg."

"I don't know how to say it. Ellis is all right, I guess. He's sort of heavy-handed, I suppose you'd call it. But that Laura is a bird of different feathers."

"Seems quiet to me."

"But what I mean is, she really doesn't *care*. Does that make any sense?"

25

"Doesn't care about what, dear? You'll have to give me more than that."

He had to stop for a light. The Randalora Club was south of the city. It made an inconvenient drive through town to get to it. Jane had turned sideways in the seat. She was frowning. "She doesn't care about the things that count around here, Fletch. You know, she wasn't pleased that we put them up for membership. Just sort of amused. As if it was some kind of a game for kids. As if she was above and beyond all that sort of thing. And when we were house-hunting, she was really almost rude."

"How?"

"Well, the house she liked, the one they took—I tried to tell her in a nice way that it wasn't a very fashionable neighborhood. She had a queer look, you know. You can't tell whether she's laughing at you or not. She told me she'd try to keep the house fashionable on the inside."

"Doesn't sound like much to condemn her for, Jane."

"Don't start defending her. I guess I shouldn't have brought it up. I have a feeling about her. She just doesn't *care* about the things that matter, and you remember what I'm saying. Because she doesn't care, she also doesn't care what she does or what she says. And it may come back on us that we put them up for membership. He's all right, but I wouldn't put anything past her."

He laughed. "Oh, come now! What's she going to do? A strip tease in front of the bandstand?"

"That's what I'm trying to say. If she decided it was a good thing to do, she'd go right ahead and do it, and I can see the look on her face while she does it. Like she was laughing at the whole club."

"Why don't you suggest it? It'll make talk for the whole summer."

"Fletch, you just aren't taking me seriously. You ought to know by now that I'm pretty good at sizing up people. Remember the gum on the hat?"

"How can I forget it when you bring it up once a month?"

She giggled. "I'll never forget how mad you got."

Fletcher remembered. A pleasant young man had come to the door. He wore a pale grey felt hat. He calmly took a

26

cud of gum out of his mouth, squashed it against the hat, then rubbed the smeared place on the floor until it was badly smudged. Then he brought out a small bottle, poured some of the fluid on a cloth and calmly removed the greasy mass, leaving no stain. Fletcher had bought a giant-size sealed bottle of that wonder cleaner for five dollars. It turned out to be a benzine solution so weak that it had no more effect on a spot than plain water. And while the transaction had been going on, Jane had managed to get close enough to Fletcher to whisper, "Dear, I don't like his looks."

"Okay," he said. "I'll be looking forward to that strip tease. Little on the scrawny side though, isn't she?"

"Don't kid yourself, my friend. That little lady is stacked. She just doesn't wave it around."

They turned into the club drive at quarter after six. He was going to drop her at the door, but she told him to head right on into the parking area and she'd walk back with him. Some die-hard golfers were teeing off. The pool was full of young people. The bastard-château interior of the club was gloomy and unpopulated. Fletcher hung his straw hat in the nearly empty check room and they walked through to the terrace, which overlooked the eighteenth green, yet was set high enough to be safe from overexuberant approach shots.

They stood in the doorway. Most of the terrace tables were filled. The white-coated waiters scurried around with trays that tinkled. They nodded and smiled at friends.

"There they are in the corner," Jane said. They walked between the tables. As Fletcher followed Jane, automatically smiling and speaking to friends and acquaintances, he was thinking of Jane's description of Laura Corban's attitude. Maybe the girl had something. Shouldn't take membership in an outfit like this too seriously. It was just one of the ways, perhaps, that people managed to segregate themselves, and preen themselves. You could be pretty well certain that in another three hours a certain immutable percentage of the members would be annoyingly and foolishly drunk. Those only partially so would be making automatic and mechanical passes at the wives of friends, or, when possible, the college-age daughters of friends. A certain number were certain to say something just far enough out of line to provide a tidbit of gossip for the coming week. And, as a result of this evening, there would doubtless be an insurance policy or two sold, a piece of real estate would change hands, a doctor would acquire a new patient, a wife would cry until daylight came. All a little on the pointless side if you looked at it, trying to ask why. It was just because people had to have a place to go, a place to be seen, a place to have fun. It labeled them as having a certain social and financial position in Minidoka, and maybe people felt safer when they were properly labeled.

As he approached the table he decided that he had better drop the clinical approach to the Randalora Club, or he would find himself ceasing to enjoy it. And he began to wonder how much he had enjoyed it in the past. To what extent, to what precise degree. The members who knocked themselves out in club affairs seemed to be the same group who went to college reunions, who sang in the bar, who took the Martini shaker along with the foursome. They got a hell of a bang out of it. He had never enjoyed it that much.

Ellis Corban saw them approaching and jumped up. His smile tightened his apple-red cheeks and flexed his tweedy mustache. He was a man who, in all situations, managed somehow to look overdressed.

"Hello, Jane, Fletch. I guess we're one up on you. Yes sir, one up on you."

They all exchanged greetings, and Ellis made quite a ceremony out of getting Jane into one of the two empty chairs. Laura wore an even, careful smile. Her dress was of a pale yellow shade that was subtly perfect for her. Once they were all seated again, Fletcher made a more searching appraisal of Laura Corban than he had previously. Her hair was no color, somewhere between ash blonde and mouse, and in the light he could see that it was silky fine, the smallest breeze moving tendrils of it. Her eyebrows were thin and strongly arched, her nose a bit sharp and with slender oval nostrils. Her mouth was curious—the upper lip a bit long, the underlip quite full, and she held her lips faintly parted. It gave her a slightly

28

expectant expression, and showed the even white teeth which were so small as to look childlike. Her ears were delicate and small and set close to the skull. He saw that his original impression of anemia was inaccurate. Her skin had a healthy glow, even though it seemed to have the texture and coloring of ivory. It was an odd face, he decided, a quiet face, yet full of a promise of passions and storms. She looked as though she could excite a man in the same guilt-laden way that a young girl could excite a man, yet capable of meeting him as a woman. He wondered how deceptive was her look of delicacy.

Even as he realized that he had stared at her several seconds too long, she glanced quickly toward him. Her eyes were clear hazel—and utterly empty. It made him remember a time many years ago when the college psychiatry class had visited a state institution. The resident used a woman patient to demonstrate one of the aspects of catatonic dementia praecox. He had taken the woman's arm and gently raised it over her head. Released it. The woman stood with her arm in that position, and remained that way until the doctor pulled her arm back down to her side. That woman had had the same eyes.

They shocked him, and then, startlingly, they changed to a bright, questioning alertness, almost birdlike.

Ellis said, "Yes, I was just saying to Laura that one of the most pleasant parts of moving to Minidoka is the opportunity of belonging to this club. We anticipate many happy times out here, don't we, darling?"

"What? Oh, yes, of course, dear." Her voice was quite deep, and almost completely unaccented. All words had the same value.

The waiter came and took their order and when he had gone Fletcher glanced toward Jane and was a bit surprised at the intent way she was scrutinizing him.

"We think it's quite pleasant," Ellis said, frowning a bit vaguely in his wife's general direction.

Laura said, "We're going to come out here at dawn and run barefoot, hand in hand, across the landscape."

Ellis laughed mechanically. "Darling," he said. "Fletch and Jane aren't used to your . . . sense of humor. They'll think you don't like the club."

Laura leaned forward, looking quite breathless. "Ah, but I do! I adore it! I'm savoring every moment. Every single perfect moment. I can also sit up and balance a piece of meat on my nose. Until you tell me it's all right to eat it, of course."

Ellis looked faintly ill. Jane had bright red spots in her cheeks. Fletcher said quickly and smoothly, "Just because we let you sit at the table like people doesn't mean we can't take you out and lock you back in the car." Ellis and Jane laughed gratefully.

Laura looked soulfully at Fletcher and said, softly, "Woof!"

"That," said Jane tartly, "is called barking up the wrong tree, dear."

Chapter Three

Laura Corban read the quick light tone in Jane's voice, sensed, beneath the pseudosophistication of the remark, a most definite "hands off" warning. Quite a handsome woman, Laura thought. A certain animal wit, but just vacant enough to be undemanding. A tawny, playful, good-tempered lioness, she decided. Certain of her mate, but not so certain that it wasn't wise to post a few warning signs. A practical executive's wife, loaded with this shoulder-to-shoulder business, and quite evidently circumspect, faithful, and sure of her values. It would indeed be a delight to be so positive about everything.

The terrace was dim in the fading day, and Ellis was talking about getting the children off to visit his parents at the Cape all summer. It made Laura think of the strange quiet day she had had, alone in the big old frame house they had rented, on the narrow, elm-shaded street where old women rocked and fanned on the shallow porches.

Ellis had gone to work that Friday morning after a slightly sticky connubial kiss, scented with shaving lotion, and the vast shady quiet day had stretched ahead of her, full of a wonderful silence after the departure of Ellis, junior, and Jean Marie. At times she thought of her children with guilt. It seemed unnatural to be so relieved that they were gone. When they were around she often had difficulty in believing that they had come from her body. Ellis, quite apparently, had possessed the dominant genes. Even at five, Ellis junior was a very sober little citizen, quite humorless—his face a diminutive caricature of his father's. With Jean Marie it was, perhaps, too early to tell. She was three, very round, very messy, very noisy. When the children were around and most usually during the evening

31

when Ellis sat working or reading, she often had the feeling that she was there in that small group as someone hired, a stranger, a person displaced.

She had thought with pleasure of her quiet day, and she had gone around and pulled down all the dark green roller shades and locked all the doors. The house retained the pleasant coolness of the night.

During the first hour after Ellis left for work, she raced through a bare minimum of housework, working fast and with an oddly expectant feeling. When everything was done, she got out her records, the ones she never played when Ellis or the children were around. The children always made noise, and Ellis always seemed to find it necessary to listen with intense concentration and make self-conscious statements when the music was done.

She sat on the floor and picked the records she wanted, sliding them out of their envelopes, taking pleasure in the look of them, careful not to handle the microgrooves. She stacked them on the spindle and sat again on the floor in front of the big speaker. Resonances of atonal brass moved through the house, moved against her face and seemed to stir her fragile hair. She locked her slim legs in one of the basic positions of Yoga, a position she could maintain for hours. She folded her arms across her breasts, eyes shut against the surge of the music, feeling the familiar restlessness grow within her, the keen honing of a slender edge of tension, half physical, half unknown.

In sudden restlessness she stripped off the light blouse, unhooked her brassiere and shrugged out of it. She stepped out of her skirt and kicked off her sandals and lay flat on the floor in front of the speaker. The hard heavy brass of the French horns was like a fluid moving across her body. The rug had a taut whiskery feel under her shoulders and hips, under the calves of her legs.

The music stopped and another disc clacked down in place under the needle. This music had more wildness and she turned slowly over to lie with lips and breasts and pelvis flattened against the rug, arms and legs spread. With each quick breath she could smell the dust of the rug, feel the stir of her hair as her exhalations escaped along her cheeks.

Restlessness grew and she jumped up to walk slowly back and forth across the rich flood of sound, her open palms brushing the hard satin of her thighs, so completely and physically aware of herself that each flex of muscle, each oiled turn of ball joint in socket, every erectile tremor was studied and weighed and observed in a coldness of excitement. She stood in front of the music, pressing the heels of her hands hard against the fronts of her thighs, then bringing them up hard and slow across the delicate intricacies of her body to cup at last the rigid breasts, and something within her was making a thin screaming sound.

She arched her body and then reached forward suddenly and turned off the music. The silence was like a roaring. In ritual silence she walked slowly through the big house, finding every mirror, pausing to stare at herself in the mirrors, realizing suddenly that she had the hope of finding one mirror in which she could look and see, at last, another face, and it would be a pleasant madness.

There was a thing that spiraled up hard within her, endlessly demanding bestialities. It wanted hurt and tearing and ripping. It wanted to race down a long hard torrent, endlessly, and it found itself in this quiet backwater, turning slowly, apart from life.

This thing within me must be killed, or allowed to feed. It is something beyond a physical tension. Were it only that, the forlorn little ceremony of self-love would suffice. Or, in much the same manner, a rough shy meter-reader, or one of those sleek and knowing door-to-door salesmen, they would be enough if this were physical, only. But this thing within me discards those solutions as being cheap, and unclean and meaningless.

And it also discards Ellis—poor dull Ellis with his apologetic love-making, his terrible efforts to keep from breathing too hard. Perhaps if, in the beginning, experimentation hadn't been killed by his quaint and Victorian reserve . . .

It isn't a need for love, because I am beyond love. Two loves had I. And one they shot and one they drowned in the Coral Sea. Sad and beautiful name, with its pictures of pink reefs and the drowned, drifting hair. And there wasn't enough of me left to ever love again. I died then, and in dying, selected a winner—coldly selected a steel-trap brain, a tool-steel ambition, and a fumbling inadequacy that does nothing for me.

And I was dead and it didn't matter. And now this thing is growing inside me. A thing that isn't love, or the need for love. Love, perhaps, was a tree on which grew many kinds of strange fruit. The tree was burned and the fruit was smashed against the earth, and it all seemed dead. But after many seasons the seed of one of the smashed fruit has taken root. It was the most exotic fruit the tree bore, distorted in its beauty. And now it alone grows. It was the thing which would have added a wildness and a madness to love, and now it alone lives and grows, and the tree itself is dead and will never grow again.

The seed grows and it is a vine looking for something which can be clasped, tendrils moving and restless. I am afraid that it will find something, someone. And when it does, God, in His infinite mercy, help the man, and help me, because it will destroy us by feeding us too well on the magic fruit.

If there were some way I could uproot it. . . . Or some intense chemical spray to make the leaves curl and char and die.

It is a fruit that grows in the filth of the bottom of the soul, and, rising greenly, takes over every clean niche.

I want to kill it, and yet, in the anticipation of fulfillment, there is an evil pride—a pride in the intricate perfection of this body, in its never-measured capacity for abandon, in its muscles that pull like silk ropes, and the flawlessness, and the wildnesses, and the lostness.

And she felt, once again, the familiar desire to punish the truant body. She snatched up the heap of clothing and hurried up the stairs. She threw the clothing on the bed and hurried to the bathroom and turned the hot water on full. It roared into the old-fashioned tub, standing on its clawed feet. Steam misted the distorted mirror of the medicine cabinet, made beads of sweat on the exposed pipes under the sink. When the steaming water reached the overflow drain she turned it off. The first time she tried to force her foot under the surface, she had to snatch it out with a small whimper of pain. Then she forced herself to keep it there, putting her weight on it, standing, forcing the other foot down into the scalding water. She grasped the sides of the tub, shut her teeth tightly, and, inch by agonizing inch, lowered herself into the water, hearing the constant trickle through the overflow as the smoothness of her body displaced the water. At last she was sitting, and the water made a line of fire around her, just below her breasts. The room rocked for a moment and she was close to fainting. When she felt steady again, she straightened her legs so that her knees went under. She slowly leaned back and the line of fire crept up over the tenderness of her breasts. Laura lay there, dazed by the heat, and knew that the feeling of acute physical suspense had been driven away for a little while, driven away, perhaps, by the orgiastic aspects of self-inflicted pain. She raised one slim leg from the water. It was fire-red and steam billowed from it. There were no long quiet days any more. Only days of a crazy wanting for unknown things.

The water was nearly cool by the time she climbed, deadened and exhausted, from the tub. The towel's harshness was increased by the pink sensitivity of her body. She lay diagonally across the big bed, face down, and felt sleep coming, moving toward her, black and silent.

When she heard the door bang downstairs she awoke instantly, knowing at once that it was Ellis. She rolled over, realizing that she had not changed her position during the long nap. She wondered, irritably, why he was home so early. Afternoon sun slanted against the green shades. The clock said four fifteen. She heard his slow footsteps downstairs, heard him call her. When he started up the stairs she closed her eyes and pretended to be asleep.

The hall floor creaked and she heard the small sharp inhalation as he saw her. She wondered what he saw when he looked at her body. Nudity distressed him in an odd way. It seemed strange that he should find it uncomfortable to look upon this body which had carried his two children, which had incubated his seed. She breathed

35

slowly as he approached the bed, and she felt the light touch of the thin summer spread as he pulled it up to cover her.

She yawned and sat up suddenly. "Oh, hello. I took a nap."

He made a half motion as though to bend and kiss her dutifully, but instead he turned to the bureau and began to empty his pockets. "I thought you might get chilled."

"Or maybe you were just covering up an unpleasant spectacle."

He turned and gave her a quick sharp look. "Please, Laura. Just please don't start anything. It's too hot."

"Did you have a lovely, lovely day at the office? Aren't you home early?"

"The air conditioning broke down. Mr. Forman shooed us out. I spoke to Fletch Wyant before I left. I wanted to make sure it was all set for tonight.

"Oh, merciful God!"

"It's something we have to do," he explained patiently. "They expect it. After all, they were nice enough to . . ."

"To stick us with an initiation fee and dues for the rest of our life."

"I wish you wouldn't take that attitude. You know we can afford the club. It will do a lot of good. It will give us a good place to entertain. And another thing, Laura. Please be good tonight. Just tonight. Make them think you're glad they put us up."

She swung her legs out of the bed and sat, scratching her arm, acidly amused to see how quickly he averted his eyes from her.

"It will be quite a trick making Jane Wyant glad, Ellis dear. She treats me as if I were a loaded pistol."

"There are plenty of good reasons for getting along with them. I don't think I have to explain all that."

"Please do, dear."

"Fletch is a very straightforward sort of man. He does his job and I guess he does it pretty well. But he misses here and there. He makes it look too easy, I think. And there are things he overlooks. If I stay on the right side of him I can make suggestions. Good ones. He'll take them, and give me credit for them, because he's that kind of a man. It will help both of us."

"Until you get a good chance to insert your boy scout knife, dear?"

"That's a hell of a thing to say!" he said with outraged indignation.

Laura yawned luxuriantly. "Oh, go take a bath or something. I could draw diagrams, dear. You know that. I could chalk a little X on his back, but you don't need that much help. Don't kid me. Just pay attention, so it won't backfire like at Tuplan and Hauser."

"If I'm like that, why do you stay with me?"

"Because I'm too lazy to get out, dear."

"Or you have no place to go."

"Don't ask me to prove anything to you, Ellis," she said in an entirely different voice.

She watched carefully as he tried to bluff his way out of it, and then broke around the eyes and the mouth, and said, "Laura, darling, we shouldn't try to hurt each other this way. God, I'd be lost without you. Don't ever leave me, dearest."

"Stop bleating, for God's sake!"

He pulled himself together quickly, gave her a cold stare and walked into the bathroom carrying his clean clothing. He always changed in there and he always locked the door. He never went swimming, never wore shorts around the yard. His modesty was pristine and unimpaired.

As Laura dressed she thought of Fletcher Wyant. She had an indistinct memory of him. Just another big man with a strong blunt face. One of those ex-athlete types, probably a whizz at a dirty story with a good snapper at the end. A smoking room card. A big clean American boy, walking like a man. A pushover, on business trips, for any twenty-year-old chippy with a lusty walk. A big, dull, simple, decent man, and no match for the subtle ripostes of Ellis Corban.

Ellis, she knew, was motivated by incredible ambition. It was the only forceful thing about him. She had learned enough of his history to understand it. He had been a weak, sickly, painfully shy child. Always on the outskirts of the games fields, always watching, never a part of life. He had found his outlet in school, in standing at the head of his class, in polishing and burnishing his quick, elusive mind. Laura remembered the odd story that Ellis' mother had told with such unwholesome pride.

In high school there had been a boy who consistently topped Ellis in the class marks. Ellis lost weight worrying about it, struggling to beat the other boy. It appeared that the other boy would become valedictorian of the graduating class in the senior year. A week before final examinations, Ellis astounded the other boy by asking to study French with him in preparation for the exams. During the French examination one of the proctors picked up a folded sheet of paper from the floor. It contained a list of French verbs, the most difficult irregular verbs and their declensions. It was in the other boy's handwriting. He could not deny that, but he did deny loudly that he had brought it into the examination room. They compromised by giving him the minimum passing grade, because of his previous record.

Ellis became valedictorian. The other boy did not attend graduation. And Ellis' mother told the story with a certain unholy glee. Her Ellis was shrewd, all right.

In the business world Ellis had found out, Laura knew, that you don't get marks. You get position and salary. And if there is a man in the job just over yours who shows no intention of stepping aside, you find some way to move him aside—delicately, subtly, effectively. Yet it had backfired rather badly at Tuplan and Hauser. The wrong man had protected himself by saving a tape recording of a singularly crucial conversation with Ellis. There was no basis on which to fire Ellis. But it had been made quite clear to him that he might be happier in some other firm.

Laura took the new yellow dress out of the closet and laid it carefully on the rumpled bed. She thought of her own childhood and how different it was from what Ellis had experienced. While he had been brought up in the prim, unchanging, middle-class environment of Fall River, Massachusetts, taking his bride back at last to show her off in the same high-shouldered stuccoed house in which he had been born, she had spent her own childhood in a dozen states of the west and southwest.

Her father, John Raymond, had been a failure of almost classic dimensions. A failure, perhaps, at everything but life itself. Her mother had died when Laura was three and her brother, Joshua, was two. John Raymond had never married again. He had taken the two kids with him on his restless, unending search. He had been a big laughing man with a raw edge to his tongue and an unhappy knack of saying exactly what he thought. Salesman, trucker, hotel clerk, carnival pitchman, restaurant keeper, builder, bulldozer operator. Nevada and Utah, Arizona and San Berdoo, Texas and New Orleans.

Somehow, he had always managed to provide food, and a bed of sorts. When the car broke down and they slept out it became an adventure, and desert sunrises had been golden indeed. They went to over twenty different schools. And life was going to be like that forever. And one evening in July—they had been living in a trailer in a park in San Antonio, and John Raymond and Josh were working on the same road job—and John Raymond came home in time to stop the silent, animal, terrifying struggle. She could remember that the most horrifying part of the struggle was within herself, fear and disgust fighting against the death wish to give in, the wish to surrender to the hard hands, to languid mysteries. And John Raymond had broken the man's face and comforted her, and sent her east to school in September.

He couldn't send much, and she had to work for the rest of it. But it was the end of a known world. School meant Tom, and he was killed in North Africa when something went strangely wrong with tank tactics. And later Josh died in Italy. And John Raymond got into a political argument with an Oklahoma Indian and died three days later of the stab wounds. And Andy, who was becoming what Tom had been to her, Andy who comforted her, drowned in the Coral Sea and all of life stopped, the way a clock will stop just before striking the hour. There was numbness, and an automatic cunning. The cunning brought Ellis, who married his deadened bride and took her back to Fall River, to the old house smelling of sachet and furniture polish. It brought her Ellis, and brought her two children, and brought her here at last to another old house in a strange city, to a time in her life when, after the deadness and the not-caring, life was coming back in a new and painful form, making her want something wild and discordant and sweetly rotten-ripe—before it was much too late.

She put the yellow dress on and settled it properly on her shoulders and the slimness of her hips. She looked in a mirror and was glad she had bought the dress. She did her hair and her nails and her lips, and then Ellis came out of the bathroom, scrubbed and brisk and confident and ready to go. In the car on the way to the club he had tried, again, to get her promise to behave during the evening. She had said, "Yes, dear," tonelessly, over and over, until he gave up in silent disgust.

She wanted holiday. Ballrooms and wine and a molten moonlight. She wanted around her the witty and incredibly beautiful people of festive cinema. And so she sat with her small hands folded passive in her lap while Ellis drove her toward a tribal conclave, toward thick sweaty bodies and suburban humor.

She saw Ellis become increasingly nervous on the terrace as they awaited the arrival of the Wyants. She sat and sipped her drink and wondered what on earth she was doing here with this man who smiled too broadly and uncertainly at waiters—and at nothing at all. . . . She rubbed the rim of her glass with one fingertip and played a child's game. I shall grant your wish, Princess. How would you like him to go, Princess? All at once, with a little puff of evil-smelling smoke? Or just steadily melting, so that at last nothing is left but the Cheshire mustache, and with one final twitch that will go too.

"What are you grinning at?" Ellis demanded crossly.

"I'm practicing my best smile, darling. And you better put yours on too, and tie the ends neatly. Because here they come. Like a refrigerator ad, with automatic defroster. The new lumpen-proletariat of the preferred stock issue. A Viking virgin dressed by Saks, escorted by her big brother-husband, smelling of Russian leather that comes in manly bottles. And . . ."

Ellis had bounded up, welcoming smile in place, and out of the corner of his mouth he said, "Stop babbling, dammit!"

They came and the usual words were said and she sat there pretending she was a robot. Very cleverly designed. The Rent-a-Wife service. Replace in Kompact Kontainer when not in use. Plug into any AC outlet. It walks, it talks, it moves its eyes. Take one home tonight. Go to your nearest . . .

And she turned her head and looked squarely into the sharply inquisitive pale grey eyes of a stranger who was calling himself Fletcher Wyant. And those eyes, which had a tantalizing familiarity, seemed to look down into hers and see a little shadow box where a woman stood nude in a flood of sonorous music. The eyes saw too much and knew too much.

And suddenly good intentions were forgotten and she became a slat-thin kid again, climbing to the tallest branch of the live oak to sway there in the wind, to impress the boy who had moved into the tourist cabin next door. She said things she knew were inane, and from far back in her mind she watched the effect of her words and actions on the three of them.

She watched Jane bristle, and stake out her claim.

And yet, it made little difference. The directionless tendrils of the green vine had found target. She knew he was brutal, and sensitive, and inquisitive, and that he felt that same oddness of being out of the proper time and place as she did.

It had been inevitable that it would happen, somewhere, somehow, soon.

Having it happen this way merely made it more complicated. More improbable, and, strangely, more inevitable.

In some half-understood way, she knew that she and Fletcher Wyant sat with two strangers—two remarkably unimportant strangers.

Chapter Four

Fletcher was quite aware of how Laura Corban, after her brief flash of life, retreated into an odd passivity during the next two rounds of drinks. Ellis talked about its being a vacation for them with the kids off at the Cape for the summer.

"Healthiest place in the world for them," he said proudly.

The last of the sun was gone and the long June twilight stretched across the fairway. The dogged players were trickling in, adding up the scores, bickering about the bets as they headed for the locker rooms.

The women excused themselves and went off. Ellis hitched his chair closer to Fletcher and said, "Look, old man, I hope you won't think I'm sounding disloyal to Laura if I tell you something I think you ought to understand."

"Go right ahead," Fletcher said, hoping his pained embarrassment didn't show.

"Well . . . she *is* odd in a lot of ways. Reads a lot. Likes to be alone. Gets a lot of weird ideas. And she doesn't mind saying them right out. Really, underneath, she's damn grateful that you put us up for membership here." He laughed a bit too jovially. "I'm always trying to soothe the feelings that Laura goes around ruffling up. Odd girl. Just don't pay too much attention to her notions, old man."

"I think she's a charming woman," Fletcher said, a little too coldly.

Ellis Corban's eyebrows slid up and froze in position. "Eh! Oh . . . well, that's fine. That's wonderful. Good God, it wasn't like this over at Tuplan and Hauser. Maybe

42

I didn't give you the whole story on why I wasn't happy there. I know we men don't like to admit it, but the little woman has a lot of influence on how well you get along in a firm. I mean there's a lot of little ways she can help. Well, I'm not saying this against Laura, you understand, because she's one in a million, but she just doesn't seem to be interested in doing those little things. She says they bore her. She says it's all a lot of nonsense, and they hire me, not her. But the really progressive firms feel that they're hiring the wife as well. Hiring a partnership, you might say. The beginning of the end at Tuplan and Hauser was when I finally got Laura to go to a party of just company people. I never should have risked it. She monopolized the dinner conversation. Lot of damn lies about her background. Kept talking through her nose. Do you know, Fletch, she actually convinced those people that she has two brothers with pinheads who travel with a side show. Got her home and she rolled around on the floor, just yelping with laughter. The next day in the office I could actually *feel* the tension. If I'd been a different sort of man I'd have thrashed her within an inch of her life when I got her home. But . . . I suppose I shouldn't sound as if I were complaining. She doesn't do that sort of thing anywhere near as much as she used to a few years ago. She's a lot quieter now. But I just thought you ought to know, and ought to tell Jane, that Laura makes absolutely no effort to . . . to be liked."

"It's refreshing, Ellis, in a way."

"Well, of course, you're looking at it from a different angle. Jane is a big help to you, I know. She tries, you see. But understand, I'm not talking Laura down. I wouldn't trade her for anything in the world. She keeps life pretty . . . interesting." Corban dabbed at his forehead with his handkerchief and smiled a bit wanly in the fading light.

When Laura and Jane came back Fletcher was pleased to see them talking and smiling at each other, and he was glad to see Jane pause by one table and introduce Laura to old friends.

As Laura sat down she smiled sweetly at Ellis and said, "Get your apologies all made, dear?"

"What does he have to apologize for?" Jane asked.

"For me. He always does. It seems to make him feel better. As though he were expiating some sin. Ellis, my boy, we'll have to go into that some day. Or right now. Lie down on the floor and relax and tell us all about your sins. I bet they're all tired little grey sins."

"Please, darling," he said.

"Oh oh," said Jane in a low voice. "Comes slow death. Don't look at him and maybe he'll go away. He's a dentist. Dr. Frike. Premium bore of the club. And a fondler. I went to him once. Never again. Even while filling a tooth he managed to take a reading in Braille."

"I have a system," Laura said. "When I get pinched, I pinch right back, and then look at them like this."

Fletcher half choked on his drink as he saw the expression of vacuous idiocy that came over her face. Jane said, in an awed tone, "Good Lord, that ought to give them pause." She took a quick sidelong glance. "Out of luck. Here he comes."

Dr. Frike was a vast lean bony old man with a peculiarly rigid way of holding his chest out and his shoulders back. He always made Fletcher think of an upended coffin. He spoke inanities in a loud firm voice, using an explosive Hah! as punctuation.

"Well, Fletcher! And Jane, my dear. Hah! I suppose this charming couple are the new members I've heard so much about? Hah!"

Fletcher and Ellis got up and Fletcher performed the introductions. "Always glad to see nice young people coming in. Hah! Now you young men just sit down and I'll walk around here. No, don't get me a chair. I can only stay a moment."

He took up a position between Jane and Laura, and put one lean old hand on Jane's shoulder and one on Laura's, squeezing in slow nervous rhythm.

He beamed down at Laura. "Hah! And how do you find our little community club?"

She looked up at him. "Why, you just drive south out of town and here it is." She paused for effect, then said, explosively, "Hah!"

The lean fingers stopped their nervous movements. Fletcher risked a quick glance in Jane's direction. He was glad it was getting dark. The squeezing began again. "My dear, I'm afraid you misunderstood me, or perhaps you were making a joke. Hah!"

"Well, if you mean do I like it here, Dr. Frike, I guess I do, because everybody is just so gosh darn friendly, you know. Hah!"

Jane made a muted strangling noise. The doctor once again began the finger exercises. Laura looked at the hand on her shoulder, and Fletcher could hear her sigh. Suddenly she laid her cheek against his hand, then turned her face quickly and began to kiss the back of the doctor's hand, making loud kissing noises. Dr. Frike snatched his hand away as though he had burned it.

"And I do so love to be surrounded by real honest-to-goodness friendly people, don't you, Doctor?"

He said, "Well . . . it's a small club . . . I mean everybody knows . . . Say, I must be getting along. Pleasure to meet you. Always a pleasure . . . to meet new members." He turned with the slow dignity of one of the larger water birds and walked away, unconsciously rubbing the back of his hand.

Jane borrowed Fletcher's handkerchief and made snorting noises into it as soon as Doctor Frike was out of earshot. Laura sat, completely expressionless.

Ellis said in a low intense tone, "Maybe you ought to realize that we're new here. Maybe you ought to stop and think once in a while. Maybe . . ."

"It doesn't matter at all," Fletcher said quickly. "That old bird is a pest. If she hadn't done that he'd have been here for an hour."

Jane said, with difficulty, "Worth . . . price of admission. God! Never forget the way . . . jumped. He'll spend the rest . . . evening down in the cellar with the . . . slot machines."

Laura sat erect. "Slots? Have we got slots here?"

"Now dear," Ellis said.

She turned to Fletcher. "Ellis has a mathematical mind. He keeps telling me that if you put eight thousand quarters in, you will get two thousand back, or something like that. I adore slots. Can I borrow him as a guide, Jane? It distresses Ellis to see money going into a hole. And that will give Ellis a chance to bring you up to date on the Laura problem."

"Go right ahead, you two," Jane said, recovering quite quickly from her speech and breathing difficulties.

Fletcher followed Laura across the terrace and into the club. He said, "Hold it while I get some change in the bar."

"Here. I've got some money."

"My treat."

"No sir. If I hit a jackpot you'll want half. I'll lose my own."

She gave him a ten. He went into the bar and changed all of it into quarters, took them back and gave her half, along with a five dollar bill from his wallet. He led her back to the stairway. "The machines are in bad repute in these here parts. So we have to keep them in the cellar. They're too profitable to give up. They just about support the club. They don't hit often, I'm warning you."

She looked back up over her shoulder at him. "Who wants to hit? I just like pulling the damn handle."

The machines were in a damp, brightly lighted little room near the furnaces. Two college boys and their dates were going partners on one of the dime machines. Laura made a beeline for the quarter machine.

She said, "Look. You've got some quarters, haven't you? Same number I have? Good. We'll put in five apiece. I'll take my turn first. Keep your own winnings and keep them separate. When the stake is gone, we'll see who did the best. Winner gets an extra five on the side. Okay?"

"All right with me."

He moved to one side, leaned his shoulder against the cement wall, the wall against which the machine was placed. He watched her. She was flushed and avid. She gave the handle a good hard yank each time.

On the third pull a win chinked into the scoop. She left it there. She hit again on her fifth coin, then counted the winnings intently. "Twelve here. Twelve for five. Not bad. Your turn."

He took her place. He pulled the handle lazily. "Nice job on the doctor."

46

"Poo, Fletcher. That was an expurgated effort. He was able to walk away."

"Rough kid, eh?"

"Not particularly. I wonder what it is that gets into the skulls of old men and makes them believe that they are utterly irresistible to all womanhood. It must be some little twist in the civilization we're living in. Somebody, somehow, is giving them the wrong steer."

"Not the civilization we're living in. Any era, I'd guess. Right back to the old bull ape, kingpin of the ape clan. You see, he's usually the oldest and the toughest, and so he has all the lady apes he wants. I think Frike just goes along with a sort of primordial instinct. The fact that it doesn't work any more is no help to him. He has to keep kidding himself."

"Hold it! You just put in your sixth. Don't pull the handle. Here's one of my quarters. My turn now. You didn't win a thing."

She was silent and intent as she played her second five quarters. She won three on the last one. He took her place.

She said, "Aren't you a little out of character too, Fletcher?"

He looked at her as he pulled the handle. The college kids were going noisily up the stairs and they were alone in the small room.

"I don't remember making any passes."

"I don't mean that. That was nice, that ape comparison. Where did you read it?"

"I didn't. I was just talking."

"You're supposed to be able to talk creatively about debentures and stock issues and reserves for contingencies. All the rest of your conversation is supposed to be either anecdotal, or a rehash of something you read somewhere."

He yanked the handle viciously. "Sweet Jesus, that line of chatter makes me goddamn sick. You're in business, so you're supposed to be an intellectual moron." He stared at the spinning wheels as he spoke. "All the little elfin bastards that never met a payroll always stick a character in their novel known as the Dull American Businessman. All the oh-so-sensitive and suffering artistes think there's nothing quite so crass as a dirty old profit-seeking businessman. It's sick-making. The dullest item I ever tried to talk to was a concert pianist. And the second dullest was a neurosurgeon, for God's sake. Maybe it started with Babbitt. I don't know. I *do* know that the quickest, brightest kids in the country go into business. And they don't stop growing mentally once they're in business."

"Like Ellis?" she asked softly.

"Hell, Ellis is one of those one-sided people they're talking about when they depict the businessman as being a . . . Wait a minute. You tricked me into that. Let's play fair."

"All right. Fair, Fletcher. I was needling you to see how you'd jump."

He grinned, a bit shamefaced. "I jumped."

"You did. Now I wonder where all that defensive strength came from. Care if I guess? Don't put that one in. That makes six."

He stepped aside. "Okay, guess."

"You got hot because there are a lot of things you want to do, a lot of things you want to read. And there doesn't seem to be time, and so you feel guilty about it."

He thought it over while she played her five coins in rapid order. "All right. I'll give you that point."

"When *are* you going to make time, Fletcher?"

"God only knows."

"If you never make time for those things, then in a few years those so-called 'elfin bastards' are going to be right about you, aren't they?"

"Women aren't supposed to be logical."

"Great little old combination we have here, Fletcher. Logical woman and intellectual businessman. We ought to be putting this on tape, wouldn't you say?"

"A weird conversation and you're a strange item."

"Part of it's a pose. I try hard to be strange. Speaking of strange, I had a strange feeling when I caught you staring so hard at me up there when you first came."

"I was staring. Is that so strange?"

She looked at him quite solemnly. "You had the look of a man who is looking hard for something. He doesn't know exactly what it is, so he won't know when he finds it."

"Maybe he knows already."

"That isn't worthy of you. That's a Randalora Club, Minidoka type conversational pass and I resent it."

"It was an automatic reflex. Around here you're supposed to say things like that. Makes you gallant. The ladies love it."

"This lady was being serious and . . . concerned. Are you looking for something?"

"I don't know. This is . . . a funny year for me. I keep losing track of myself, and wondering where the hell I've been, and where I might be going."

She shut her fingers hard on his wrist. "And a funny, greedy feeling? As if the world is a big table all covered with food, and you've lost your appetite, but still you want to eat, and can't?"

"You've been reading my mail."

She released his wrist. "That's another cheap, pointless remark. Some sort of a defense, I guess."

"It could be a defense against you. I have a yen, Laura. Closely allied, perhaps, with the rape instinct. But I'm not pursuing same any further. Not in the market, thank you."

"Implying that I am?" she demanded, her voice rising.

"I'll rephrase it. We're both in the market for something, and we don't know what, but this isn't it."

"Jane is sweet."

"Apropos of what?"

"I don't know. Sweetness. Which I am not. Ellis, the humorless wretch, keeps imploring me to be sweeter to people. I always ask why. That usually stumps him for a few minutes. If I keep on asking, it usually turns out that he wants me to be sweet so he can be president of General Motors. And I refuse to pimp for a corporation."

"Are you sure that little state of mind isn't just delayed adolescence?"

"You have a real nasty habit of picking at weak spots, don't you? I keep wondering that myself. Give me time. Maybe I'll grow up. Move over. My turn."

They played doggedly and in silence. He won a little,

but not enough to catch her. At last she was down to her last quarter.

"Last one," she said. "Kiss for luck?"

Her perfume had an odd spicy flavor. Her hand was on the machine lever. He took her hand and pulled her quickly, almost harshly, into his arms. In his arms, with his lips driving down hard against hers, she felt neither frail nor fragile to him. She felt almost sturdy, and exceedingly alive. They swayed and bumped awkwardly against the slot machine. He released her. She was looking at him intently. "I meant the quarter, not me."

"There are germs on money."

"You just babble on, don't you? Open your mouth and out comes bright sayings. Don't you get tired?"

"It was a stupid thing to do and I'm sorry. I don't go around doing things like that."

She smiled. "I go around clawing big chunks of meat out of people who try it."

"But you didn't."

"And I'm not entirely sure why, Fletcher. What are we getting into?"

"Nothing."

"Repeat. Nothing. But it rocked me. It curled my stupid toes, and I have the horrid feeling that a bra strap popped. It shouldn't rock me, Fletcher."

"Nor me. Not on such short acquaintance."

"There you go again."

"I insist on a few clichés, for God's sake."

"Okay. Wipe your mouth. Let's see if the magic spell worked." She put the coin in the slot. "Put your hand over mine and we'll both pull the handle."

Somehow he had a feeling what was going to happen even as the handle was going down. He guessed that she did too. For while the wheels were still spinning, she reached down and picked up the front of her skirt and made a place for the coins which would overflow the scoop.

He saw the first bar snap into place, and the second, and at last the third. The machine made an agonized clanking, and then the coins showered down, overflowing the scoop, cascading into her skirt.

She looked at him with an odd expression. "That star-marks us, Fletcher. That marks us good."

"Don't get carried away."

"You owe me five."

"With that lapful you still want five?"

"I play for a lot of reasons, and I always play for keeps, Up with the five."

He followed her slim straight legs as she went up the narrow stairs, holding the wealth in the yellow skirt. Ellis said, at the head of the stairs, "Oh, here you are? Good luck, I see."

"All kinds of luck," Laura said.

"I'll bet," Jane said a bit grimly. Fletcher resented her tone, but felt guilty.

Chapter Five

Fletcher drove slowly back home from the club, through the hot night and the empty streets. Jane sat far over on her side of the front seat, sat in her party dress, sat with a silence that made him dread the inevitable quarrel, yet angered him just enough so that in some curious fashion he found he was looking forward to it. It was very late. Nearly quarter to three.

Usually she chattered brightly on the way home from such an event. From time to time she lifted a cigarette slowly to her lips. The street lamps swept across her calm face in regular cadence.

It was going to be a bad one, he knew. There hadn't been a bad one since . . . since that trip he had made to Chicago in forty-eight. It had been a damn fool trip. He and Stanley Forman had gone out there to look over a small company which made thermostats with the idea of working out a merger agreement, based on a stock transfer. In the company offices Fletcher Wyant had shed his coat and dug into their figures. It took him three days to find the padded inventory figures, the falsified raw material position. He had said nothing to them, had spoken quietly to Stanley when he had a chance.

"Rigged books, Stanley."

Stanley had given him a sleepy look. "Thought so. Which is worse, Fletch, cheating or being so stupid you get caught? I wonder, sometimes. We'll let them wine us and dine us tonight and give our regrets in the morning. One year, I'd guess, and we'll make an offer to the Receiver in Bankruptcy."

With the pressure off him and transferred to Stanley Forman, Fletcher unwound a bit too far. The application of intense concentration over a three-day period had left him in a state of nervous exhaustion. And the drinks had hit too soon, and too hard. The executives of the thermostat firm had spread the royal carpet. The evening, for Fletcher, had soon begun to blur, with one club, one night spot, merging into the next with no memory of going from place to place. Stanley disappeared somewhere along the route. Fletcher found himself with a tall, knowing redhead, and he found that he was being exceptionally witty and charming. He was entrancing her with very little effort. It gave him a feeling of vast power. The other men were gone and he was alone with the redhead in a small place where the music was too loud, and he had his hand on her under the table.

And then, again without memory of transition, they were in his hotel room. There was a towel to subdue the bedside lamp, and she lay beside him, a wise-eyed, sleek-hipped girl with astonishingly small hard breasts, set wide apart. In a moment of clarity he accused her, fumblingly, of being paid off by the thermostat firm. She asked him if, at this particular moment, it actually made a hell of a lot of difference. It was an argument he couldn't seem to answer.

She was patient, and practiced, and adept. She got to him, through the mists of alcohol, and he slid from her into sleep. The jarring sound of the telephone woke him in the morning. He had the feeling it had been going on for some time. His head was a blue-white agony as he groped and found it and mumbled into it.

Stanley's voice was sharp and angry. "Goddamn it, Wyant, where the hell are you? This plane is going to take off in ten minutes. I've been calling you all morning."

Fletcher looked behind him. The redhead was gone. He tried to make his voice clear and decisive. "Sorry, Stanley. I can't make the flight."

"And just why the hell can't you make the flight?"

"Because, goddamn it, I got drunk and I just woke up, and if I stand up right now, it's going to kill me."

Stanley was silent for a few moments. "All right. Catch the next one if you can. Better phone your wife, or she'll meet the plane. I wired this morning. The office will let her know. I told them the deal is off. You should have heard the tears and sobs of anguish. See you later this afternoon then, Fletch."

He hung up the phone and barely had time to lurch to the bathroom before being wrenchingly ill. He went back to the bureau and looked at his wallet. His money was all there. His watch was running. It was fifteen minutes after ten. He groaned with semirelief as he lay back on the bed. There was a faint scent of the redhead in the room. A scent of her, mingled with the faint odor of love. He hoped he wouldn't be sick again. He rubbed his eyes. Time to call Jane. Better think of something, first. And his voice had a telltale huskiness. While he was wondering what to say, he fell asleep again. He woke up at three. He felt better. But his health began to dissolve as he realized that Jane had already met the plane, had talked, no doubt, to Stanley Forman, who might be just mad enough to tell the truth.

He phoned his home. Jane answered. Her voice was chilly.

"I've been trying to get you, darling. The circuits have been busy."

"Is that right?"

"Of course, darling. And I missed the plane this morning because I had a slight touch of food poisoning. Thought I'd better lie down here in the room for a while."

"With whom?"

"What? Aw, honey, don't say things like that. You know they're not so."

"Where do the lies stop, dear?"

"What do you mean?"

"I met the plane at one. Stanley Forman told me you had told him you'd call me. I waited and waited. I phoned the hotel there an hour ago and asked if you'd checked out. They said you hadn't. I asked if you'd placed a long distance call to Minidoka and they said you hadn't. Keep talking, dear."

"You've got a hell of a nerve checking on me that way!"

"Don't bluster, dear. It isn't becoming. I'm not upset. You're just a big boy, dear, and you're six hundred or so

54

miles from the flagpole. Isn't that what they used to say in the army? I'll expect you when I see you."

He started to counterattack and found the line was dead. He banged the phone up. He called the airport. "Sorry, but all the flights are booked solidly, sir. Perhaps tomorrow morning, if that wouldn't be too late. No, I'm afraid it will have to be tomorrow afternoon."

He took a long shower, ate too heavily, checked out too late to save a day's rent, climbed morosely onto a train at five of five. He sat alone in the smoking car with his long, savage thoughts. His face felt grainy and abused. His hands still trembled with hangover. He thought of what he had done, and of how it had happened. Those thermostat people had set her on him, like sicking a dog on a lame horse. Or, he thought with a faint glimmer of objective humor, like sicking a Sabine woman on a Roman soldier. The ultimate of service. The American merchandising ideal, combined with the farmer's definition. It was a hell of a thing, he thought, to remember so damn little about it, now that the price was apparently going to be paid.

He had never made a particular fetish of faithfulness. Yet, during the years of his marriage—twelve at that time —there had only been three women besides Jane. And two of those had been overseas, over in the crazy wartime wonderland of London. Many months with a warm, loyal little FANY—what was that again?—First Aid Nursing Yeomanry—though they claimed quite happily that they hadn't done any nursing since the Boer War. Code work, you know. Silly little hats with the round fuzzy button on top. Sturdy legs in impossible stockings. That had been Beatrice. And the other, of course, had been Hannah, the Ingrid-faced OSS typist, who had the little flat, and who had cooked those gargantuan meals for him, and after the heavy, spicy food each evening, they had tumbled into bed, leaving the dishes on the table just three feet away. Then she had been sent home, and after that he had found Beatrice, and then he had been sent home for discharge and a terminal promotion to Major.

Now the third was the redhead and she had no name that he could remember, and she was in this country. He had never told Jane of the women overseas. Yet he guessed that she suspected and had, in some coldly feminine way, checked it off to wartime and absence. He knew, obscurely, that this was much the worst, for Jane was in this country too, only three hours away by air. You did not need others when you had Jane, he thought. You didn't need anything else at all. But he had taken something else. Or been taken by something else. He preferred to think of it that way.

He and Jane had watched the intrigues among many of their friends. One of the intrigues had culminated in a double divorce and a double marriage, with a switch of partners. All good friends, of course. Jane had said it was dirty. In his heart he agreed. So they had prided themselves on being so well mated that there was no need of dirty little subterfuges.

He rode through the night, wondering what he would do, what he would say. He arrived in the Minidoka station that night, three years ago, at quarter of four in the morning. He'd had the crazy idea, during the taxi ride to the old house, the one they had left two years later, that Jane had gone and had taken the kids. He unlocked the door and carried his bag in, carried it upstairs. He risked the hall light and his heart gave a great leap when he peered into the dimness and saw the high warm mound of her sleeping hip, the rest of her, from her waist up, in darkness. He had been quiet in the bathroom, and had undressed in the hall, turned out the light, carried his clothes in in darkness.

He had slid cautiously into his half of the double bed—twin beds now, though pushed close together always—and had lain back and risked a long deep breath of thanksgiving. She said, in the darkness, in the voice she used over the telephone, "Have a ducky time, dear?"

"Just dandy, thanks."

"Good night, dear."

"Just like that?"

"Just like that." And, after a time, he had slept. She had been dressed almost formally for breakfast the next day. For three days he had tiptoed lightly around her. But it couldn't go on. Then the fight came one evening, when both kids were at the movies. One of those bitter, almost meaningless, destructive quarrels.

And, he thought, God forgive me, I lied to her and finally made her believe it, because I didn't have the guts to tell the truth and risk losing her. Because her ideas of integrity are one hell of a lot higher than mine. I made her believe it, and then we had to be together again, right then and there, because it was something we both needed as a kind of proof. Right then and there, with the lights out in the living room, there on the couch, and with as much heat and heart in it as though we had been separated for years instead of days.

And now, three years later, there had not been anyone else since the redhead, and Jane sat over in her corner of the car, remote, unapproachable. He let himself fill with righteous anger. Goddamn it, he hadn't done anything. What the hell kind of a jail was she trying to keep him in?'

"You seem pretty quiet," he said mildly.

"Do I? I'm sorry."

"Get it off your chest, Jane."

"What in the world do you think you're talking about?" She looked out the window. "You're going right past our street!"

"I know it," he said grimly.

"Isn't it a little late for melodrama, dear? I need my sleep. I'm very tired."

He drove on in silence, parked in windless tree shadows, lit two cigarettes, handed her one. He said, "Jane, I've lived with you for fifteen years. I know you pretty well. I know when something is eating on you. There is something eating on you right now. I think I know what it is. Let's get this over before we go home."

"It isn't important, really."

"How do you mean?"

"Well, it is a little silly of me. I'm an adult I guess. Or should be. I ought to get used to such things. Other women do."

"What things?"

"Oh, things. Going out for cocktails and dinner and a dance and watching your husband glow and hover all evening."

"Just how did I do that?"

"Glowing like a two-dollar lantern every time you looked at Laura Corban. Hovering around her as if you were afraid something might swoop in and damage her or something. You were a fool and everybody in the club saw it. They'll be whispering all week. Going down there into that cellar with her and spending hours alone down there with her, while I tried to talk to that hideous Ellis Corban, and neither of us could say what we were thinking. Then seeing you come up with her, and she all flushed and excited and her skirt up around her waist. What was I supposed to think, Fletcher?"

"That I'd backed her up against a slot machine down there and she was very tasty."

"Don't be coarse and ridiculous!" she snapped.

"Coarse—I'll stand still for that, but I think you've won the ridiculousness medal. She was flushed and excited because she hit the jackpot. There were college kids down there with us. As far as my glow is concerned, that was a glow of apprehension. I didn't know what she'd do next. And as far as hovering is concerned, I was trying to be able to get there in time if she did go off her rocker."

"Oh, you make it sound perfectly all right, don't you?"

"Possibly because it was perfectly all right and you're in a big tizzy about nothing at all. Damn it, they asked us out tonight. They paid the shot. I paid some attention to her. I even danced with her, you may have noticed. I think that was expected of me. She doesn't dance well, if that makes you happier. She's too stiff. Inhibited or something."

"Hah!"

"What does that mean?"

"Calling that woman inhibited hands me a big laugh. She's about as inhibited as Max Baer. I know that type. It was written all over her, and all over Ellis, too, the poor man."

"I guess I can't read that kind of writing."

"She's a floozy, Fletcher. God, you ought to be able to see that. She's tail, Fletcher. Every other man in the club could see it, if you couldn't."

"Now who's coarse?"

"Sometimes there's only one name that fits. And what's

more, I bet she doesn't even get any pleasure out of it. I bet she just rocks back on her round heels just to see how much trouble she can make. You told me Ellis wasn't happy with that other company. It's as plain as the nose on your face what happened. She just ran through all the men in view and got restless. I don't see what you see in her, frankly. That long upper lip and her mouth open all the time. Adenoidal, I'd say."

"I tell you, I *don't* see anything in her. I'm *not* attracted to her. And I don't think she—as you so deftly put it—is tail."

"But you're going to find out, aren't you?"

"Oh for Christ' sake, Jane! You talk like a crazy person."

"*I'm* not crazy. But you better watch yourself, bud. You're getting to that age. You've got to prove you're a man or something. Like that time in Chicago."

"Let's stay on the subject."

"You find the subject pretty attractive. You *want* to talk about her. You're getting some kind of filthy pleasure out of talking about her, aren't you?"

He held his teeth tight shut for the space of three breaths. Then he said slowly, "We don't get anywhere bickering, Jane. She's an odd woman. Not like others we know. I'm perfectly willing to admit that. I don't envy Ellis. It looks as though he's got himself a hell of a problem. I don't know what makes the woman tick."

"But you'd like . . ."

"Please let me finish this. I'm trying to be as objective as possible. If I seemed to pay too much attention to her, I'm sorry. Maybe I did. But it wasn't an attempt to make passes. It was an honest, though perhaps misguided, attempt to find out what motivates her. It interests me, because I want to be able to depend more and more on Ellis as time goes by. I want to know if she is going to cut loose and give him so much personal hell that he won't be of any use to us down at the shop. I do not think we ought to see too much of them. You know I don't like to be too close to anybody who is working for me. I seriously doubt, and I believe you do too, that there's going to be any whispering due to my actions tonight."

"You don't know . . ."

"Please, honey. Just let me finish and then you can give me some more hell. I want to talk about how I feel about women. I like them, dammit. I enjoy looking at them. I inspect every pretty girl who passes me on the street. I like to look at the eighteen year olds. But God forbid that I should ever get involved with one. You can't spend all of your time in bed, and I would have absolutely nothing else in common with a young girl except that. Now, how about women? How about Mrs. Corban? I think she is an attractive woman. You know she is. In her own way, she's witty. Now, let us suppose that I suddenly had to go to New York, and I met her on the street there. Assume, further, that she was anxious to have me take her back to my hotel room. This is getting a bit fantastic. I don't think I would, dear."

"I'll say it's getting fantastic."

"Not in the way you mean. I'm getting older and I'm getting smarter. I knew some girls before I met you. I've learned something. The first time is no good. You aren't adjusted to each other. You know absolutely nothing about the other person's wants or needs or tempo or anything else. It takes a lot of times of being together before you're—damn it, I hate to sound so clinical—proficient. And that means just from the physical angle, without thinking of any emotional or spiritual aspects.

"We've been together a long time, Jane. I love you and I don't want to lose you. Both of us have a strong streak of the voluptuary. So with us it's good. I'm not a kid. I'm not looking for illicit thrills. I'm not trying to prove anything to myself, or to anybody else. To make any deal with Laura worth while, assuming that I *could* seduce her, or, as you might say, vice versa—a long long time would have to pass before we could do each other any good. And frankly, I'm too old and too weary and too lazy and too damn set in my ways to embark on any campaign like that, believe me."

There was a long silence. He decided he did not want to plead any longer. He stared glumly ahead, sucking hard on the cigarette, seeing, against the slant of the windshield, the reflection of the glowing red end of his cigarette. It was the dead still part of the morning. The time when old people died. The time when hospital corridors were empty echoing places, smelling of pain.

He felt Jane move close to him, the long warm length of her thigh against his, her hand light on his knee.

"God, I'm silly," she said in a small voice.

"I wouldn't say that."

"Yes you would. I rattle on and on and you listen to me half the time and I hardly blame you for that. I guess I've got everything in the world I want. I forget that. I let the little darn things pile up on me—things that aren't important. And then I give you a bad time because I get stupid jealous of you. But you *did* spend an awful long time down there with her, and I guess the old gabby-noses will find somebody to talk about. Mostly I didn't like being left with that Ellis creature. He's so ponderous. And we've got to bear with them on Sunday, bless us."

"Let's not make them a habit, hey?"

"I'll take opium first. Now kiss me and let's go to bed."

He smiled in the night and kissed her and she made her arms tight around his neck, and then whispered in his ear that she was sorry for saying so many nasty things. She sat close to him on the way home.

He was in his bed and she was in the bathroom and he fought to keep awake for her. Weariness ran like molten lead through his veins. She came into the bedroom, silhouetted for a moment against the bathroom light before she reached back to turn it off. And then she was heavy and sweet-smelling against him. The night was warm, and he channeled his thoughts to maintain his awareness of her.

Long after she had gone to sleep and he could hear her breathing deeply in her own bed, he thought of Laura Corban, thought of the thin, clear, delicate articulation of her, the clever intricacies of knee and ankle and oiled socket of hip. She moved lightly across the backs of his eyes, and, on the very edge of sleep, he thought that she was a symbol of some subtle depravity, that there was something about her which was unclean, and yet something that he had to learn. With Jane he had gone through the accustomed rites of their love, and all the time it had been happening, he had seen the watchful face of Laura

61

Corban. She had watched them with remote, indifferent interest. With a faint trace of amusement. As one might watch the antics of the clumsier beasts at a zoo, filled with self-awareness of her own more motile deftness, more astringent delights, and degenerate devices.

He slept and his dreams were full of unnamed fears, of running—but never fast enough; of hiding—but never cleverly enough; of fighting—with awareness of defeat. Ellis Corban romped woodenly through his dreams, and in one memorable sequence he held a tiny doll so tightly in his fist that only the thin white feet showed.

Laura rode home beside Ellis from the club, sitting silently and remembering. Remembering the look of him, the awareness of his heavy muscular body beside her slimness. The deep slow tones of his voice. And she remembered that first feeling of awe when she sensed his vulnerability—sensed that he by some other path, alien to her, had come at last to stand at the same place where she had stood since the first warm days of spring. It would be good to run, she thought. Safer and better. But a thought as forlorn as that of the child on a mountaintop thinking how good it would be to fly.

She squirmed a bit in the car seat as she remembered the cheapness and obviousness of the way she had maneuvered him into kissing her. And she knew that up until the instant of contact of their lips, she had half believed and half hoped that it would be as meaningless as other kisses on other nights at other clubs.

Yet, in contact, his lips had been hard as oak roots, his arms strong enough to break her body. Her tongue returned to the small raw place on the inside of her upper lip where it had been bruised against a tooth. Her lips still felt swollen.

And the driving, punishing kiss had weakened her oddly, had driven her back to that afternoon time of lying white and naked on the stubbled rug in the bath of music. Then they had swayed, awkward as adolescents, bumping against the slot machine.

And then she had put the last quarter in, knowing as she pulled the lever that it was jackpot, knowing it was and wishing it wouldn't be, and holding the yellow skirt ready for the coins that streamed down the scoop and overflowed to chink together in the yellow fabric.

For the rest of the evening he had been near her. Even when he was across the room, he had been near her, and she knew that he felt as she did, that they were the only two living things, moving among automatons in a strange game of charades.

She sat and remembered while Ellis talked cheerfully and endlessly about the success of the evening, complimenting her on her excellent behavior after a bad start.

"Fletch seems quite taken with you, dear," he said complacently. It jolted her out of a pleasant reverie.

"What? What is that supposed to mean?"

"Nothing in particular. He just told me he thinks you're charming and quite unusual. You seem to have gotten off on the right foot here. I'm really pleased."

"Jane doesn't seem to be quite so enthusiastic."

"Well, you never have gotten on too well with women. Just so long as you don't make an enemy out of her, that's enough. And I think if Jane tries to criticize you, it will just put Fletch further on your side. It will even help your relationship."

"Relationship! What are you talking about?"

Ellis laughed comfortably. "Don't be so naïve, darling. It doesn't hurt a man at all to have his pretty wife flirt a little with the boss."

"I'm supposed to dangle? Like a carrot in front of a mule, or whatever they put carrots in front of?"

"Do it right, dear, and you'll earn yourself the other kind of carats. Pretty good, eh? The other kind of carats. I'll have to remember that."

"Please do."

"You don't think it's funny?"

"It's an absolute howl. But isn't the whole idea dishonest, darling? I mean dangling like that. To be fair, I better go off on a business trip with him. It would really be business, and if I spent anything, we could deduct it, couldn't we? If a little flirtation will help you at the office, just think, darling, what a long honest-to-God weekend in the hay could do. You might get to be president."

"Why do you have to spoil everything?"

"Why would it spoil anything? Aren't we all sophisticated people? If you think you're being left out, maybe we could work a four-way deal and include Jane."

"Get your filthy mouth off her! She'd understand what I mean. I've watched her talking to Stanley Forman. She doesn't think there's anything degrading about being merely pleasant."

"Men like you ought to have two wives. One to handle the promotional aspects."

"What makes you think you're too damn pure to play the game the way everybody else does?"

"Any game I play, I play for keeps."

"You're always saying that. I've heard it a hundred times. Frankly, I can't see as it means anything. It's just one of those meaningless comments that make you sound as if you were loaded with integrity or something."

She didn't answer him. He turned into the drive and she got out while Ellis took the car back and put it in the garage. She hadn't brought her house key so she waited in the night for him to come back. She had a sudden strong urge to call a truce, to put a temporary end to the pointless bickering. She wished, suddenly, that she could be everything he wanted her to be, even if it would mean a minor death. The night was warm and the stars were out, and she wanted to cry, for no special reason.

She heard the scuff of his foot on cement as he came back along the walk. He came up to her, making no move to unlock the door. They stood close in the night and he said in what she secretly called his "marshmallow fudge" voice, "Kits, we shouldn't fuss at each other. Things are getting better between us. You know that. You've steadied down a lot, believe me, and don't think I don't appreciate it and love you for it. And I was really so terribly proud of you tonight."

Laura wanted to make up to him, and yet when he took the initiative she felt both repulsion and rebellion.

She leaned closer to him and whispered the vilest word she knew. It was as brutal and meaningless as a blow. The moment she said it, she wished with all her heart she could take it back. He unlocked the door with rigid dignity.

They did not speak while preparing for bed. Once the lights were out he turned over on his side, his back to her. She lay in the darkness for a time and then, as penance for her own brutality, she slid close to him and caressed him. She half smiled in the darkness as she sensed his shock at this rare and unusual incident. And then he turned to her with such a bumbling eagerness that she was at once sorry for her impulse. She automatically performed her suitable portion of the joyless act, while her mind roved far from the tangled bed and the labored breathing, far from the broken words of adoration. When she was quite certain that he had slipped into heavy slumber, she got quietly out of bed, took a quick chill bath, dressed in the darkness in slacks, a light sweater, comfortable moccasins.

She locked the door behind her when she left the house. She walked slowly toward the river, her hands shoved deeply into the pockets of the slacks, fingertips against the soft roll of her thigh muscles as she walked. There was a crumpled dollar in the slacks and she bought a Coke from a sleepy counter boy at an all-night drugstore.

A block from the river a group of young drunks came up behind her, promising her unspeakable delights in fuzzed voices. The pack chases a prey that runs, and she turned and faced them and told them off quietly. They went on down the street, looking back, mumbling about "wise bitch" and "goddamn smart-pants dame." She walked slowly out onto the old Town Street bridge, aware of the darkness under it, the shadow bank where she could have been dragged by them, down there in the rusty litter, by the river smell. Maybe a thing like that would be in part an answer, to be dragged down by a pack, half strangled, used by each one of them, left at last in the broken moaning silence, with all the memories of pain.

The sky was getting light in the east. She climbed up onto the broad concrete railing and sat with her feet dangling over the dark water of the Glass River, her arms braced, a cigarette hanging from the corner of her mouth.

Half an hour later the police car stopped. The man was heavy, balding. He wore a summer uniform that smelled sharply of sweat, and he clinked and creaked as he came over to her.

"It's against the law to sit on that there railing, girl."

She turned a bit further, so he could see her face. "I'm sorry. I didn't know." She swung her legs over and slid down onto the sidewalk, dusting the seat of her slacks with her hands. "I couldn't sleep so I wandered down here, Officer."

"What's your name and address?"

She told him, and his manner changed a bit. "Lady, this isn't such a healthy part of town, not since the war. You want we should give you a lift home? That sun'll be up in another couple minutes."

"If it wouldn't be too much trouble, Officer."

"Glad to do it. Today's going to be another boomer."

The sun was coming up as she got out in front of the house and thanked them. The color was brass, and the early heat was beginning to slant against the stone sides of the city. They waited until she unlocked the front door, turned and waved at them. Then the grey car with its gold decal on the door moved softly down the street, grey as what was left of dawn, and almost as silent.

She made coffee and sat at the kitchen table and drank it. Whenever she was up this early she found herself thinking of her father, remembering another world.

Things would be going pretty well. And slowly his usual good cheer would fade away, change by degrees into irritability, into moroseness. And he would complain about the job of the moment.

She and Josh would know when it was due, almost to the day. A loud clap of the big calloused hands. "Kids, let's get out of this crumby town. There's nothing here. It's dead. Let's pack up and hit the road."

Then, on the highway, with the car loaded heavy on its springs, the three of them would sing, and there would be a black heat mirage on the highway far ahead. She could remember the good chill taste of the orange pop when they made stops, the way he always wanted to turn down side roads, his outraged and fluent protests when an old tire would let go.

Those were the good days because you had no doubt that all the rest of life was going to be just as wide and fine and free. Life was going to taste like that first gulp of iced pop, was going to look like a desert sunrise, was going to feel like a party dress, slick and nice against your skin. You were going to grow up and live in a house all redwood and glass and decorator's colors, with a round bed, and a French maid, and a convertible the color of your eyes, and a dark lover-husband, strong as bulls, sensitive as artists, who would make you want to faint when he touched you, and handsome children and laughter and moonlight parties and . . .

She could go no further. She could stay no longer with that lost child of the wandering years. She pressed the heels of her hands tightly against her eyes until she saw green and blue pinwheels of flame.

"Bitch," she called that child of long ago. "Simple, inane, trusting little empty-headed bitch. Why didn't you die then . . . with all the rest of them. . . ."

Chapter Six

Jane felt rested and festive when she awoke at nine, Saturday morning. She glanced at the clock. The hair at the nape of her neck was damp with sweat. This day was going to be another killer. She lay there, permitting herself the Saturday luxury of drifting aimlessly up out of sleep. Fletch was purring softly. She looked over and saw that he had kicked his sheet off in the night.

The kids made some kind of unidentifiable thumping noise and she cocked her head to listen as she sat up. It was not repeated. She sat on the edge of the bed and shoved her feet into her slippers, wishing that it was a cool Saturday. In this weather golf was uninviting, tennis was impossible. Maybe it would be a good day to go up to the lake. Bust in on Dolly and Hank Dimbrough. Their kids were about the same age. And it would be fun to try the skis again behind the big fast Chris-Craft. They could take drinks along. Fletch always seemed to enjoy Hank.

She padded into the bathroom in her old slippers, kicked them off and stepped into the shower, pulling the glass door closed. She kept her hair out of the spray, soaped abundantly and kept the water as hot as she could stand it for a long time. By then the bathroom was too steamy to get dry in, so she went into the bedroom and scrubbed herself vigorously with one of the harsh towels. She tied her blonde hair back with a scrap of yarn, put on a crisp white play suit and sandals, and glanced fondly at Fletch before going to the kitchen.

Judge and Dink had fixed their own breakfast and they began begging permission to leave for the pool. Jane said, "You better wait until your father gets up. I don't think he wants you going off to that public pool. He didn't like it because I let you go yesterday." She felt a little qualm of guilt at passing the buck to Fletch.

"Aw, poo!" Judge said in a snarly voice.

"Easy there, my friend," Jane said.

"*Everybody* goes, Mother," Dink said.

"Now you two find something to do and stop pestering me. Maybe we'll all go to the lake this afternoon."

"Can I try the water skis this time? Can I?" Dink demanded. "Judge tried them and he fell off every time."

"That's no crime. Your father fell off too."

"That's because he was a little crocked," Judge said.

Jane whirled to face him. "Judson Wyant! What a way to talk!"

"Well, it was true, wasn't it? If a thing is true, is it wrong to say it? Is it?"

"Now run along. Don't bother me, and remember, don't bother your father until he's had his second cup of coffee. Turn on the sprinklers, Judge. I don't think the sun is high enough yet to scorch the grass."

They went off, with Dink insisting hotly that she'd be able to stand up on the water skis and ride fine, just like mother did.

Summer camp started for both of them on the fifth of July and lasted until the twenty-first of August. A week from today they'd be driving the kids to camp. Their two small trunks were in the utility room, filled with the items listed on the camp literature. Just one more week to endure the restless energy of the little monsters. That Laura Corban was lucky. She got hers off early, and was able to park them with relatives at that. I guess we seem to have a sort of inhuman attitude toward kids these days. Then, it isn't like it was generations ago. Gadgets do everything now. Kids had chores then, and knew the importance of those chores. Chores, these days, are just make-work, and the kids know it and resent it if you start to pile on needless work. Thank God they at least keep their rooms picked up now. That was more than a moral victory. And they weren't really bratty, like Sue's kids. Always demanding the center of attention, screaming and throwing tantrums, so that you actually hated to go over to their house, it could be so embarrassing and so exhausting.

She sang in her small true voice as she measured the coffee. She decided it would be too hot and buggy on the terrace, so she set the table in the nook. It was odd how the memory of the quarrel would drift across her mind, like a small cloud cutting out the sunlight. And then she would remember how it had all ended, and the cloud would be gone. Certainly there was nothing to fear from poor little Laura Corban. In a way she was quite pathetic. It must be wearing, married to that dull man. She guessed that if she were married to Ellis Corban, she'd get a little on that weird side too.

She turned, smiling, when she recognized Fletch's step. But her smile faded a bit when she saw how he was dressed.

" 'Morning, darling. You going to the office today?"

"There's a report I want to finish before the Monday meeting. It will be quiet down there this morning."

"Will it take you long?"

He sat down and unfolded the morning paper she had put at his place. "Not too long, I hope. Why?"

"It looks like another of those days. I thought we might go out to the lake. Dolly was disappointed that we didn't come out last weekend."

"Oh, Christ! I get sick of being patronized by Hank Dimbrough."

She felt her cheeks flush at the sharp tone of his voice. But, recognizing his morning mood, she compressed her lips and turned back to the stove. She heard the hard snap as he pulled the folds out of the morning paper, and then he mumbled something about ". . . and his goddamn Chris-Craft."

Despite her warning, the children came roaring in before he had touched his first cup of coffee. He said good morning to them in a dangerously level voice.

Dink said, "Today can I try the water skis? Can I? Judge tried them last time and Dotty Dimbrough does it and she's only ten and I'm eleven."

Judge started to say something and then changed his mind. Fletcher looked at them and Jane saw the expression on his face and saw both the children instinctively move back a half step and stand closer together.

Fletcher folded his paper and laid it down. "In the first place, it is considered common courtesy to respond in kind when someone says good morning to you. In the second place, don't come through the house like a herd of buffalo. In the third place, *if* we should go to the lake, which is highly doubtful, and if there should be any water skiing, neither of you is going to do any. Is that clear? Now go to your rooms."

The children left silently. Jane heard Dink's muffled sob as she went through the door.

"Aw, Fletch!" Jane said in a tone the children couldn't overhear. "That was awfully rough, darling."

"They need a good lesson in manners, those two."

"Not *that* kind of a lesson."

He stared at her. "Just what kind of a lesson do you have in mind?"

"Well . . . fairness, at least. I mean they've been up for hours and they've been terribly quiet and good, and I told them about going to the lake to take their minds off going to that pool again."

"They're *not* going to that pool."

"What would you like them to do? Stay nicely in their rooms all day? You want to give them sleeping pills? Darn it, Fletch, be reasonable."

"Do you want them to get polio?"

"Now you're trying to get difficult."

He finished his cup of coffee and stood up. "I'll be back as soon as I can."

"Don't you want your second cup?"

He kissed her lightly on the cheek. "No thanks. See you."

He went out and she watched from the living room window while he backed the car out. He turned down the street without waving or looking back. The small cloud had drifted into the center of her mind, and the world was darkened. She hoped he would be contrite enough to phone. And suddenly she became more angry than when he had been the most unpleasant. Just exactly what sort of a little king did he think he was? She walked quickly to the phone before she could change her mind. She phoned Martha Rogers and said, "Martha, dear? Jane. It looks like another stinker of a day and Fletch has gone to the office with the car. I can't phone him there because it's Saturday and the switchboard doesn't work. How about you and I and the three kids going out to call on Dolly Dimbrough and taking a dip in the lake? I can leave a note for Fletch. Hud has to work on Saturdays, doesn't he?"

"Hey, not so fast, woman! Are you sure the Dimbroughs won't have company?"

"What if they do? It's a big lake."

"Well . . . then okay. I'll put beer in that cooler thing. It will take me twenty minutes to get ready and get over there. But let's not sponge lunch. They've got a good little restaurant up there this year, you know."

Jane hurried and told the children. They cheered up at once and scrambled to get suits and towels. She opened her own drawer and hesitated over the new suit, then decided to take it, as a gesture of defiance. It was made of two scant panels for front and back, and laced up the sides with black. She put it, and sun lotion and dark glasses and cigarettes and a towel, in her beach bag.

Martha Rogers honked in front and the children ran out to get in. Just as she was closing the door Jane heard the phone start to ring. She stood still for a moment and bit her lip. Then she slammed the door a bit harder than necessary and walked down to the car with her head high.

The three children were in the back. Martha's girl was named Joanna and she was twelve. She and Dink started whispering and giggling at once, while Judge maintained an aloof and haughty male calm.

Martha Rogers said, "Jane Wyant, how on earth do you do it? In that play suit you look about eighteen."

"A clean life, kid. Gawd, is that lake going to taste good."

Lake Vernon was only eighteen miles north of town. The last three miles were over a narrow, winding dirt road. It was a small pretty lake surrounded by gentle hills. There were about twenty-five camps ringing the lake and the one belonging to the Dimbroughs was the most impressive. Before the war Hank Dimbrough had been the owner of a rather small automobile agency. During the war he had branched out into machine tools, and later into

72

scrap. The standard word around Minidoka was, "Ole Hank made himself a pile, boy." He still maintained the agency, but he was seldom there.

They went down the drive and Martha said, "Good! No strangers."

They piled out and hammered on the door. The cars were there, but there was no response. They went around the camp and down to the big dock that extended out into the lake. Tanned forms were prone and supine on the weathered boards. Children splashed around in the shallows. Far out on the blue water a slim girl was being towed on the water skis.

Jane firmly fought her sensation of guilt and disloyalty. She said, "Hi there, suckers. You would have a place so close to the city."

Hank lifted his long narrow head, shaded his eyes and said, "By God, it's a mirage. I was just thinking about a tall beautiful blonde and there she is. And don't move anybody, or it'll go away."

Dolly sat up and said, "Darlings! We love you. What a tan you've got, Martha! Hello, Joanna, Judge, Dink. You kids go on up to the house and change so you can get in the water. Have a cocktail, darlings, before you change."

They went down to the dock. There were two strange young men, very husky and very young men, with surprising poise for their age. Hank said, "My lambs, we have here some talent from State University. Footballers. My nefoo is running the boat, trying to dunk his intended in the drink out there. He brought these two mammoths here on a house visit. They all go to work on a road job next week to keep muscular during the off season. Boys, Mrs. Rogers and Mrs. Wyant. Martha and Jane, to keep it formal. Girls, the big one is Steve Lincoln, and the bigger one is Sam Rice."

The one named Sam Rice was truly vast. He had startling shoulders and he narrowed down to cowhand hips. His legs were long and lithe and powerful. He had a small-boy grin, butch-cut brown hair, and he looked at Jane with such bold and uncompromising admiration and speculation that she was annoyed to feel herself blush.

She said, knowing she was babbling to cover her confusion, "Do you boys drink too? I thought they kept you on rules or something."

"Gee," said Sam Rice, not taking his eyes from her, "we drink and we dance and tell jokes and laugh like anything. Actually, Mrs. Wyant, this is a break in training. I'm working up to big black cigars."

"He's our pet wolf," Steve Lincoln said proudly. Lincoln was dark, and built like a piece of road machinery. "Don't even talk to him, Mrs. Wyant. He's what they call disarming."

Still without taking his eyes from Jane, Sam Rice jabbed suddenly at Steve's face, his palm open. Steve whooped and went sprawling off the dock to send up a geyser of water, most of which landed on Martha.

Both boys were immediately apologetic. Steve climbed puffing out of the lake and tried to dab at Martha with a towel. Just then the big fast boat came swinging back by the dock. Jane remembered Hank's nephew as an overgrown boy named Dick something. He waved at them. The girl on the skis released the tow bar and came skimming toward the shallow water. She had timed it beautifully. When she was in a foot of water she lost all momentum and the skis sank under her weight.

She was a dark, vital-looking girl, a bit too heavy in the hips and legs. She slung the skis up onto the dock and said, "Yow, my legs. He kept hitting our own wake at an angle. Who's next? You go next, Steve."

She came up on the dock and was introduced. Dick brought the boat back and stood up and tossed the tow bar to Steve. He said, "Yell when the rope is just about taut, hambone."

"You just drive your little boat, sonny," Steve bellowed.

Steve sat on the end of the dock, braced and ready. He yelled as the rope came taut, and Dick gunned the boat. Steve went down onto his heels on the skis and wobbled dangerously, then came up triumphantly, skimming fast over the water. He cut expertly out of the wake, waved back at the dock.

Dolly Dimbrough said, "Jane, Sam Rice would be real competition for you. He's good on the darn things."

"Hey!" Sam Rice said. "You know how?"

"She's good at everything, darn it," Dolly said. "Me, I haven't stood up on the damn things yet."

"Go change, then," Sam said, "and we'll have some fun."

Jane, on impulse, gave him a lofty eyebrow. "Change, my dear boy? Whatever for? I'll change when I go swimming. When I ski, I don't swim."

She saw the clear, bright, competitive look in his eye and knew at once that this boy who was ten, or eleven, or twelve years younger than she took the same quick joy in contest as she did. He turned away from her and said, "Hank, you said you had another set of skis and a rope and tow bar?"

"Over in the pump house, son. Only watch that woman. She'll try to drown you."

Sam Rice got the other pair of skis. Steve had been spilled far out in the lake. He got back up onto the skis again from deep water. Jane, watching him, felt the exciting thudding of her heart. She drained the chill cocktail from a paper cup and accepted half of a refill. Martha Rogers had gone up to change. Jane watched her children in the water. Judge wallowed along in happy puppy fashion. Already Dink was developing a crisp, clean crawl.

As the big boat came booming back Steve Lincoln swung wide to pick up speed and let go of the tow bar as he came opposite the boat. He went around in a wide curve, edging the heavy skis, and ended at the end of the dock just in time to turn with heavy grace and plant his hips on the edge. He grinned at the involuntary applause.

Sam signaled Dick in with the boat and explained that he was going to tow two this time. Dick's girl got in the boat with him. Sam fastened the two ropes at the two corners of the transom and tugged them tight. Jane sat on the end of the dock and worked her bare feet into the rubber harness. Sam sat beside her and handed her a tow bar and put his own skis on.

"Are there any special rules?" Jane asked sweetly.

"Dick and Deena will be the judges. Okay, kids? The award to the fanciest performance, and a bath to the loser."

"Hope you brought your soap," Jane said.

"I love that overconfidence, Mrs. Wyant. After I dunk you I'll have no more respect and I can call you Jane."

"Let's roll!" Dick yelled, and the big boat moved slowly away from the dock, the exhaust burbling powerfully. Jane gave Sam Rice a quick grin. Slowly the rope tautened.

"Yo!" Sam roared and the big motor blasted and the boat lifted up onto its step and Jane leaned back, crouching against the hard yank on her arms. And then they were both skimming out, side by side. The sense of great speed was exhilarating. The hard wind flattened the white play suit against the lines of her body. In a very short time the speed boat was up to full speed. Jane worked the skis to test the fit of the rubber bindings, veered out to her right away from Sam, crouched and jumped the wake slapping the skis hard. The wind fluttered the short flared pant legs of the play suit.

She smiled over at Sam. She saw him laugh but could not hear the sound. She saw him shorten the tow rope, then cut across the wake toward her. She sensed that he was going to try to grab her tow rope ahead of her bar. She cut sharply in toward him, lifting her bar high. He gave a quick startled look, and ducked barely in time and she rode far out on the side where he had been, laughing over at him. Their ropes were now crossed. She shortened her rope a bit, nodded at him, and swung in. They performed the same maneuver and then again, taking turns passing under the other's rope, and it became a sort of a dance rather than a competition. They rode side by side. She put the tow bar behind her neck, rode with her hands on her hips. He did the same, then worked the bar down to the small of his back, his body through the triangle of bar and rope. She laughed aloud and did the same and worked the bar down to the backs of her knees, leaned back against it, feeling a little chill of fear as she realized that if she spilled in that position, it might ruin her legs forever. She laughed over at him as he did the same. His face was changing, the bones looked more prominent, ridges of muscle standing out on his jaw.

They had made a wide sweep of the lake and they were heading back toward the dock. They both slid the tow bars up and held them normally. She laughed at him again and pointed down at her feet and kicked off one ski as they passed the dock. She saw him do the same and then look over at her. She crouched and balanced carefully and worked her foot out of the bindings. She had never tried this before, but she had wondered if she could do it. She balanced with one foot ahead and one foot behind the rubber bindings. The ski veered dangerously and she caught herself just in time. She stood on the balls of her feet and then, with infinite caution, turned slowly until she could set her heels down again, her feet reversed on the skis, the tow bar behind her. She slid her right foot down and wedged it into the bindings, then slowly raised her left foot behind her, hooked her heel over the middle of the tow bar, let go with both hands and rode that way for five seconds, backwards, on one ski, her arms outstretched, bent forward from the waist, before she felt herself going. She hit the water hard, plunging down into green depths, then surfacing, shaking the water out of her eyes, bruised and breathless from the impact. She swam over to the single ski. The boat turned in the distance and she saw it coming back toward her at full speed. It was towing Sam Rice. His position was awkward. He was on one ski and tentatively bracing his free foot in the water. The rigid foot sent up a high gout of spray. And then she gasped as she saw him put more and more of the weight on his free foot and kick off the other ski. The tremendous water resistance slowed the big boat. Yet he rode that way, at a perilous angle, skiing on his bare feet. She had heard of it, but had never seen it done. The strain made the muscles across his back stand out like hard cables. As he went by, his face was a mask of strain and then, fifty feet from her he overcompensated for the drag and fell backward.

He came up and she heard his hard laugh and he came over to her, swimming powerfully.

He grinned at her. "One ski, no skis. How about us?"

"Exhibitionists, Sam. That's what we are. Who won?"

"We both dunked. I can't do what you did, God, that was lovely!"

"And I can't do what you just did, Sam."

"All that takes is brute strength and awkwardness,

Jane. Dick is going to collect the skis we left all over the lake. You're quite a gal. You ought to get yourself a job down at Cypress Gardens. I call it a draw."

"Okay, Sam. A draw."

There was something about the vital young strength of him that made her feel absurdly girlish. She looked at him and knew that her face had shown too much and that this was not a young man with whom you turned the cards face up. He moved closer to her in the water and put a big hand on her waist and pulled her over against him. She was conscious of the way the play suit was plastered to her, of how the cold of the water had made her nipples swell, sharp against the thin wet fabric.

She put her hand on his big square wrist and tried to push his hand away. "Don't be a damn fool, Sam. Good Lord, I'm . . ."

"Old enough to be my mother. I doubt that. Look, dear, a whole lake all to ourselves."

"They're watching us. Now stop! I mean it!"

"Jane, you're the nicest thing I've seen, anywhere."

She turned suddenly away from him, spinning in the water, moving away to tread water and stare at him with what she hoped was severity.

"Don't get carried away. I've got two kids there at the dock. I don't think you're more than six or seven years older than my boy. Now don't handle me. I don't like it."

He smiled ruefully. "That's the hell of it, Jane. When I find what I want, it turns out I was born just a little too late. Or you came along too soon."

"The cry of the junior wolf."

"Come on up and I'll show you my merit badges, honey."

"Fool!"

"At least you're smiling again. I like that smile. Look, this is vacation. A nice day. Nice people. A nice place. Fair warning, now. I'm after you."

She stared at him. "What do you mean?"

"It certainly won't hurt me any, and I know it won't do you any harm. A little bonus for both of us, and nobody talks, and who knows about it but you and me."

"That's pretty damn direct and insulting. What gets into

you kids these days? Good Lord, when I was in college nobody ever had the nerve to come right out and . . ."

"Don't get yourself in a froth, dear. Pretty soon you'll start talking about the nasty moral standards of the new generation. What's nasty, dear? Asking for it like a civilized human being, or mooching around and trying to sneak up on it? The result is the same, but the anticipation is better. And just think how well co-ordinated we both are. Now slap my sassy face."

"Stop grinning like an idiot. What gives you the right to talk to me as if I was cheap enough to . . . to play around with a college boy?"

"You did."

"How on earth . . ."

"You said people were watching, Jane. That was your first reaction. So it makes me wonder what happens when we get where nobody is watching."

"Two-bit psychology, and it's all wrong. Now get away. Don't touch me again. Here comes the boat."

The boat came up and Dick took it out of gear and it rocked near them burbling softly. Deena called to them, "We decided it was a tie."

"So did we," Sam said. "We decided she's going to try to ride back on my shoulders. So after she gets on my skis, pull her tow rope in, hey?"

"I am not!" Jane said in a low heated tone.

Sam gave her a look of blank amazement, and said in a low voice, "Darling, this is for the amusement of the people, not us."

"I won't do it," she said.

She recovered her other ski, put it on, got herself in position in the water, ski tips elevated, Sam beside her. The boat started up and they came dripping up out of the water, skimming along as before.

Sam swooped near her and before she could move away, he grasped her tow bar. He yelled into her ear, "I'll shorten my rope and you put one ski between mine." He moved forward, holding onto her rope as well as his. Then he let himself back toward her and she had to slide one ski between his or be spilled. He reached back and took her tow bar and twisted it. When she knew she had to let go, she grabbed wildly at his waist. He dropped her bar and Deena reeled in the rope.

He yelled back over his shoulder, "Get on my skis."

"I know how, dammit," she said. She kicked her skis off, one at a time, and was standing on his skis, her feet behind his. He squatted and she held his shoulders, got on him piggyback, then worked her way up, swinging her right leg over his right shoulder first, then swinging the left leg up. She hooked her feet back around him, let go of his head and balanced there, sullenly angry at him and at herself, but smiling for the benefit of the admiring Dick and Deena. Once she was firmly balanced, Sam began to cut slowly back and forth across the wake.

She felt, under her thighs, the smooth roll and coil of his warm shoulder muscles. She was saddled on the nape of his neck, and his head was against her stomach. And slowly, as he swayed in slow rhythm back and forth across the wake, as her play suit began to dry quickly in the warm wind, she sensed the beginnings of sensual physical pleasure within herself. She cursed him inwardly, knowing that he had planned it in this way, knowing that he already had a frightening knowledge of her. She fought against the slow melting within her. She had the crazy feeling that she was going half asleep, that her eyes and head were getting heavy. Her lips felt warm and bruised, even in the wind. And then she had no urge or will to fight against the warmnesses in her, wanting only that they should go on and on, that she should remain here, skimming sleepily under the bright sun, the masculine warmth under her, swinging back and forth across the blue and white of the wake, with the sun gleaming on the dark wood and polished brass of the boat. She knew that she had tightened herself against him and she did not care any longer whether he knew it.

And then the dock came toward them, and she felt a sharp disappointment and they slowed suddenly as he released the tow bar, then the water of the lake closed over them, its chill bringing her back to self-knowledge, and self-disgust and a kind of despair.

She came to the surface and his head was near her. He turned and looked at her and she felt that if he had laughed, if he had looked at her with knowing slyness, she would have reached for his eyes with her nails. But he looked sobered, and concerned and distressed, and he said so softly that those on the nearby dock couldn't hear, "I'm sorry, Jane."

"N-never mind, Sam."

They swam to the dock, each pushing one ski. Jane hauled herself lithely out of the water. Martha Rogers looked at the way the play suit was pasted against Jane's body and said, "Well, *really,* dear!" And Jane ignored her and smiled at the praise of all the others, and then stood up and said, "When you see me coming in a suit, Hank, pour me another. That's my cup."

She stripped off the wet play suit, the sodden nylon panties and bra, in Dolly's bedroom. There was a full-length mirror set into the front of the closet door. She stood and looked dubiously at the rich femininity of her body. She had the strange feeling that her body had betrayed her. She had treated it well, kept it brisk and clean and firm and young. It had been an ally, and loyal, and she had trusted it. In a strange sense it had been something which only she and Fletcher shared, both taking pleasure from it, both proud of it—and now, in revolt for some unknown reason, it had let itself be stimulated, had let itself become warm and frighteningly willing, merely because a muscular college boy had known how to seek it out, had known, somehow, that her trust had been naïve, that all along the traitor body had given the impression of faithfulness, while waiting for a chance.

She put the suit on, wishing she had brought the older, more sedate one. She was troubled. She had believed with all her heart that there were no circumstances possible which would cause her to be unfaithful to Fletcher. She had believed that no man except Fletcher would ever possess her, and she was content in that belief, wanting nothing else.

Yet she was painfully honest enough with herself to know that had that last ride ended, not in chill water, but on some dry and grassy bank in the warm sunshine, she might have given herself quickly, completely, to that big bronzed child, without scruple or hesitation, and that afterward she would have found herself in a peculiar hell of her own devising. It was especially sickening that her children should have witnessed, even without realization, her shame and her new self-knowledge.

It was a difficult thing to accept—that given the right circumstances, despite all her previous belief in her own staunchness and character, her heels could become as round as those of any tramp. Because it was not love involved. And Fletcher left her with no tensions of dissatisfaction. It was only a physical, inexplicable lust. A wish to be possessed.

She gathered up her wet things and remembered the sound of the phone as she had closed the front door of the house. This was punishment for not answering it. She found a line beside the house and hung the wet things up neatly, lit a cigarette, walked slowly and casually around the house toward the dock. She looked first for Sam, saw his brown length sprawled on the dock, felt the increased tempo of her heart, and felt, anew, a sick despair.

Chapter Seven

Fletcher Wyant drove toward his office, nursing a dogged anger and a sense of self-righteousness. Damn kids think they own the house. Think we're there just for their pleasure and amusement.

He had awakened with a dull headache, a distant throb behind his eyes that had banged harder when he had bent over to lace his shoes. He had awakened feeling more weary than when he had gone to bed. He knew his dreams had been weird, but all memory of them was gone. He knew that he had handled the argument with Jane very cleverly, but he had done it by skirting the truth.

That damn Laura Corban. This was no time for any interest, speculative or otherwise, in another woman. Couldn't help wondering what she'd be like. And it was pretty evident—she'd made it evident—that she'd be willing. No time for one of those tasteless suburban infidelities. No time to join the summer Minidoka game of musical beds.

He nursed his anger, but despite all he could do it began to fade, leaving him filled with uneasy remorse and self-doubt. God, they were good kids. Better than most. And no harm in asking about the water skis. He was half tempted to turn around and head back to the house, but that seemed too great a loss of dignity. You had to maintain some consistency. He drove more slowly, planning how he would do it. Call from the plant and tell them the lake would be fine. Then, on the drive out there, give the kids a talking-to about common courtesy and rescind the order about no water skiing. Hank was a fool, but he could be amusing enough. And it was a nice attitude at the Dimbrough camp. Relaxed and easy. And there was no

83

pleasure exactly like watching Jane out there, graceful as a bird on those skis. She would flash by in her trimness, and he would watch her and begin to want her, and know, with fatuous certainty, that there was nothing in the world to stop him from having her.

Certainly was an oaf this morning. Ashamed of myself. That little sob that Dink let out as she left the room. Hell of a note, being an ogre on a Saturday morning, when it's their last week before camp. To be perfectly honest, I don't have to come down here to the office at all. Got up and decided to come here because I wanted to punish the whole world and myself too. For some crime. Kissing that Corban bitch, maybe. Or perhaps the crime of not sleeping well. God, will I *ever* grow up?"

He parked in the slot with his name on it, and went into the offices. The watchman was sitting inside the door, his chair tilted back, reading a comic book.

" 'Morning, Mr. Wyant. They got the air conditioning fixed."

"That's fine, Mike."

"Maintenance says the oil cooked right out of a bearing. Sure feels good to have it back on. Going to be a worse day than yesterday."

"Who's in, Mike?"

"Some of the girls in Purchasing, and that new fella in Personnel, and Mr. Corban. I don't right now recall anybody else. Is it true we're going on two shifts in the shop, Mr. Wyant?"

"That's hard to say, Mike." He glanced over at the live phone on the reception desk. "Say, could you plug my phone in? I've got some calls to make."

"Sure thing."

He went on to his office. It was comfortably cool in the office building. He wondered how much it cost to keep it running for just a few people on Saturday morning. Better do a little watchdogging about that.

He heard the clatter of a mimeograph machine in Purchasing. The new man in Personnel glanced out at him as he went down the hall and gave him a careful smile. As soon as he was in his office, Fletcher tested his phone and got a dial tone. He dialed his home. After it rang ten times, he hung up, annoyed. All right, so she got huffy and took off with the kids. I better not find out she took them down to that public pool. Maybe she went shopping, took the kids on the bus.

He felt oddly relieved to have a new justificaton for his anger. He got out the figures he had been working on when Stanley had shooed him out. Anger obstructed his concentration for a few minutes and then slowly he worked his way into the world of symbols. At the Monday meeting he would be expected to report what would have to be done to enable Forman Furnace to take on a subcontract, a large one, for parts of a field kitchen. The defense production program had finally, after many warnings, begun to pinch materials. The working capital position was shaky. There were two reasons for it. First, there were a lot of units of the regular line warehoused, waiting for the thermostat controls. Those almost completed units represented capital tied up. Secondly the prime government contractor could not give them an advance for the subcontract on field kitchens. It was mostly metal stampings, heavy-gauge work, but nothing they couldn't handle. The trouble was the outlay for materials. There were many ways of getting the working capital position up to where the subcontract could be safely undertaken. The problem was the choice of methods. Comparative expense of each method of borrowing. Forman was sound and healthy. He worked patiently on a schedule of borrowings that would keep them in the clear, yet not obligate them too heavily for the interest payments. All this would not have to be typed for the Monday meeting. He could speak from rough notes, distribute information copies later.

As he was beginning to feel satisfied with his conclusions, Ellis Corban came into the office, hearty and smiling.

"The wife and I certainly had a good time last night, Fletch."

"Well, I want to thank you for inviting us, Ellis."

"That's the sort of thing we ought to do more often, believe me. We old married characters ought to date our wives more often. They get a real kick out of a dance like that. And I must say the club serves wonderful food. Say,

85

what I wanted to ask you, Laura just phoned me. She was trying to phone Jane and there's no answer at your house. Laura wants to know what sort of thing to wear when we come over tomorrow afternoon. Jane forgot to say, and Laura forgot to ask her."

"Well, if it's hot like today, it's pretty informal. Sport jackets and slacks, and the women wear cotton dresses or blouse and skirt and some of them bring sun suits and change and lie around and toast."

"Fine, that's just what we want to know. About three?"

"Somewhere around that time, Ellis."

Ellis studied a thumbnail. "Say, I hope I wasn't out of line when I . . . sort of briefed you on Laura."

"Not at all."

"She . . . well, she seems to think this corporation executive setup has some silly angles."

"She's not alone."

"Eh? Oh, I see what you mean. Sure. Funny kid, though. I really don't think it would make any difference to her if I was a . . . plumber or something. She'd probably like it better. Quite a background, you know. Her father was a widower. Pretty much of a bum, from what I can gather. He dragged the kids all over the country. They adored him. He got killed during the war. Got knifed in a drunken brawl in Oklahoma. There was just the two kids. Her brother, Josh, I never met him, was killed in the war. And there were two boys she was engaged to—and they both got killed one after the other. Hard lines."

"Where did you meet her?"

"Oh, right after the war. I was with another firm, the job I had before I went with Tuplan and Hauser. We farmed out some work with the GE labs, and I went there to follow it up. She was working there. I don't know. She seemed . . . like in the fairy stories when you were a kid . . . enchanted or something. Neither alive nor dead. A good worker, though, they told me. I had the feeling that I could . . . make a lot of things up to her. I . . ." He flushed and smiled too broadly. "I'm talking too damn much."

"I shouldn't ask so many questions."

"You must have married Jane when you were both pretty young, Fletch."

"I was twenty-two and she was nineteen. I guess it's one of those traditional kind of things, Ellis. Grew up on the same block right here in Minidoka. I started taking her out when she was fifteen, and I used to come home on vacations from college. There just never was anybody else for either one of us. Funny, we both used to talk about getting away from this town. We were away, for a while, but we came back."

"You seem so well suited to each other, Fletch."

Fletcher glanced up quickly, slightly annoyed, and surprised a look almost of longing in Ellis' eyes. A kid with his nose against the toy window. Though he didn't like the man personally, he had a sudden warm feeling of pity for him. Except in his keen financial understanding, Ellis seemed to be one of those men who are but half alive. And Laura, no matter what else she might be, seemed as intensely aware and alive as anyone he had ever met. A keen, roving, inquisitive mind, a constant appraisal of environment and its interaction on her. Whereas Ellis accepted his environment, asked only comfort, while he exercised his specialist abilities. In that moment he saw Ellis as a mother hen, standing and flapping and tukkawing on the bank, while the duck child paddled in blithe circles.

Out of embarrassment Fletcher changed the subject quickly. "Take a look at this schedule, Ellis. What do you think?"

Ellis sat on the corner of the desk and studied the pencil notes. As always, he seemed to come intensely alive when he studied figures. His expression and his manner changed.

"Just an additional two hundred thousand for the first quarter?" he asked sharply.

"We can decide where to overlap it. If it bunches up on us, we can take it up to three by the end of the second month, and up to four or five by the time the quarter is over. Then the repayment will knock it back down to two fifty. By that time we ought to be getting in the returns on the subcontract, and have the warehouse emptying."

"It keeps us close to the line. It is predicated on almost no difficulties in production."

"But on a pessimistic guess as to when we can ship the stored units to dealers. It ought to even up."

Ellis handed him back the sheet and, smiling, suddenly took on his customary air of overjovial insincerity. "I guess it is all just educated guessing."

"Not much more than that. But Stanley likes to have a plan, even if we do change it to make it fit better as the problem develops."

"Well . . . we'll see you tomorrow then, Fletch."

"Sure thing."

At the door Ellis turned, winked a shade too broadly at Fletcher. "Good thing, boss, I'm not the jealous type."

"What do you mean?" Fletcher asked too sharply.

"Laura spent the breakfast hour telling me what a great guy you are."

Fletcher relaxed inwardly. "She's trying to make you glad to work for me, Ellis. Tell her I keep my hoof on the back of your neck."

Ellis went whistling up the hall. The office was very silent. Fletcher put the finishing touches on his notes, rechecked his figures, then looked at his watch. Twelve thirty. He phoned his house and once again the phone was not answered.

Outside the heat of the day was almost overpowering. His shirt was stuck to him by the time he reached his car. He drove home doggedly and unlocked the silent house. The note was in front of the door, held down by an ash tray. His head throbbed a little as he picked it up.

Dear—We decided to go to the lake with Martha. You can call us there when you get home, or just drive on out. And bring your suit if you come.

It was signed with a sprawling J that ran off the edge of the paper. He knew that she had been intensely annoyed with him when she wrote it. "Bring your suit if you come." And be damned if you don't. The more casual her notes sounded, the angrier she was when she wrote them.

He went into the bedroom, the note still in his hand. He crumpled it and threw it in the wastebasket, stripped to the waist and sat on the bed, wondering what he ought to do. It would be a little too childish to neither call nor drive up there.

He waited for a few minutes, and then phoned. Hank Dimbrough answered on the third ring. "Hank, this is Fletch. Jane handy?"

"Hi there, boy. What are you doing down in that stink hole? Get your ass up here and put it in the lake. A buck says it'll steam."

"No bet. Can I speak to Jane?"

"Here's the way it is. They loaded the boat with kids and everything, and the whole gang has gone over across the lake to the restaurant to eat. I'm sitting here alone drinking my lunch, because I'm expecting a long distance call. Come up and help me drink my lunch."

Fletcher thought for a moment. So she was too mad to stay anywhere near the phone. Okay, there can be a limit to that, my girl. Have a happy time for yourself.

"Hank, I'm sorry as hell, but I can't make it. That's what I wanted to tell Jane. Please tell her a couple of things have come up, and I'll try to get home as soon after dinner tonight as I can."

"I'm sorry to hear that. I got nobody to talk to around here. Women and college boys, by God. Look, as long as you can't get home until after dinner, I'm going to keep your woman and your kids here for some special steaks I've got in the deep freeze. Say, we'll save you a steak out, and you come up if you can make it. Tomorrow's Sunday and your kids can sleep on the way home. Moonlight tonight, old man, and maybe you can paddle around in the water. Bring your suit."

"I'll do that if I can make it, Hank."

"Well, phone me if you can't, hey, and I'll eat that steak myself. Triple A. Had them flown air express from K.C. They cut like butter."

After he hung up, Fletcher had the feeling that he was the kid who hadn't been invited to the party. He realized wryly that it was his own fault. If he weren't being so stuffy, he could be on his way up there right now.

Hell, let her sweat it out. Just because I popped off too

much at breakfast doesn't mean I've got to come around on my damn knees. I'll go up there when I get damn good and ready to go up there.

As he showered, he wondered what he'd do for the rest of the day. Maybe a late lunch at the Downtown Club and there might be somebody around for some handball. The courts were air-conditioned this year. Some fast games for the waistline and then a swim in the pool. Some lazy drinks and then drive out to the lake for a steak and a reconciliation.

The Downtown Club had once been a vast private residence, a Georgian structure with wide lawns. But the widened city streets had swallowed the lawns and now the entrance steps were flush with the sidewalk. The white columns were soot-stained. It was primarily a man's club, with not more than three functions a year when women were admitted. In Minidoka the social lines were drawn firmly, but since the war more and more exceptions had been made. In the old days, if a man belonged to the Randalora Club, he definitely did not belong to the Downtown Club. If he was a member of the Downtown Club, his country club was the ancient, slightly ratty, socially impeccable Christopher Golf and Tennis Club on the hills east of the city. But, since the war, a few of the younger businessmen, professional men and executives who were members of Randalora were asked, discreetly, if they would care to join the Downtown Club. It had created a rather odd attitude on the part of such young men. It gave them a slightly condescending attitude toward the Randalora Club, and it also made their wives look hopefully across the horizon toward the weathered roofs of the Christopher Club. And, as the Randalora-Downtown contingent grew larger in the Downtown Club, they, feeling, and rightly, that the Christopher-Downtown contingent formed a rather impassive clique within the Downtown Club, formed a clique of their own. Yet any one of them would have left it willingly should they be put up for membership in the Christopher Club.

Thus, whenever Fletcher went up the wide steps and into the dim, high-ceilinged interior of the Downtown Club, he had the feeling of being a slightly second-class citizen. And he knew that their membership in the Randalora Club and his membership, particularly, in the Downtown Club, was due primarily to Jane's inherited social standing. Her father had been an almost notoriously unsuccessful and unlucky doctor. Yet, he had been a doctor, and in the tribal hierarchy of Minidoka, that counted. Dr. Tibault had been dead for many years, but that pretty Jane Wyant was still old Dr. Tibault's younger daughter. Mrs. Tibault, a regal and forbidding woman, who had never forgiven Dr. Tibault for dying poor, lived in southern California with Jane's older sister, who was a nervous, childless, arrogant, pathetic woman married to an industrial designer.

Fletcher's father had been, until his death in 1947, a successful merchant who had made a better than average living from his large hardware store. And Fletcher knew that, had he married the daughter of another merchant, he might very possibly, because of his position with Forman, have belonged to the Randalora Club, but the world had not yet changed sufficiently to assure him of membership in the Downtown Club. He knew, also, that Jane wanted, with all her heart, to belong to the Christopher Club. She had only mentioned it once, and that was several years ago. Aside from that one slip, she had maintained an air of pure and perfect indifference to the Christopher Club, and on several occasions had begged out of appearing in interclub tennis matches there. And Fletcher knew that Jane's attitude of indifference was, perhaps, the only effective weapon at her disposal, the only attitude which might conceivably result in an invitation to join at some future date.

The desk man gave Fletcher a servile superior smile as he walked in. Fletcher looked into the dining room and saw that with the exception of a few very elderly gentlemen, it was deserted. And no one was eating in the bar. So he took a new magazine and went into the dining room and took one of the tables for two beside the wall. The sound of city traffic outside was muted. From time to time a horn blared faintly. The catfooted waiter took his order for cold cuts and presented the check for his signature.

Fletcher ate slowly as he read the magazine. There was a nervous irritable edge somewhere within his mind, fraying the thoughts that rubbed against it. When his coffee was brought it was not hot enough, and he sent it back with a bit more irritability than the situation demanded. Christ, this club was dead in the summer! A pasture for aged bankers.

He replaced the magazine on the lounge table and looked in the bar again. Still empty. He wandered down past the bowling alleys in the cellar to the small gym and the handball courts beyond. It was as silent as a tomb. He looked at the pool. The water lay like green glass, with every tile on the bottom showing. He quickly repressed an astonishing impulse to spit into it.

When he went upstairs the bar was still empty. He held his thumb on the buzzer until a white-coated man with an aggrieved expression came through the door behind the bar and said, "Yes sore?"

"A double Scotch and plain water on the side, if it isn't too much trouble."

"No trouble, sore."

Slightly ashamed at the snap in his voice, Fletcher said, "Nice and cool in here."

"Yes sore. Is Pinch all right, sore?"

"Fine."

"If there's anything else, would you ring the buzzer, sore." The man drifted away and the door swung shut behind him, rocked once and was still.

Fletcher tossed the drink down, eased the throat burn with the water. He banged the glass down and walked out, down the lobby, out the big doors without glancing at the man behind the desk. Liquor heat spread out from his belly, meeting the burning heat of the sidewalk. He turned away from his car and walked down the street with a rapid stride, as though he were going someplace. He turned down by the theater district and slowed and read the ads. He went into a nearby bar and got another double Scotch. The bar was too frigidly air-conditioned. A ratty-looking young girl in a soiled dress gave him a tentative, yellow-toothed smile. He looked away before the smile reached full flower. The girl went to the juke box with an exaggerated sway of her pulpy hips and put a nickle in a ripe flatulent baritone who sang of what we did last night. There was a faint pink lipstick smear on the rim of his chaser glass.

He went out and walked directly into the first movie. He took a seat near the back, on the side. His long legs were cramped. It was an old movie, a biblical spectacle. The dark heroine emoted with her breasts. The two heavy shots of liquor dulled him. He sat there, and let the music and the meaningless words and the rich colors of the picture drift across the surface of his consciousness. He felt far away, and lost from everything of meaning. He looked woodenly at the silken flanks of the actress, ten times life size on the screen. She wiggled, and the pimpled public whistled in shrill awe.

He sat and stewed in sourness and nameless regret and dark purposeless gloom and when he looked for the raw flanks again he found that the pictures were no longer colored and that, without his noticing, the picture had changed to a western. Pistols banged flatly in the stale movie air and he put his chin on his chest and fell asleep, his knees aching where they pressed against the back of the seat in front of him.

Chapter Eight

They came back across the lake at two o'clock, the big fast boat loaded with adults and screaming children. Jane lay on her stomach on the bow deck with Martha beside her. The children were shrilly demanding their proper turns steering the boat. Sam, Steve, Dick and all the children were crowded in the seat behind the wheel. Dolly and Deena were in the stern. Once Jane looked around and met Sam's glance. There was an odd impact as their glances locked. She turned back, retaining the memory of limpid brown eyes. Setter puppy eyes.

They had no chance to talk, and Jane had resolutely blocked every attempt he had made to get her aside from the others. She lay there knowing his eyes were on her, knowing that he was staring at her, and knowing, also, that she was taking pleasure in that knowledge.

A child. A kid somewhere around twenty. Child's mind, in a body of heroic proportions.

"Gloomy, or just silent?" Martha asked, putting her lips close to Jane's ear.

"Both. I'm wondering if Fletch has gotten here yet. And, if so, how many drinks Hank has poured down him."

"Gee, I wish Hud could get off Saturdays."

"Fletch had a little work to do this morning. He probably got home around noon and got my note and got up here just in time to miss us." She had a twinge of guilt as she remembered her note. It had been pretty chilly. She put her lips closer to Martha's ear. "Pal, if anybody should ask you, coming up here was your idea."

Martha gave her a quick, wise look. "Sure. Any time. Sometimes I can use favors like that myself."

Jane rested her forehead on her crooked forearm. Every

94

dip and movement of the boat made her conscious of her body, conscious of flux and flow and that raw little edge of wanting which, once aroused, would stubbornly not recede until sated. Yes, Fletch would be there, waiting. He'd be irritated, and they'd do a little genteel snapping at each other, without letting the others know—because that united front you presented to the world was very precious and very necessary. And then you would find a chance to get away from the others for a few moments and then you would kiss and make up, and the instant he kisses you, he'll know just how you stand because he always seems to sense that, always. And it will be a game to get away from the others, and it will be like that time last summer. Sun shining down through the leaves, and oh, those miserable deer flies, but good anyway, as this will be good.

When the motor slowed she lifted her head and saw the dock close by. She got up and balanced and picked up the bow line and jumped to the dock, turned and fended the boat off with her bare foot, then sat on her heels and made the line fast to the dock. It seemed silent and hot after the roar and wind of the boat.

Judge said, "Mother, Johnny Dimbrough says there's a very easy mountain right over there with a trail and everything and we can't go swimming for an hour anyway, so all the kids are going and can we?"

"Of course, dear. Be careful. Watch out for Dink."

They ran off whooping. Dolly grabbed her little one and carted it, objecting, off to the midday nap. Hank came out on the dock with a drink in his hand just as Jane stood up and turned toward the house.

"Is Fletch inside?" she asked, a funny feeling of catastrophe pinching her heart.

"He phoned, darlin'. He left a message. A couple of things have come up, he said. He said he'd try to be home as soon after dinner as possible, so I told him to come up here for a steak tonight and he said he'd call if he couldn't make it."

Jane frowned at him. "That's funny. He *never* works Saturday afternoon."

Hank beamed. "Tell you what. We'll set spies on him and get her address. Then we'll raid the joint."

She turned to Martha. "Gosh, I think maybe I better go back to town."

"Why don't you phone him?"

"I don't think I can get him at the office."

"Go try, dear. It's a lot easier than rounding up the kids and dragging them back into the heat."

"Go use the phone, dear," Dolly said.

Jane phoned the house, and then the office. After six rings a man answered hesitantly. "Yes?"

"Is this Forman Furnace? Who is speaking, please?"

"Glover, M'am. I'm a watchman."

"This is Mrs. Fletcher Wyant. Do you happen to know if my husband is in his office?"

"He was, Missus Wyant, but not any more. He left here I'd say about twelve thirty. Around there. Drove off and he hasn't come back. Nobody's here. The air conditioning is all turned off and everything. I don't expect nobody back on an afternoon like this."

"Well . . . if he should come back, will you tell him to please phone the Dimbrough's camp? Can you do that?"

"Glad to. Dimbrough you said? I'll tell him, but like I said, I don't expect nobody will come back today."

"Thank you, Mr. Glover."

"You're certainly welcome, Ma'am."

She sat by the phone for a few moments, snapping her thumbnail against her front teeth. She took a cigarette and flicked it angrily against the back of her hand, lit it with a hard sweep of the match against the striking surface. She broke the wooden match between her fingers. He'd started it, hadn't he? Waking up in a bestial temper. Abusing the children. Growling at me. Taking the car without a word or an offer. Nobody would blame me for getting the children out of that heat. Heat like that can make them sick. And me too. He'd never think of that. He goes to an air-conditioned office every day, while I slog around that house with sweat dripping off me, trying to keep it decent for him and the children. Oh, Fletch, why are we doing this to each other just when I . . . when I need you near me. . . .

The sharp yell of the phone made her jump. She picked it up. "Is this Lake Vernon aye-yut seven nye-yun?"

"Yes, it is." And bless you, my darling, for calling me.

"I have a call from Washington, D.C., for Mr. Henry Dimbrough. Is he there? Hello! Is he there?"

"Yes," Jane said dully. "Just a moment, please."

She went out and called Henry in off the dock. He was jubilant at getting his call. He patted Jane on the fanny, a familiarity that she despised, and said, "You just earned yourself an orchid, baby." He snatched up the phone. "Hello? Hello? Johnny? You bastard! Jane honey, shut that door there, will you please?"

Jane went back to the dock. Martha was sitting up, oiling her legs. "Still want a ride back? I was thinking, I could leave all the kids here and drive you in and drive back out myself. I could do it, with luck, in less than an hour."

Jane sat down. She knew she should say yes. She knew that it might be terribly important to say yes. She managed a smile. "He's big enough now to take care of himself, Martha. I like it here, and here I stay."

"Smart gal!" Dolly said, peering through her sun glasses at her knitting. She stood up. "You two can soak up that heat all day if you want to. Me for a cool nap with the rest of the young children."

Jane spread her towel out, put her cigarettes handy. "I'll take mine right here," she said. She rolled onto her face and surrendered herself to the bright hard weight of the sun. The boards under the towel were sun-hot, and she could feel the heat of them against her breasts through the towel and the swim suit. She felt on edge. She felt as though she were trembling inwardly. Why should this feel like such an irrevocable decision? She shut her eyes against the glare. The lake lapped the pilings of the dock. She could almost smell the brassy heat. She made her muscles go flaccid, and she felt as thought, with each exhalation, her body flattened itself a bit more against the heated boards.

The voice awakened her and she felt bleared by heat, swimming in heat, afloat in tides of hot light. "Wha'?" she said, through thickened lips.

"I said you might be getting too much, Jane." She half

turned and squinted up into Sam's face. He was massive against the sun, kneeling beside her. She saw the incredible symmetry of his broad chest, curved hard as a warrior shield. She lay back again, face down, trying to force her way up through the daze of sun and light.

"Where's . . . everybody?"

"Let's see. Hank is napping and so is Dolly. The kids are up the mountain. Steve and Dick and Deena are doing some slow trolling in the boat. Jane, your back looks almost crisp. Let me put some oil on it."

"Don't, please," she said weakly.

She heard him unscrew the bottle cap. Then she felt the warm slick of oil on her back, felt the gentle pressure of his big hand. He rubbed it up from the small of her back toward her shoulders. The sun and sleep had beaten down the hard wiry edge of desire in her, and now it all came back, but not as before. It came back as a floating warmness, and she abandoned herself to it completely, breathing through her open mouth, and his touch was a caress, and his hand was strong and warm.

"My darling," he whispered.

"No," she said, her thoughts incoherent, knowing only that she must stop the touch of his hand. "No! Oh, damn you! Oh, God, Sam!" And she rolled away from him, sitting up, her eyes squinched with brightness and with tears, and saying, "Leave me alone. Please leave me alone."

He was kneeling, sitting back on his heels. His big hand gleamed with the oil. He stared at her and said quietly, "I know."

"You don't know a damn thing. You're too young to know anything."

He deliberately capped the bottle, lay face down and washed his hands in the lake, picked up her towel and dried them, without speaking.

"Okay, Jane. In the lake it was a gag. Hell, you're female. You're pretty. You're stacked. So you're fair game. Nothing ventured, nothing gained. That's the way I figure. And, baby, I'm not one of your wet-eared prep-school kids. I've picked coal and driven trucks. So it was a standard approach. You see that? If I made out, fine. If I didn't, better luck next time. But something went wrong."

"How?" she whispered.

"You tell me. That crazy ride with you perched on my shoulders. I don't know. Like floating. Like dreaming. Like nothing ever. It scared me. In a way that nothing ever has before. I kept thinking it had all happened before, somehow. I don't expect you to understand what I mean. So I'm sunk. Damn it, I think I'm in love with you."

"You're not."

"I don't see how I could be. What's the other answer? What is it, then?"

She squared her shoulders. "Young boys often get crushes on older women."

He leaned forward a little. "All right lady. Then tell me what it was that got to you? Tell me."

She was gaining control and she knew it. "Sam, I'd like to say it was your sterling character or your big shoulders or something. But it was purely physiological. Nothing more than that. Ask any neurologist, if you don't understand what I mean."

He stared at her and then shocked her with a great brassy bray of laughter. It made the cords in his strong throat stand out. "Now—believe me—I've heard everything."

"Why are you laughing?"

"Let's go for a walk along one of these trails."

"No."

"Don't you want to prove you're stronger than what any neurologist can explain to me?"

"That's not the point. I don't have to prove anything."

He sobered at once. "I'm sorry I said that. Jane, I think you're one damn fine person. I know what I am. I don't want you to have any part of me."

"Never fear."

"But I can't guarantee that I won't make passes. That's almost instinctive."

"No character?"

He grinned that small-boy grin. "No training, maybe. So promise I'll get a cold shoulder every time."

"You will. That's a guarantee."

"Because, Jane, I think this could be trouble. I think it ... might mean too much."

"Nonsense!"

"We're a hell of a lot alike, basically. That's the trouble with us. You could be my sister."

"Big sister."

"Stop smiling at me like that or I make the next pass right here in front of God and everybody."

"Control yourself, sonny. Lie down and tell me your personal history."

He rolled onto his back. "Let me see now. Where do I start? The pass I made at the nurse in the maternity ward? I think I was four days old at the time."

"That might be interesting."

"Well, she leaned over my cradle and you understand I was too young to have developed any taste at that point. She had red hair and teeth like a beaver. And when she saw what was I up to, she was filled with outraged indignation. She told me she was old enough to be my mother, and what was I thinking of, anyhow. God, Jane, you've got a lovely laugh. Like bells."

"Get back to the nurse."

"Well, she reported me to the doctor and he told my mother and she said she wasn't at all surprised, as that sort of thing seemed to run in the family. From then on I was under a cloud. I was the scourge of the kindergarten, and by the time I got to the first grade, I was a tired old roué, but I still had a fine fond eye for a shapely ankle. Girls used to follow me wherever I went. I made them line up in columns of twos and hired a fife and drum corps. We were quite a sight on the streets of Nanticoke. I insisted on nothing but music from *Scheherazade*. Now tell me all about yourself."

"Dull, sonny. Dull. A housewife. My husband is the treasurer of Forman Furnace. I have those two children you met. We live in a new house. We love each other, and we're good for each other."

"He a nice guy?"

"Fletch is a honey. He has his gruesome moments, but don't we all."

"The script is wrong, Jane. You're supposed to be married to some half-dead old crud. And you love life, see. So we get this sequence, see. We make it like a dream, and we put you in something all shimmery and white, coming down these pink marble stairs see. With a full orchestra and heavy on the violins. I come walking out from the side to where the camera can pick me up, and at first I don't see you. Then suddenly I look up and there you are. Your eyes go wide. We stare at each other. Lots of violins right there. You come down the stairs hesitant-like, your fingers at your throat. I can't believe what I'm seeing. I take a step toward you. We reach out. Our fingertips touch. And we dance. Oh, hell! Cut. I just remember I don't dance good enough."

"Sam you're a wonderful fool!"

"Oh, sure. Good old Sam. Tell you what. I'll be a friend of the family. Raid your icebox on Thursday nights. The three of us, we'll sit out in the kitchen and tell lies and laugh like anything."

"What are you going to be, Sam?"

"When I grow up, you mean? It's like this. That fellow that steers the back end of the hook and ladder, there's a job!"

"Seriously."

"Hmm, she's got to be serious," he said. She was propped on her elbows, looking at him in profile. His eyes were shut against the sun. He said slowly, "This I usually keep to myself. Don't know why you should all of a sudden seem like . . . well, like another part of myself. I clown, kid. Strictly for the kicks. When I lock my door, I hit the books. We beef-trusters aren't supposed to do that, not with the money they pay us to play ball. Honey, I've got to find myself something I can believe in. We've built a fat shiny world, and we've built it so tall, it looks like it wanted to fall on us. I know I could make myself fit my natural environment—which is maybe that good old Community Plate, Rusko Windows and a Forman Furnace in the basement. I have the right touch, somehow, with people. So I can make the living, according to *their* rules, but believing in it is something else. Mr. W. Chambers, it seems to me, simplified the problem. Be a pinko or a Christer he says, with nobody in the middle. I personally can't get up a hot sweat over either answer. That Walden gentleman comes close, but I haven't got a green thumb and I like modern plumbing. You see, I somehow don't wa to live my life with my tongue in my cheek. Corny as sounds, I want a cause, and some good reasons."

"Well," Jane said uncertainly, "I don't think I know exact what you mean, but doesn't *everybody* feel that way at son time or another?"

"Could be. How about hubby? Bright guy?"

"Oh, yes."

"Ever hear the same general thing from him?"

"A long time ago, I guess. We had some crazy ideas. W were kids. I started going with him when I was fifteen. Th depression was a pretty real thing then. We had a vague ide of going someplace in the world that was full of .. superstition and poverty and disease and . . . doing what w could. Changing the world a little as much as we could. Bt that was a long time ago."

"What happened?"

She laughed and it had a slightly flat sound in the sunligh "Oh, you have to earn a living. You take a job you don really want, and then you have kids and you have to get ahea in the job as best you can."

"Is he happy?"

"Fletch loves his job. And I guess he's proud of his hom and his family. We belong to nice clubs and we have goo friends. It's a good life, Sam."

"That's what I want to know," he said, turning onto hi side, leaning on one elbow. *"Is* it a good life, or do you ge to a point where it turns into just a hell of a lot of compro mises, and it doesn't seem to mean a hell of a lot? It's this I guess. Should a man have a real sense of dedication, o can he get along without it, and make his buck with the least possible fuss?"

"The way you talk you're trying to make our life sounc . . . oh, sort of silly and pointless. But it isn't, you see. can't talk this way very well. Maybe I don't think this way often enough. But always there have been men and women and they've lived together and they've had chil dren. And isn't that the point of the whole thing? A sort ol a unit, and you're together. And that's enough. I've me some of those people, those strange people with some kind of a mission. They're always a little weird. And they make

102

me uncomfortable. And don't try to tell me it's guilt that makes me uncomfortable, either."

"Okay, Jane. Try this for size, then. Five more years, and your kids will be out of the nest. You'll still be a young woman with a lot of spunk. So what do you do? Bridge? Red Cross Drive? Social work? Friend husband will be plugging away for another twenty years at least."

"I'll find something to keep me busy."

"And out of mischief?" Will it be something satisfying? I mean all that is just another phase of the same problem, isn't it?"

"Sam, now you're making me uncomfortable. I just asked you what you were going to do with yourself after you're through school."

"One more thing, honey, and then I'll shut up. I'm afraid that if I turn into a nice steady insurance agent or something, I'll stick it out for fifteen years or so and then blow my top. Either that or pop off from a heart attack, or nurse an ulcer, and don't tell me all the heart jobs and ulcer jobs don't come from that sort of tension you get when you don't like your work."

"Fletch loves his work. I told you that."

"I wasn't talking about your Fletch. I was talking about me. You know, I think I'll be a soldier of fortune. I'll be a general in some banana republic and take the midnight plane out with the Presidente's daughter and the Inca emeralds. Then I'll turn up in Persia, only I guess they don't call it that any more, and I'll sell the Presidente's daughter to some roving Bedouin tribe and as they ride off on their camels into the sunset, I'll chuckle heartily. Later the Presidente's daughter will turn up in a Paul Bowles novel, and a 20th Century-Fox agent will find her and give her a screen contract, and I'll turn up again to collect the usual agent's commission. You know, a guy could make a career out of just turning up at the dramatic moment. I'll be the poor girl's Errol Flynn." He stood up quickly, hooked his toes over the edge of the dock, gave her a broad wink, and went off in a flat racing dive.

She sat and watched him swim out, thankful that her sense of proportion had returned. He was a spectacular male, but basically just a kid, and of no danger to her. He

had stirred her physically, but that was the end of it. T
lake was utterly still in the afternoon heat. She sat cros
legged, her elbows on her knees, chin on her hands, watc
ing him swim out. Darn him. First he makes i
uncomfortable one way and then another way. Fletch
happy. He gets moody. That's just the way he is. May
he's seemed a little further away this year, but it's probab
the office. He's good at his job and he knows it. He's not
crusader, for goodness sake. And neither is Sam Rice. Sa
is just in a phase. It's part of growing up. God, I was goi
to be Florence Nightingale, junior. A dim ward, and n
rustling in starch, and laying my cool hand on the fever
brows of the wounded, while I could hear cannon in th
distance. Kid stuff. Dreams. Self-dramatization. You g
over that. I got over that dream fast the time I went wi
Daddy when he didn't want me to go. That boy, screami
and screaming, and oh the blood and the smell. I'm where
belong. Wife and mother. It sounds so dull when you fi
out a form and have to write housewife. But it's good. Th
kids and the love and the fun. It's what you're after. A l
of people miss. We didn't. Those Corbans. They misse
You can see it. Contempt when she looks at him. Sh
doesn't know how much it shows. Or maybe she doesn
care. Those hills are the right misty blue. That's what
wanted, but when I got the drapes home they were just to
damn blue. They've faded and maybe they'll fade more an
be right for the room. Fletch, we're being childish toda
Our day to be childish. Our year, maybe, to have a littl
trouble. Like that second year we were married. And th
year after the war when he was so irritable. Trouble end
and we're always closer. God, if this heat doesn't end m
golf is going to be shot. The kids should be back by now
Dink will get tennis at the camp. She needs work on he
backhand. She could be good, really good, starting so early
I know she lets Judge beat her every once in a while. Is h
going to swim all the way across the lake? No, he's floatin
out there. I'm baked. I'll swim out to him. It doesn't mea
anything now and he knows it. We're friends now. A gri
like a little kid, and then all of a sudden so serious. He'
quick. He picks things up. I wonder what sort of family h
came from.

She dived from the dock and slanted up through the green water, and swam out toward Sam Rice, swam with a slow effortless crawl, gliding like an otter through the clear blue water of Lake Vernon.

Chapter Nine

When the moon came up out of the east, full and golden as a lantern, it turned the last of the lingering grey dusk to night. Only a few coals were left to glow in the grey bed of ash in the outdoor fireplace. Someone far down the lake was singing. Jane sat alone on the dock, dangling her legs, huddled and miserable. Hank was in his usual form, loud and lewd by turns. She could not hear some whispered comment he made, but she heard Dolly and Martha's scandalized laughter.

Martha came down the dock and squatted beside her. "I got hold of Hud all right. Dolly and Hank say there's plenty of room. And Hank says that Fletch must be coming out or he would have phoned. So let's do this. It's after nine and the kids are bushed, so let's drop them in the sack. If Fletch gets here too late, your kids can stay overnight and Hud and I will bring them down in time tomorrow. We have to be at your place around three, so we'll drop them off on our way home to change, say about one thirty or two. Of course, if Fletch gets here before they cork off, you can take them back with you. But there is plenty of room."

Jane stood up. "Okay, Martha. Let's put them to bed. Where are they going to be?"

"Girls in the bunk room and boys upstairs. Your glass empty? So's mine. Let's take a break for a refill."

They walked up by the big picnic table beside the house and Hank, under the light of the yellow mosquito bulb, jovially mixed them drinks. Every once in a while Jane would listen for the sound of the car, for the sound of Fletch's arrival. She knew she had drunk more than usual, had drunk enough to, under normal circumstances, give her an infuriating attack of giggles. But Fletch's continued lateness left her with a hard core of sobriety. All the drinks had done was to make her lips feel numbed, her legs a bit uncertain.

She helped Martha round up the children and then, with dire threats about going to sleep and not yammering all night, they got them assorted in the proper beds with a single blanket apiece and another handy, and turned out the lights. As they left they could hear the whispering start.

Jane stood out in the night and drained the glass. Ice clinked against her teeth. She was still in her swim suit. The night breeze was turning a bit chill. She shuddered violently.

Steve Lincoln came over to her, looming wide in the night. "Jane, we're trying to drum up some business. They got a little band in the pavilion at the end of the lake. Come on."

"Thanks, Steve, but I don't think . . ."

"Break down," Sam said, close beside her, startling her. He moved like a big cat. "I square dance like a fool. While I was learning I used to throw my women right through the side of the hall."

"No thanks, Sam. I'm expecting Fletch any minute. I want to be here."

"Well . . . okay. Sorry," Steve said and they went away into the night. She heard their low voices and then they laughed together. Jane made herself a fresh drink and took it out to the end of the dock. She tensed as she heard a car motor, and then realized that it was the young people leaving for the dance. She sat on the dock again and Hank came down a bit later to lower himself awkwardly beside her.

He said, "It is one damn beautiful night, isn't it? I love this place."

"It's pretty here, Hank."

"Why so sad, sugar? Tell old Hank all your troubles."

"Don't paw me, for God's sake!"

"Well, I'm certainly sorry," he said with drunken dignity. "I really am. I had no idea that a little gesshure of affection . . ."

107

He started to get up and she turned and put her hand on his shoulder and forced him down. "I'm sorry, Hank. I didn't mean to snap. I'm just all . . ." She stopped, unhappily aware that she was very close to tears, and that if she started it would turn out to be a sodden crying jag.

"I accept your aplo . . . apology," Hank said stiffly. "See what you mean. Husbands are bad things. Give you a rough time. Ask old Dolly. She's been over the jumps. Man . . . a man gets a little restless. Artificial situation. Know what I mean?"

"Not exactly. What's artificial?"

"The whole thing, baby. Woman's monogamous, man is polygamous. Got to bust out every once in a while. Hey! You ever see a pasture where they got as many bulls as they have cows?" He gave a hard grunt of laughter and smacked her on the back. It stung and it nearly knocked her off the dock.

"Hey, take it easy!"

"Me and Dolly, we been married a long time. To us you two are just . . . just a pair of kids. We both love you both. I guess you know that, huh? We just love you both like the dickens. And I'm not being sloppy either. Finest pair of young people in Minidoka, bar none. Swell kids. What was I saying?"

"About man being polygamous, I think."

"Well, baby, you just use your head. That's all you got to do. Use your head. If ole Fletch takes off, you just remember it's man's nature, that's all. He'll come back like a kid been in the jam. Women make a mistake. Toss the old bastard out for good. That's no way to do. Spoils everything. Little piece of tail isn't that important. Sure, make him suffer a little, but don't bust up the happy home. Dolly tossed me out once. Right in the winter, by God. Got drunk for a week. Came around and it was snowing and blowing and she wouldn't let me in. Nossir. Through for keeps. All on account of a little tramp who got ideas and called her up. I'm there in the snow and the cold and I'm crying. Me, crying. And I'm tight, see. I had to go, so I go over to a big snowdrift, and while I'm going, I write in the snow, you know what I mean. Hank loves Dolly, I write. Crooked letters, but you could read it. She turns on the porch light and comes out to see what the hell I'm doing. Had the damnedest case of hysterics you ever saw, and pretty soon I'm inside and we're hanging onto each other and both crying. Nossir, busting up a home is bad business."

Jane said, "I don't want to seem dull, but why the lecture? Just because Fletch happens to be late. Do you happen to think he's been running around?"

"Me? I don't know a thing. I was saying to Dolly how we love you kids. And you're glooming around, so I guess that maybe that's what it is, him not being here and all."

She patted his hand and made her voice bright. "Now don't worry about us, Hank. We're fine. He's just late and I know he couldn't help it, and I'm gloomy because it's Saturday night and I miss him. That's all, really."

"Well, I'm sure glad about that, baby. You two never been mixed up in all that yak yak down in the city. Nice clean kids. Hey, knock that off and I'll build you a good one. Peace offering." He reached out and snapped the rim of her glass. It rang sweetly. "Hear that? Dolly bought 'em. Danish or something. Four bucks a copy and we bought two dozen and I think we got seven left."

She knew she should not have another, but alcohol had wedged caution down into a part of her mind where she could ignore it.

"Sure, Hank," she said. She finished her drink and handed him the glass. He trudged off. Jane turned and looked up toward the camp. The lights were on and through the window she could see Dolly and Martha just beginning one of their interminable variations of Canasta. She shivered again, reached and found a towel and draped it around her bare shoulders.

Hank called her and she went up to the table. He said, 'B'er mix your own, honey. Hit me allofa su'n. Drink'n all day See'f I can make that porch swing. Love you kids. Really do."

He lumbered away. She heard his feet fumbling on the steps, heard the porch creak, and then heard the springs and chains as he stretched out on the swing. It thumped once against the wall and creaked softly and then was still. She made a stiffer drink than before, telling herself that it would last longer. She went back down to the dock and lay flat on her back and put the towel over her. The dock seemed to sway under her. The stars circled and she shut her eyes hard and opened them and squinted, trying to make them stop moving. They would stop and then begin to move again. She rolled over onto her stomach, awkwardly placed the towel across her bare back. Drunker than a skunk. Puh-lastered, Janey. All your fault, Fletch. Anything I do, it's your fault, all of it. Every bit of it. Might as well do a good job of it, now I'm started.

She sat up and drank the stiff drink down without a pause. She tried to throw the ice out of the glass, but the glass slipped out of her fingers. It made a funny thumping sound and she puzzled about the sound until she had to crawl over on her hands and knees and look down off the dock at the waterline. Though it was in the velvet shadow of the dock, she could see that the glass had hit the yellow rubber life raft that the children had been playing with. It was drawn up on shore.

"Good thing," she said aloud. "Four dollar glass. Ought to have a life raft around every time you drop a glass."

"Be pretty handy wouldn't it?" a deep voice said.

She sat back on her haunches and peered up at him. "Sam! Gee, I thought for a minute there it was going to be Fletch. Everybody came back from the dance, huh?"

"I didn't go. Changed my mind at the last minute. Darling, what's wrong with you?" He sat on his heels beside her and took her hand.

She giggled. "Rebellious wife. Got myself stinky. Serve'm right. Hank says men're polygamous. That right, Sam Rice? How'd you get a name like Rice? Sea food and rice is very nice."

He stroked her hand. "Poor baby. He's giving you a bad time, isn't he?"

It was comforting to have somebody stroke her hand and murmur to her in such a nice soft deep masculine voice. She knew that it was just a little bit too pleasant, but she pushed that thought away from her. "Cute Sam Rice. Oh, God, I think I'm going to throw up."

"I know what will fix it."

"Don't want to fix it. Want to throw up and stop spin-

110

ning. You're spinning and the dock is spinning and all the stars are going around. See?"

"We'll stop all that spinning," he said in that nice low voice that made the back of her neck feel furry. He dropped easily off the dock to stand in the water. He reached his arms up to her. "Sit on the edge, honey, and I'll lift you down."

"Why?"

"We'll take a little moonlight swim, that's all. Clear out the cobwebs."

"You promise things will stop spinning, honey? I don't call you honey. I call Fletch honey and you're not Fletch."

"If Fletch was here he'd take you swimming."

"Really? Would he?"

"Of course he would."

"Okay then. Catch. I'm heavy as lead, Fletch says. Solid as a rock."

He lifted her down. "Like feathers. Come on now. Hold onto my hand. We'll wade out."

"Gee the water feels warm."

"That's because the air is cold," he said patiently.

They waded out. Water was a warmth moving up her thighs. She pulled her hand free and lunged forward. She could not time her stroke properly, and she wallowed and splashed and took in a mouthful of lake water. She stopped and coughed, treading water.

"You okay?" he asked.

"It's wonnerful. Really."

She tried again, counting grimly to herself until her stroke seemed to adjust itself and she began to slide through the water properly. Sam came up beside her and she said, "Race you, sonny." She kicked off before he could say yes or no, driving hard toward the center of the lake. Water flashed white in the moonlight. She saw him out of the corner of her eye as she breathed, and she drove herself to greater effort.

Suddenly, as she reached forward, his hand closed on her wrist. "No fair," she sputtered.

"I can't race you, darling. You're making a big circle."

She stared at him. She was winded. Suddenly swimming in a circle was the funniest thing in the world. She guffawed and gasped and laughed until her stomach hurt, laughed there in the moonlight until again she gulped water and coughed it out.

"Better float before you drown yourself, Janey."

"Janey. I haven't been called that since I was a kid." She rolled onto her back, lazing on the warm water, fluttering her feet each time her legs started to sink. Sam floated beside her.

"How are the stars doing, Janey?"

"They're standing still like good little stars. My, it's a lot better."

"Dr. Rice took care of you." He moved closer and slid his arm under her neck. She was too happy and warm to object. Sam was a nice boy. It was moonlight. And it would be just too darn stuffy to get stuffy out in the middle of a lake.

"Say," she heard herself say, "I haven't been called Janey since I was a kid. And I haven't been kissed under water since I was thirteen."

"Then take a deep breath."

She laughed and turned toward him in the water and his arms were around her tightly and his lips were on hers and he held her close and they drifted under water, turning slowly, bobbing up again. She was facing him and she laughed, leaning back, her arms around his neck, laughed up at the stars and the moon, and felt his hands slide down to her waist. And he pulled her close again and they kissed and his hands were learning her body, and she laughed again and heard the lost shrillness in her own voice. And somehow he had gotten the top of her suit down around her waist, and she was turned so that she floated again, and he was beside her. She looked down and saw the fullness and the startling untanned whiteness of her breasts, and saw his huge brown hand on her right breast, and she turned and made a crazy whimpering sound as she looked into his face that was like brown stone in the moonlight, feeling his other hand working gently as it peeled the tight suit down, pulling it off over her unresisting feet so that she floated there, naked in the moonlight, her body bone-white where the sun had not touched it, and whimpering again as he turned her, and again the kiss, and the water

112

folding them under, and the hardness of him against her, and the craziness of the moonlight. And he held her and she felt the long tug of his muscles as he swam slowly toward shore, towing her, his hands on her, touching, moving on her, keeping her in that warm whimpering helplessness. And she saw the edge of the dock against the sky. He stood up, lifting her in his arms, and she held tight, holding her face against him to keep the world from seeing her. He walked with the water whispering around his legs, then slowly set her down in the velvet shadows, laid her down in the rubber raft, and she kept her eyes tight shut so that no one could see. And he was over her with his breathing hard against her cheek. She held him and her hands slid up across the broad hard shoulders and the neck and touched, then, the wet stubble of the cropped haircut, and it was wrong because her hands, doing that, always touched the softer hair of Fletcher. Fright and realization exploded in her and she suddenly writhed hard, twisting and writhing to get away from sudden incredible nightmare.

They fought almost without sound in the black dock shadow, and he was frighteningly strong. He lay pinning her down with his long hard body. She had fought this way in dreams. He caught her right wrist and pinned it down on her left side, her own arm across her chest helping to hold her down. Her left hand touched coolness and her fingers closed on it and she knew it was the glass that had slipped from her hand. She held it like the haft of a knife and hammered the solid base against the side of his head, expecting him to go slack, as she had hit him as hard as she could. He grunted and groped for her hand. She hit him again and as she tried to strike the third time, he found her wrist and his fingers slid down to the glass and twisted it out of her hand and threw it aside. She could not scream out in her fear and terror. She felt as if her throat had closed. She hit him weakly with her left fist and he caught her hand again and pinned it and then he moved upward a bit and she tried to twist out from under him, but she was caught there motionless in the deep shock of invasion.

She lay with the slow tears squeezing through the lids of

her closed eyes. And she felt as though she were apart from herself, as though she had died and her soul was high in the night over the dock, looking down with cold detachment, so that it could see the lighted windows of the camp, the stringy man who snored on the porch swing, see into the black dockside shadow where a woman lay impaled in traditional sacrifice, accepting in numbed slackness.

She lay there making no sound while he was heavy against her, his breathing slowing and deepening. She kept her eyes shut and he went away from her. The rubber raft shifted a bit as he got to his feet. She turned half onto her side, knees bent and pressed close together. She opened her eyes and saw him. Just his head and shoulders were in the bright moonlight and his back was to her, the black shadow making a diagonal line across it. He bent over and he was invisible, just something moving in the darkness. He straightened up again, a bit unsteadily, and she realized he had pulled on his swimming trunks. He put his hands on the edge of the dock, leaped lightly up, turning to sit on the edge of the dock, facing her. His head and torso were a silhouette blocking the stars. The moon made a faint highlight on the top of a hard thigh. She watched him and saw him look and lean back and find cigarettes. He lit one and the match flame shook as he held it to the end of the cigarette. He tossed it toward the water and the night was so still that she heard the faint hiss of it striking the water. She did not want to move or speak ever again. Her mind would move to fit itself around the enormity of what had happened, and then slide uneasily back into the nothingness of just lying there.

"Better put your suit on," he said in a low casual tone. His voice had a surprising flatness. "It's by your feet."

She said, almost wonderingly, "Why . . . why did you keep on when you knew I . . . when you knew I didn't want you to?"

"You were asking for it, honey. Don't try to kid me and don't try to kid yourself. If you had objections, you should have kept your suit on."

"Oh, God," she said softly. "God!"

"Don't hoke it up. It isn't the end of the world. Put on your suit, will you?"

She sat up slowly. Her body felt pulped and bruised. She reached down in the darkness and searched until she touched her wet suit. It was inside out and she straightened it slowly and found the front and got it over her feet and pulled it up her legs. She lay back and arched her body and pulled it over her hips.

The top edge of the strapless suit was elasticized. She stood up slowly, pulled it up over her breasts. It fit snugly.

He was fingering the right side of his head. He said, "I'm beginning to get a bitch of a headache." His tone was petulant, abused.

"Sam . . . all that talk this afternoon. The way you talked to me. I thought you were . . ."

"Were what? Setting you up, maybe? I don't know. For God's sake, let's drop the subject. Maybe it was a mistake. You weren't what I'd call co-operating, anyway. Keep up this line of chatter and I'll be curling the ends of my mustache and sneering. What the hell got us onto this Victorian scenario anyway? You trying to make a big deal out of this or something? Relax, even if you couldn't enjoy it."

"But I . . ." She had to explain to him, to let him know, somehow, that it was more than that to her. Much more. And before she could find the words, the nausea came again, and the stars wheeled. She turned blindly toward the water and stumbled on the rounded edge of the inflated raft and went down heavily onto her hands and knees in the shallow water.

She was blind sick. Wrenchingly. Gasping for air. And she was aware that he was beside her, that he held her head, dispassionately helpful. When it was over he lifted her and made her sit on the bulbous rim of the raft. He got a towel and dipped it in the lake and wiped her face with a rough tenderness. She sat huddled and miserable and began to cry, struggling to cry silently, yet unable to keep from articulating her sobs. Through her tears she could sense his irritation and frustration. He put his arm around her and she dug her head into his shoulder and, after long minutes, brought the tears under control. The infrequent sobs sounded like hiccups. She found a clean part of the towel and dipped it in the lake water and bathed her eyes.

"That," he said, "I guess you didn't fake. Dammit, Janey, what gives with you?"

"I . . . don't know. I just don't know what I'll say or do. I can't face Fletcher. He'll sense it. Everything was so . . . g-good between us and . . ."

"Don't start again, for God's sake. Look, honey, I'm beginning to get a hint of what the hell you're talking about. Haven't you ever cheated before?"

"Nobody ever had me before. Except Fletch. Nobody."

He was silent for some seconds and then he said, "Sweet Jesus!" His voice was full of awe. "I thought you were . . . well, just trying to give that impression. You know. A standard line. Not at all unusual."

She was quite suddenly aware that his arm was still around her shoulders, that he was sitting there, holding her calmly, twisting words around, turning it inside out so that it was somehow going to end up all her fault, her fault entirely.

She twisted away from him, hating him with a sudden frightful violence. "You . . . you filthy bastard!" she said. Her voice broke.

"Now wait a minute! Ease up. So I figured you wrong. God . . . I mean how would I figure you? That suit came off without a murmur."

"You knew I was drunk. You knew just what to do, didn't you? You knew exactly how to do it, too. Before I knew what was happening. That's the way you did it. It was filthy. It's rape, that's what it is."

He stood up slowly. His voice was angry. "Okay. Call the cops. Dear Officer. Gee, I was stupid. I took off her suit and I was so stupid I thought she was willing. How did I know she was so drunk she thought it was her old mammy undressing her for bed?"

"I fought. I hit you. You can't deny that."

"I wouldn't want to deny that, dearie. Lumps I got."

"You did it to me, and you've spoiled everything for me," she said, trying to hurt him, and yet make him understand at the same time.

116

"Come sit on the end of the dock and have one of the last two cigarettes and cool off, for God's sake."

"I don't want to be anywhere near you. Just looking at you makes me want to be sick again. You're so darn smart. What did your friend call you? Wolf, wasn't it? Sure, you know everything about women. Why did you think I was hitting you? Sadistic pleasure?"

"Come on and sit on the dock."

"Don't touch me. I can get up myself." They walked out to the end of the dock. She accepted one of the cigarettes.

He sat down too close to her and she moved away. He said, "To answer your question, lady, by the time you started clubbing me with that glass, I was in a state of mind where you might just as well have been using a handful of feathers."

"Then it *was* your fault."

"Janey, look."

"Don't call me Janey."

"Mrs. Wyant, then. Look. It happened. It's done. I believe what you say . . ."

"Oh, thanks!"

"I believe what you say, and if it's any use to you, I'm sorry it happened. But all this yakking about whose fault it is isn't going to help you."

"What do you mean, help me?"

"Are you going to run to your husband yelling rape? So this is the first time you ever cheated."

"The first and the last."

"Okay, okay. The point is, you're making too much of a whing-ding out of it just because it is the first. I'm looking at you. You don't look any different. It doesn't show. Don't be so stupid and try any dramatic confessions or accusations. He'll hate you either way. Just keep your very pretty mouth shut and forget it."

"You can forget things like this because they don't mean anything to you. With you it's like . . . shaking hands. You can't understand how much it means to me, how much it ruins everything, because you're too damn coarse and callous to understand."

"So maybe I feel some responsibility. So maybe I want to see you get out of this without taking a beating. Go off half-cocked and it'll blow your happy home all to hell, and once you stop trying to kick me around, you'll know I'm right."

"What am I going to do?" she said in a barely audible tone.

"I told you. Just shut up about it. Your conscience shouldn't hurt any. Lord, you were less co-operative than anything I ever saw in my life. It doesn't show on you any more than it does on those gals who take their fun on the side as a regular diet."

"If I had a gun in my hand, I'd kill you. I mean it."

"I'm glad you haven't, because you probably would, and all my friends tell me I'm a nice guy, so it would be a tragic loss to the world at large. And I'll go along with your hating my guts as long as we both shall live. It doesn't rankle. I certainly will not talk. You can count on that. I learned that early. If I don't talk and you don't talk, what proof is there? I ask you? If you can't carry it off all the way and he gets a little suspicious, deny everything until hell freezes over."

"Do . . . you really think I can get away with it?"

"Jane, you're a backward type. Good Lord, what kind of a world have you grown up in? And you *look* so sophisticated. That's what kills me."

"I . . . wish I looked like a mud fence so you'd never noticed me. I wish there was a clock I could turn back to before it happened. Even if I do get away with it, nothing will ever really be the same again. Not really."

"How middle-class can morality get?"

"Smart talk. Words. What have you got to offer a wife? And what will she give you? Like shaking hands. That's what it is with you kids. God, how I wish you were dead!"

"I'm just a handy object to hate. That's fine with me. Go right ahead. Blame me all the way down the line. But for your own sake, never mention this to anyone. Understand? No dear friends. They all talk, sooner or later."

In the stillness she heard the thud of a car door behind the camp and her heart stopped.

"That's . . . that's Fletch, Sam. He came too . . . soon. I'm not ready to face him."

"Stand up and face the moonlight. Let me get a look at you."

"You've got no reason to . . ."

"I'll help you carry it off. I'll do what I can. Maybe I owe you that and maybe I don't. But I don't want your loving husband hunting me with buckshot either."

"I'm not going to thank you, because all this is your fault."

"Sure, sure. I think the eyes are a little red. Swimming could do that. Stay out of strong lights. Now I'll be clean-cut American youth in action. Loaded with respect and veneration. Come on. You're fine. I'm leaving here in another week and you won't ever have to see me again. That make you happy?"

"Extremely."

"Stay mad at me and maybe you'll handle the husband problem better."

She followed him along the dock toward the shore. Her body felt sore and used. She thought of Judge and Dink, asleep not over a hundred feet from where it had happened. She looked at the slant of moonlight on Sam's brown powerful shoulders, and she relived the terror of the fight and then the hopelessness of submission. He had done it. He had ruined every damn thing in the whole world. He had made her feel rotten inside, filthy-sick.

She dreaded the moment when she would have to look into Fletcher's eyes, and she wished that this dark walk toward the camp would last forever, even if it did mean spending forever in the company of this young, arrogant, brutal stud.

Hank still snored on the swing. She saw, through the windows, Dolly and Martha at the card table, smiling up at Fletch. He stood looking down at them, and he seemed to be a bit rumpled, a bit pale, his expression showing uncertainty.

Chapter Ten

The usher had been concerned about him and had awakened him in the dark movie to find out if he was ill. It had taken him a long embarrassing few moments to realize where he was. He reassured the usher. Liquor was a stale taste in his mouth. Both legs had gone to sleep. On the colored screen an army with banners was on the march, and the sound track was brassy and triumphant. He worked his legs and feet and felt the slow electric prickle of returning circulation. He walked heavily out through the lobby. The street shocked him. It was full night. A thick, hot summer Saturday night, with the young girls parading in their thin dresses. Sleep had left him with a dazed, far-away feeling. He could not shut his hands tightly enough.

He looked at the clock in the ticket booth, above the head of a girl with hair the color of new pennies. It was ten minutes of ten. No small wonder that the usher had awakened him. He had gone in sometime before four. His big body was cramped. His shoulders ached and his hips felt as if he had been beaten.

He was forced to grin wryly at himself. Lord, Jane would be livid with rage. There was no time to go home and freshen up. His car was parked up beyond the Downtown Club. The night had brought no coolness to the city. Sweat pasted his shirt to his back and he took his jacket off as he walked, pausing outside the club to slip into it again. He went to the men's room, stripped to his waist, used one of the clean hand towels to sponge his body. The cool water against his face helped quite a bit. He dampened his dark hair, combed it down with his fingers. His lightweight suit was badly wrinkled from the long sleep in the movie.

Back in the lobby he debated calling the Dimbrough number at the lake, then decided against it. He'd said he'd call if he wasn't coming, so he would be expected. But too late to get one of Hank's steaks. According to Hank's immutable routine, he would be passed out by now. As he got in the car he remembered a drive-in on the way up to the lake, one that stayed open until after midnight. Now that sleep was out of his system, he felt hungry.

Traffic was much lighter than he had anticipated. He was able to make fair time. There were three other cars at the drive-in. There was a big speaker which blasted juke box music out across the parking area. A girl in slacks took his order for hamburg, milk shake and cigarettes. Her face had a grey tired look in the floodlights, and she walked heavily on her heels as she went back to put in the order, her buttocks jouncing in the tight slacks, her shoulders slumped.

When the hamburg came at long last, it was lukewarm. The milk shake had the consistency of mud. He ate too quickly, turned on his lights. When the girl did not come, he blatted the car horn in irritation. She walked out looking angry, and snatched the tray off the car, turning it so she could see the amount of the tip. She mumbled thanks and he drove on, grateful as the cooler air came into the heated car as the road climbed.

The food he had gulped sat in a greasy wad in his middle. It now seemed extraordinarily silly to have stayed in Minidoka when he could have been up at the lake. The half-quarrel seemed banal and pointless. A Saturday shot completely to hell. Well, part of it was the damn miserable heat. Made people jump at each other's throats. Jane didn't deserve that kind of treatment. And, the way it had come out, he had merely punished himself. She'd had a fine cool day at the lake with the kids. He drove, worried about how she'd greet him. If it was with that impassive, cool politeness, he would be in for a bad time. Outright indignation would be better. Something dark and furry streaked across the road, and he wrenched the wheel and missed it and cursed heartily.

When he thought he should start looking for the Lake Vernon turnoff, he saw it flash by. He went up the road, turned around in a farm drive and came back. His headlights illuminated the long tunnel of the dirt road under the overhanging trees. The springs rocked the car over lumps in the road. He found the Dimbrough sign and turned down their drive toward the lake shore. He came around the last bend and his headlights swept across the back of the camp. He turned off the lights and motor and got out and chunked the door shut. The lake breeze felt good as it touched his face. There was a dim light in the back entryway. He went in and down the short hall to the cluttered kitchen and through into the living room. Dolly and Martha were in the middle of one of their viciously competitive card games.

"Who pays?" he asked.

Dolly looked up from her hand. "Well, so it came at last! Greetings, stranger. That rattling sound you hear is Hank sleeping it off in the moonlight. Had anything to eat, Fletch?"

"Yes, thanks. Where's Hud, Martha?"

"He's coming out in the morning to get me, plus the kids, yours and mine. They're all bedded down."

"Isn't that kind of a nuisance, Dolly?" Fletcher asked.

"No. They're good kids. Honey, you have a familiar guilty look. You're about to catch hell from your bride."

"I thought so. Couldn't be helped though. Call of duty. Where is she?"

"Out swimming in the moonlight with a very attractive young man, and it serves you right, my friend."

The screen door opened and Jane came in wearing a swim suit he hadn't seen on her before. Her blonde hair had been wet and it was beginning to dry. The damp suit displayed every line of her body, just a bit too flamboyantly, Fletcher decided. A very big husky young man followed her in. A young man with a pleasant open face, a brown butch haircut, a relaxed manner. Fletcher typed him at once as both pleasant and able. A good kid to hire. Sales end, or public relations. But most of his attention was on Jane, trying to find out how she was going to react. He saw at once that she had been crying, and that made him feel guilty for having thought of her day at the lake as being pleasant. She was almost expressionless, and she seemed to be walking with an uncertain shyness. He guessed that it was the suit that bothered her. And no wonder.

"Hi, Fletch darling," she said. Her voice puzzled him. It sounded both blithe and uncertain, and did not match the woodenness of her expression.

"Sorry it took me so long to finish up, honey," he said, casually. He put his hand on her shoulder, bent and kissed her cool lips lightly. He felt her tremble. It probably was a bit cool out there in the night wind in a suit that skimpy.

"Fletch, this is Sam Rice. He's a friend of Dick's. You know, Hank's nephew."

"Glad to meet you, sir," the boy said. His grip was strong, and he had a nice manner. Not too deferential, and yet respectful. "Mrs. Wyant is quite a swimmer."

"I gave up racing her a long time ago."

"Sam is awfully good on the water skis, darling," Jane said quickly. "We had a contest and it was a tie."

Fletcher still couldn't figure out how she was going to react when they were alone. She seemed to be wearing her company manners. He looked over at the table and thought Martha was looking at Jane a bit oddly. Probably getting catty ideas about Jane out swimming in the moonlight with this boy, he thought.

"What are the plans, Jane? Do we wake up the kids and head for home?"

"Now, Fletcher Wyant, you let those children sleep," Dolly ordered. "They're no trouble at all, and Hud and Martha will return them safely tomorrow, you hear?"

Jane said, "I . . . I guess that will be all right, Fletch. It's awfully nice of you, Dolly."

"Nonsense! Martha, are you going to take a card, or are you going to sit there like a bump on a log? Make yourself a drink, Fletch."

"It's pretty late. I think we ought to head back. You better change, Jane."

"All right. My play suit is still out on the line, I guess." She went off quickly.

The card game continued. Fletcher stood and chatted

with Sam Rice. "Didn't you get an All-American mention last fall, Sam?"

"Just one little one. The competition was rough."

"I thought I heard the name before."

"I'm up here with Steve Lincoln. He made most of the lists."

"Oh sure! Defensive guard. Is he around?"

"No, he went up to the dance with Dick and Dick's girl. I was going to go, but I thought I'd rather stay and swim with your wife."

"Glad you did. She doesn't like cards, and Hank doesn't sound like he'd be much company tonight. I'm grateful to you for keeping Jane entertained, Sam."

"It was a pleasure, sir. She's a lot of fun."

Jane came back into the room with her beach bag in her hand. She wore the white play suit and her sandals.

Dolly said, "Say, you'll be cold riding in that skimpy thing. I'll get you something to put on." She started to get up.

"No, really, Dolly. I'll be all right. We have a robe in the back end I can put around my shoulders if I get cold. And thanks for taking the kids. And thank you, Martha, for driving me up. See you tomorrow, hey? Why don't you and Hank come down, Dolly?"

"I couldn't drag Hank away from here on a Sunday. And somebody always shows up. Thanks anyway, dear."

Fletch shook hands with Sam and, as he was saying good night to the women, he heard Jane say, "And thank you, Sam. I hope . . . we'll see you again sometime."

"I hope so too, Jane. Good night."

Dolly was melding furiously as they walked out, and Sam was moving a chair over by the table. They let themselves out the back door and got into the car. Fletch backed it around in a quarter circle and then headed up the narrow drive in low. She sat far over on her side of the seat and she did not speak. He did not say anything until he turned out onto the paved road, headed south.

"Jane, I guess I was a plain damn fool today."

"Yes?"

"I didn't have to go to the office. I just woke up grouchy. I snapped at the kids and snapped at you, and I'm sorry.

Then I was just too damn stubborn to drive up here after I got your note."

"What did you do?"

"This sounds silly. I went to the Downtown Club. It was dead. I had lunch there, a late lunch, and then had a drink, and had another drink in a dive, and went to an air-conditioned movie. I was pooped from not sleeping last night. So I fell asleep in the movie and slept in that damn tight little seat for about six hours. I've never done anything like that before in my life. The usher woke me up. He thought I was sick or dead."

"You . . . you were *asleep* . . . in a *movie?*"

"Yes, dammit," he said miserably, yet feeling the pleasant release of confession.

She made no sound. He glanced over at her, but he could not see her face. Suddenly she made a small strangled sound, and another. And she began to laugh, gaspingly. He laughed with her and then stopped as he became aware that she had become hysterical.

"Jane!" he said sharply. "Jane! Cut it out!"

She got worse. He swung onto the shoulder and stopped the car and set the brake. He took her shoulders and she was limp and helpless, making the great raw sounds of tears and laughter. He shook her hard and she did not stop. He held her and, measuring carefully, slapped her hard. The sound stopped abruptly. She lay forward, her head on her knees, crying softly.

"What in the world did that?" he demanded.

"I . . . don't know."

"Lord, I haven't seen you like that in years. What happened back there today, anyway?"

"Nothing, Fletch. Nothing at all. It's just . . . I was miserable. And imagining you doing . . . all sorts of things. But . . . asleep in a movie!" She made another harsh sound.

"Watch it! Don't get going again."

"I'm . . . going to be all right now."

"Shall I start the car?"

"Please." She opened the glove compartment, dug around for Kleenex. She blew her nose lustily.

"You got pretty emotional about all this," he said stiffly.

"It always upsets me when we have a . . . misunderstanding. You know that."

"Not this much, honey."

"Oh, I guess it was the heat and all, and working too hard yesterday, and that gruesome evening last night. This sort of . . . topped it all off."

"But the hollering hysterics. That rattled me. I thought you'd had a fight or something back there. All I could think of was that Hank had gotten out of line or something."

"No. He wasn't any more sneaky than usual. I guess that . . . the time of the month has something to do with it."

"Oh."

She blew her nose again. She moved over close to him, almost shyly, it seemed to him. He reached down and patted her bare knee. "We're okay now?" he asked.

"Sure, darling, Everything is fine."

"You're not sore?"

"No, darling. Not the least bit."

"I think you mean that," he said wonderingly.

"Am I usually so nasty about something like this?"

"No . . . but . . ."

"Hush then," she said.

The miles went by, the warm night flowing by the car windows and the city pink on the sky ahead.

"That Rice boy seems like a pleasant sort."

"I suppose he's all right."

"Didn't you like him?"

"Yes, I guess so. But he is . . . a boy. A sort of a mixed-up boy, I guess."

"In what way?"

"Oh, we were talking on the dock this afternoon. He doesn't know what he wants to do with his life. You know what I mean. Sort of restless and discontented. I guess he'll settle down someday."

"Nearly everybody does. It isn't such a bad fate, is it, darling?"

"No."

As he turned into their street she said suddenly, surprisingly, after a long silence, "I love you, you know. I love you very much, Fletch."

"Well! What brought that on?"

Her laugh sounded a bit nervous. "A statement of fact, I guess. It just seemed like a good time to say it, that's all."

"I give you a bad time, and still you say that out of a clear sky. Lady, your deep and sincere emotion is reciprocated in toto."

As he undressed, he was puzzled about her. She was acting quite strange. He tried to relate it back to something that could have happened at the lake, but that didn't make much sense. He guessed that it was due to the quarrel the night before. Things had gone bad too quickly after a quarrel. And then, as she said, the moon was also involved. A funny kid sometimes. Think you have her cased, and she comes up with a brand-new reaction. What did the man say? Infinite variety. He was about right. Damn hot in this bedroom. Open more windows. In spite of that sleep, I'm still bushed. And she looks weary. Too weary, maybe. And yet I want her. In a funny way. As though she was a stranger, almost. A stranger I saw walking into the Dimbrough's camp in that skimpy suit, and that tall kid behind her, with the pair of them looking darn near the same age.

He was in bed first and she came in the darkness and sat shyly on the edge of his bed, half facing him. He took her hand and felt her tremble. For some zany reason she seemed to be acting shy as a bride. Her shyness made him more gentle with her than usual. He was gentle with her and it took her much longer than usual to achieve her fulfillment, and when it happened, it was a shy and gentle fury with her. Then she wept almost silently and he did not know why, and did not want to ask. He held her close and kissed her salt eyes and murmured to her, comforting sounds with few words. He held her until she slept, and after she was asleep she sobbed twice more and once seemed to strike out with her hand. As he did not want to disturb her he stood up slowly, spread the light sheet over her, walked around and got into her bed. She had been as passive and humbly eager as in the very first months of their marriage. He lay in the darkness wondering about it, wondering about her. And he felt sleep coming for him, coming like a warm tide that started at his toes. He welcomed it and knew, from his feeling of utter relaxation, that the sleep would be good, and deep, and healing.

Chapter Eleven

Jane's sleep was so deep that when she slowly came awake on Sunday morning it was with an odd disoriented feeling. The sun was bright and even before she looked at the clock, she knew from the slant of the sun that it was mid-morning. Sunday morning, she realized. And suddenly she thought of all the things she had to do.

She swung her legs out of the bed and sat up, suddenly feeling the muscle soreness in her shoulders from holding the tow rope behind the fast boat. The memory of the lake, and of the night, flooded into her mind, the very impact of it making her gasp. She sat on the edge of the bed, shocked, startled, almost terrified. Last night she had been possessed by a man not her husband. It had happened almost without warning. It was something that had never been going to happen to her. Never.

She put her hands hard against her eyes and relived that shocking moment, that sharp and unbelievable moment of bitter realization that it had happened, that he had incredibly taken from her both the will and the ability to resist. As though, in that sense, the act of union was all of the act itself, a deed accomplished, and the remaining time while she had lain flaccid under his possession had been merely a further affirmation of the conquest he had expressed in that first deep linking.

She took a deep, shuddering breath and then turned slowly, timidly, to look at Fletcher in her bed, more than half certain that he would be staring back at her, his eyes full of hate and knowing contempt.

But his back was to her and she saw the slow lift of his breathing. She remembered last night. Remembered her terror as Fletch had possessed her, a fear that somehow he

129

would know. That he would sense the use to which her body had been put, that he would detect some alien motion, some vile residue. And she remembered how his tenderness had made her cry, and how he had held her and kissed her eyes and how terribly close she had come in that moment to telling him. She knew that if he had asked her why she was crying, she would have told him. She would have been unable to stop her own lips. But by some merciful chance he had not asked. She stood up, feeling old and somber and soiled. Her body felt worn and heavy. She went into the bathroom and began her morning routines, finding in their homely necessity the satisfactions and faint forgetfulness of habit. She showered and, standing in the hot water, remembering, she scrubbed her body with dedicated fury.

When she came out of the bathroom Fletch was sitting up in bed, yawning mightily. He scratched his chest and gave her a sleepy grin. "God, if I'd slept like this Friday night, we'd have had no trouble."

"A good sleep? I'm glad."

"You look lush and lovely this morning. Either put on some clothes or come back to bed."

"Don't brag, dear," she said primly, taking comfort in her traditional response. She dug out a blue denim halter and shorts, put them on and tied her hair with a scrap of matching blue ribbon. Fletch was shuffling into the bathroom as she left for the kitchen.

Her kitchen was shiny and new and spotless and comforting. She startled herself by humming above the metallic drone of the squeezer as she held the orange halves against it. She was both pleased that she could hum, and guilty about it. Was it going to mean that little, after all? Perhaps that was the best way. It happened to some other woman. To a stranger there in the deep shadow. Yet she could remember the rubbery smell of the yellow raft, the feeling of the cool glass in her hand.

Forget it, Jane. Put it out of your silly head. It happened to me but it was like . . . like getting run over. Or drowning. It happened so it happened and there's no harm done, so skip it. Maybe it did some good. Maybe it taught you that it mustn't ever happen again. Did it happen because I had some tiny rotten place in me? A sort of curiosity? After all, there never had been anyone else. And you wonder, sometimes. Not seriously. Just idly. Now I know. It's no good. It's a snare and a delusion. It makes you feel dirty. It's . . . an invasion of privacy.

The coffee began to make a good smell. When she heard the shower stop she put butter in the frying pan and got the eggs out of the refrigerator. She thought of how she had looked in the mirror. Just the same. Like Sam said. It doesn't show. You don't have to tell.

Fletch came out in a startlingly vivid sports shirt and pale grey slacks. He came up behind her and grabbed her around the waist and kissed her behind the ear.

"No paper yet?"

"I forgot to look," she said.

"What good are you?" he muttered and went off to the front door. She served his juice and bacon and eggs. He came back and they solemnly split the Sunday paper down the middle. She pretended to read and from time to time she glanced over at him. There was a heaviness of flesh under his firm jaw. Where the shirt was opened one button too far she could see the sprinkling of white hairs amid the dark thatch on his chest.

"They're getting bids for repaving Lamont Street," he said. "Oh, fine. They wait until we move off it, *then* fix it up."

"Want to move back, dear?"

"Not right this minute. Later, maybe, when we can get a sucker to give us our price on this place."

"Over my dead body," she said firmly. "I love every inch of this place."

He grunted and they read in silence. She got up and brought the pot and refilled his coffee cup. He smiled up at her. "Know what's wrong around here?"

"What's wrong!"

"Don't jump like that. Your nerves are going bad. I mean the great silence. None of your monstrous children clumping around."

"Don't look so happy about it. When they're gone most

of the summer you're going to miss them. Now why don't you take your coffee in the other room so I can clean up here? Today is going to be one of the rough ones."

His smile faded. "Oh, Lord! I'd forgotten them. Who did you say is coming? Martha and Hud I know about. And the Corbans. Who else?"

"Midge and Harry, Sue and Dick."

"Hmm. Ten counting us. Not too bad. Oh, Lord, I forgot to check the liquor.

"I did that Friday when I decided to ask them. You were short, so I phoned and they delivered it. A mixed case. Gin, rum and bourbon. And I bought some more glasses last week, remember. The only things you have to do are get the chairs out, set up the bar, and then go down and get a bag of cubes before they get here."

"We're eating in?"

"Just the two of us, so it won't be much trouble. Martha said the kids would be fed before they drop them off on us. And I noticed that there's a good movie. You could take them when you get the cubes and that'll get them out from under foot."

"Where is it?"

"At the Palace. They can come back on the bus."

He took all the paper and carried his coffee into the living room. He stretched out on the couch with the coffee on the low table near his elbow. She went in and looked at him and got another pillow and said, "Sit up a minute. This will be better."

"Such service, my love."

She felt herself blush and she turned away quickly before he could see it and wonder about it. "You go blind and I have to go to work. It's enlightened self-interest."

As she walked back out into the kitchen she wished there was more she could do for him. Some way to make up to him for something he would never know. She would do it in little ways, she decided. There would be a lot of little things she could do. And there were years ahead in which to do them. It made her feel better to decide that, as though she had measured out a portion of the payment for sin. Expiation of guilt. One day, perhaps, when they were

132

both very old, when they were far beyond any physical relationship she could tell him, and tell of how it had changed her, how she had spent all the years trying to make it up to him in a thousand little ways. And perhaps, together, in the wisdom that comes with age, they could laugh softly over the panic and terror of a silly woman who was so unpracticed and so ignorant in her faithfulness to one man that she had been fair game for another, seduced by a college kid twelve years her junior.

She sang in her small true voice as she packed the breakfast dishes into the dishwasher. Panic and terror were far away. Nothing like that would ever happen again. Indeed, already it had begun to seem as if it had never happened once.

Midge and Harry Van Wirt were the first ones to arrive at ten after three. She was a birdlike woman, very nervous and jumpy, with a startlingly loud harsh laugh. Her face was seamed and simian. Harry Van Wirt was a big pasty man with a bloated look. He was always short of breath. He made every banal comment sound like confidential information. He was the general agent of one of the largest insurance firms in town, and made a handsome living out of it. In spite of their slightly irritating mannerisms, they were good guests, and good hosts.

By the time Fletch had made them their drinks, Sue and Dick Hosking arrived. Neither he nor Jane cared much for Dick, Sue's second husband, but they were fond of Sue. Sue's first husband had died, leaving her a large wholesale grocery firm. They had been childless. She had tried to learn the business, and in the process had fallen in love with Dick Hosking, who was twenty-four to her thirty-seven. Dick had been working as an order clerk in the firm. It took Sue three months to promote him to general manager and marry him. To the surprise of everyone in Minidoka who knew the score, Dick took hold of the job well. He was a rather pretty young man, a bit on the frail side. Sue adored him, and was most pathetically anxious to equalize as nearly as possible the difference in their ages. She made Dick grow a rather discouraged-looking mustache, and she dressed far younger than her years. She became a bit kittenish, which did not become her, as she was a rather raw-boned woman with a slightly somber expression. Dick had appeared to be wilting under the force of her determination and her love, and then, in March, she had discovered she was pregnant.

This fact had eased their relationship entirely. Sue gave up her kittenish mannerisms, dressed more sedately. Dick acquired a manly strut, and spent most of his time at parties seeing that she was comfortable. She followed him with her eyes whenever he was within sight, no matter whom she was talking to. Pregnancy had ripened her rather spare figure and given her a blooming look. Everyone in Minidoka said it was just dandy, even if it was perhaps a little dangerous for a woman her age to have a first baby, and who would have thought that prissy little citizen would have turned the trick when big, booming, jovial Carl, her first husband, had labored strenuously and to the limit of his resources for fifteen years without a single jackpot. They said you never could tell about these little fellows, could you, but then remember Papa Dionne.

Jane kissed Sue and told her how well she looked while Fletcher shook Dick's rather limp hand and took the drink order.

The Corbans arrived bare minutes after the Hoskings. Fletcher looked over Dick's shoulder and saw them coming across the yard. Laura wore something strapless in a pale blue-green. It fitted tightly to the slim waist then flared out into yards of skirt. He saw her and magically all his good spirits of the morning and of the day thus far ran quickly out of a ragged hole in the bottom of his soul. The wind ruffled her no-color cobwebby hair, and she walked with the stride of a trained model, and she looked directly at him across forty feet of green lawn and smiled in a way that made them both alone with all these people, both strangers and aware.

Fletcher turned gratefully back to the outdoor bar and let Jane handle the introductions. She was very good and quick and easy with introductions and he was most likely to foul them up, forgetting a well-known name at the crucial moment. Martha and Hud Rogers arrived just in time to be included in the introductions and to remind Jane that they were the only ones who had met the Corbans the previous evening. Hud Rogers was a big tow-headed man with the ineradicable look of a dirt farmer, though he was at least four generations removed from the land.

Harry, Ellis and Hud stood and talked together. Dick hovered protectively around his aging bride. The women made a small group of the terrace chairs.

Laura appeared at Fletcher's elbow. "Greetings, sahib. What comes in those copper mugs? I can't remember the name, but I want one. And Ellis will have his usual bourbon and water. He doesn't like it at all, but he likes the sound of it when he orders it."

"A Moscow Mule comes encased in copper. I was just about to make one for myself. You recovered from Friday night?"

She gave him a prim look. "What part of Friday night?"

"Wasn't it you who resented my suburban innuendoes?"

"That was Friday. I've decided to conform, now. A nice little lecherous corporation wife. I'm supposed to entice you, to help Ellis get ahead at the office."

He looked at her, slightly startled. Her face was calm and her smile was measured and careful, but the clear hazel eyes looked bright with malice.

"But you aren't supposed to tell me, are you?"

"Who wants to be sneaky?"

"Here. This one goes to Sue Hosking, and this one to her husband."

She took the glasses dutifully and walked off with them. Fletcher saw Jane give her a rather startled look, and then turn and stare at him. He turned back to his duties as Hud came up. "Something tall and cold and full of gin, Fletch."

"Sir, keep my wife out of this. By God, I've been waiting for a chance to use that line ever since I read it."

Hud looked at him mournfully. "I was going to stand around and talk to you. Not if you keep up that sort of thing. Martha wants the same thing too. I was going to stand here and help you feel sorry for the pair of us."

"Why?"

"While we labor in the city, our wives dally with younger men at a woodland lake."

"We've gotten middle-aged and unexciting, Huddleston."

Hud nodded sadly. "Life goes by. But before the last juices are gone, old boy, I should like a fast hack at the Corban woman. She exudes an aura."

Fletcher kept his tone casual. "You've noticed it too?"

"She has brightened these rheumy old eyes. She has reactivated sagging hormones. Yes, as a man who in years past has made an intensive study of such things, I recognize the type. Wives bristle when she walks by. She has that deceptive tranquillity, like a blast furnace with door closed. A highly specialized organism, I should judge. Do you suspect that yon elderly cub-scout is able to cope? One wonders. She bemused me, my boy. Feature by feature she is almost plain. The little body has all the usual parts and configurations, but not in any particularly startling manner. Yet somehow the whole effect is that of something barely able to contain live steam at a pressure of four thousand pounds per square inch."

Whenever he was with Hud, Fletch found himself talking in Hud's florid manner. "Jane expresses that mysterious element by declaring that the woman just doesn't care. But her analysis stops there."

"A not inadequate analysis. I suspect that an explosive element has been added to our little sewing circle, Fletcher. Remember Dorry Haines? Lovely little girl. She broke up three marriages before departing for points unknown with one of our most promising young attorneys."

"Do you really think she's another Dorry Haines, Hud?"

Hud nodded solemnly. "Note the walk as she approaches. Very indicative, my boy. When they walk as though they were carrying a silver dollar clenched between their dimpled knees, they're invariably hell on wheels. And note the hands. I haven't had a look yet, but I would give odds that you will find a pronounced curvature of the nails over the tips of the fingers, plus very plump pads at the base of the fingers. And, should you ever get close enough, Lord help you, you will detect a slightly heavy personal odor—not at all unpleasant—but a bit on the musky side."

He dropped his voice on the last few words as Laura approached them. Fletcher squeezed the quarter of lime in on top of the vodka and ginger beer in the copper mug and handed it to her with a slight bow. "Give the ice a chance to work before you start on it, Laura. Hud was just telling me the results of years of research."

He saw the look that she slanted up at Hud, knowing and speculative. "I didn't think you were the research type, Mr. Rogers."

It was one of the few times that Fletcher had seen Hud discomfited. "I . . . I was giving Fletch the benefit of my vast experience, Mrs. Corban."

"Do you think I would profit by it, Mr. Rogers?" she asked, wide-eyed. And, as Hud gulped, she turned and gave Fletcher a bawdy wink and said, "You see, I need a lot of practice, Fletch. I'm making a study of innuendoes, Mr. Rogers. I've been told they're the favorite indoor sport in Minidoka. Is that Ellis' drink? I'll take it to him, thank you."

As she reached her hand for the glass, Fletcher looked at it and saw that it was precisely as Hud had said it would be. She walked off with glass and copper mug, turning to smile brightly back over her shoulder.

"That," said Hud solemnly, "is an infernal machine and it's set to go off in your face, sir. I hope you brought your Bandaids."

"I have a strong character."

Hud waited while Fletcher finished making the two strong Collinses. He took them and started away, then stopped and turned and said, "I don't think she has any interest in your character, Mr. Wyant. She is in a phase. A female Samson. Somebody cut her curly locks and they have just grown back and you are a temple and she is about to push you down, just to test her strength."

"Didn't the temple kill Samson?"

"She's the type to push and run. Or vice versa, as the case may be."

Fletcher made his own drink last and then wandered

over and joined the group. Martha was giving a spirited account of the water skiing. Midge Van Wirt was competing with a more spirited account of a bridge hand with eleven hearts in it, and a partner with holes in her head. Ellis was sitting gingerly on the edge of the terrace on the grass, beside Laura's chair. His sports jacket was vivid and hairy, and his slacks were a peculiarly unpleasant mustard shade. The faint breeze was dying and Fletcher saw the dew of perspiration on all the polite faces and knew that they would have to move out of the sun or melt. Next year, he decided, he would have a lattice roof put over half the terrace, and Jane could train something green to climb and cover it, so that the sun worshipers could at least sit near people who wanted the shade.

The conversation suddenly turned itself, like an aimed cannon, on the weather, and nearly everybody began to talk at once—as though they had diligently suppressed weather talk as being dull, and now found that through restraint it had become the most fascinating topic in the world. ". . . seven dead of heat prostration they say . . . worst in the history of Minidoka . . . I say it's those damn rainmakers seeding the clouds . . . feels like there's a thunderstorm coming, but it never comes . . . move out of this bastard climate for good . . ."

Fletcher made another round of drinks, two at a time, and heard Jane inviting all sun bathers to don their costumes while she got the blankets from the garage. Of the women only Sue Hoskings sat where she was. The others began to drift toward the house. Fletcher saw Laura walking with Martha Rogers. Dick murmured to Sue and she got up and he carried her chair over into the shade for her. She gave him a warm grateful look and he bent down a bit awkwardly and kissed her. The men, except Dick gathered around Fletcher as he prepared refills, and they all decided that sun bathing interfered with serious Sunday drinking, and it was a woman's sport at best. Harry Van Wirt said, in his most confidential voice, that the last time he'd been naked in the sunshine was when he was fifteen, and it had only taken him one time to find out he didn't like it. Hud said that as long as the bar was in the shade he, personally, planned to sit down right beside it. Ellis said it only took ten minutes to burn him so bad he'd have chills, but the sun didn't seem to bother Laura at all. Didn't burn her and didn't even tan her very much.

Jane spread the blankets on the grass in the place where they would get any available breeze, should one happen to come along, then hurried into the house to change. Ellis was at his most affable state. His manner filled Fletcher with dull annoyance. Damn the man, he was like a puppy which had been kicked too often and figured that if you wagged your tail hard enough, they wouldn't kick you again. He saw Hud examining Ellis with mild disapproval. Dick came over and got another very light drink for Sue and took it over to her chair.

It was Hud who gave the low grunt of surprise. Fletcher looked at him, then turned to look in the direction of Hud's startled glance. Martha, Laura and Midge were walking out together. Both Martha and Midge wore sun suits consisting of shorts and halter. They were both quite brown. Midge was thin-limbed, spidery. Martha was round and buttery. Both of the women seemed to be making a ludicrous attempt to pretend that they weren't with Laura, and had never seen or heard of her before. Laura wore a Bikini suit improvised out of four dark blue bandannas. There was a knot between her small rather sharp breasts, and a knot at each side about two inches below where her slim waist curved out quite abruptly to form the lyre curve of hip. The taut blue fabric bisected the satin flatness of her belly. She was all of a piece, a perfect even shade like milk tea, and the texture of her was like cream. She was flawless and tight in her skin, and she made Fletcher think of a tiny figurine he had purchased in London during the war. The dealer said it had once been a toy made for the favorite daughter of a maharajah. It depicted a fragile, nude Indian princess, and, with typical Hindu literalness, each anatomical detail had been carved with almost embarrassing exactitude. The child for which it had been made was long dead, and the ivory of the figurine had yellowed, and the saris of the doll wardrobe had long since mouldered away. Yet the figurine remained in its eternal resilience of youth. He had paid far too much for it and later it had been stolen out of his room in the BOQ in Paris.

Laura, in her clothes, had walked with a restraint that was near awkwardness. Naked, her stride was long and lithe and free. Her face was expressionless, but Fletcher had the vivid impression that she was laughing inside, laughing at all of them.

Almost instinctively, he turned to glance at Ellis at the same moment Hud did. Ellis' face had darkened and his eyes were uneasy. He laughed a bit nervously and said, "Laura likes to get plenty of sun."

"And that, class," said Hud in an awe-stricken tone, "is an example of a self-evident truth. The lady will get plenty of sun."

"They wear those all the time on the French beaches," Ellis said defensively.

"I'll stay to hell out of France," Harry rasped huskily. "My blood pressure, you know."

Ellis acted like a man who wanted to be offended, and didn't know exactly how to go about it. He took his drink and wandered out toward the blankets where Laura was in the process of spreading herself out.

Hud said, "I request permission to retract a statement, Mr. Wyant. I mentioned Dorry Haines previously, somewhat in the nature of a comparison. Even in my myopic state, I can see that the comparison was inept. Scratch Dorry Haines, please."

Harry giggled, a bit damply. Dick was staring over toward Laura, rigid as a setter at Bok Tower. Sue was aiming a rather cool glare at the nape of his neck. Jane came across the yard from the house, and from the depth of the black and ominous look she tossed in his direction, Fletcher knew that Jane had seen Laura before she came out. Jane wore a yellow terry-cloth sun outfit, and that particular shade of yellow, Fletcher noted with annoyance, was as wrong for her as Laura's yellow had been right for her on Friday evening.

There were two refills to take over to the blankets, one for Jane and another mule for Laura. He made the drinks and took them over. Laura lay a bit apart from the other

140

three. Midge and Martha and Jane chatted with just a shade too much animation about meat prices. Laura lay on her back, with two little plastic cups, joined by a nose-piece, on her eyes. The little cups were dead white.

"Another mule, lady," he said with hostlike joviality. She rolled up onto one elbow and took the chill copper mug with a quick smile.

"Thanks loads, Fletch. They're awfully good."

He felt the stir of his blood as he looked down at her. She was just naked enough so that it was embarrassing to look at her, and almost impossible to look away. She sipped from the mug, and her eyes were bland and mocking. In the delicate intricacy of her, satin textures over the small bones, body-down sun-bleached to white against the flawless gold, she made the other women look distressingly coarse-grained and meaty. She made Jane's a peasant body, made Martha's bounciness into glutinous obesity, turned Midge into a hideousness of brown strings and knots. And Fletcher guessed that the other women were uncomfortably aware of their disadvantage. He handed Jane her drink a bit blindly, and then walked back to the bar, the song of Laura running hard through his blood. He told himself he wasn't an adolescent any longer. A naked woman was merely that, and nothing more. But he remembered the feel of her in his arms, and the quickness of her response. And she was a woman who didn't give a damn. She was making that obvious. There would be no arduous campaign, no move and countermove. Perhaps she would like best a plain statement of intent, and respond best to that.

Harry had wandered over to talk to Dick and Sue. Hud moved close to him and said, "Have you got a claim staked, or can anybody play?"

"Try your luck, Huddleston. I'm not having any."

"Then you better stop trying your smirk on her. It shows, my boy. Jane has willed you to drop dead twice already. In my case, it's different. Martha knows I'm weak. And I don't think another set of horns on that fatuous husband will make any particular difference."

Fletch dropped ice in a glass and turned and looked at Hud with a sudden anger out of all proportion to the situation. Suddenly the farmery look of his best friend annoyed him. The big plow-jockey hands and the seamed neck.

"I suppose all you have to do is snap your fingers and she lies on her back."

"No. I bedazzle her with witty sayings and homely philosophies, and before she knows my foul design, bingo. And why is your back hair standing on end? I asked, didn't I?"

"Oh, skip it, for God's sake!"

Hud stared into his glass, picked up the bottle and made the drink much stronger. He set the bottle down. "One would suspect that there is enough over there to go around, my old pal."

"Don't you ever talk about anything else?"

Hud's eyes narrowed a bit. "What would you like? An analysis of the Korean truce talks? The infamy of the Minidoka City Council? Take any card."

"I'm sorry, Hud. I mean one topic of conversation can get tiresome."

Hud smiled sleepily. "Then get yourself another boy. I've got one of those one-track minds." He walked away in a long half-circle that inevitably took him over to Laura Corban. He sat down beside her and a few minutes later, as Fletcher was making a stronger mule this time for himself, he heard her laugh. It was a good, rich, bawdy, throaty laugh. She had laughed at the club, but not like that. He was jealous, he realized, of Hud Rogers, who could make her laugh in a way that verified his immediate estimate of her.

Jane went toward the house and signaled him to come along and help bring out the trays of snacks. Once she was in the kitchen alone with him, she exploded.

"Understand I'm no prude, Fletch, but *that's* the limit. What does she think we're running here? A peep show? And you made it worse, you and Hud and Harry over there snickering and drooling. If I were Ellis Corban, I'd smack her bottom good and take her home. Showing off like a nasty little kid. Waving her bare ass in the breezes! I suppose you think that's cute and adorable. Maybe she thinks next time she can get away with a G string and two rosebuds. Well, there won't be any next time. I've got a thirteen-year-old boy, and I don't want him coming home to goggle at that spectacle. She had the nerve to tell us those four handkerchiefs cost nineteen cents apiece, and that she liked the outfit because it's so comfortable and inexpensive. You ought to see her put the darn thing on. She had the four folded bandannas in her handbag. You should have seen Midge's face. What in the world are we going to do?"

"I don't think there's anything we can do."

"You men don't want anything done. It's a free show for you, and don't think she doesn't know it. Little bitch!"

"Look, what do I do? Put on my policeman hat and go tell her to get off the beach? Or do I pray for rain, for God's sake?"

She stared at him with an unpleasant accusing expression on her face. "You don't have to bite my head off."

"Well then, make sense. There isn't anything we can do."

"Then stop getting off with Hud and you two nudging each other and snickering."

"Sure," he said wearily. "Sure."

"I told you she'd make trouble. I knew it right away. I know the type, believe me. A troublemaker from the word go."

He carried the trays out. Laura and Hud had moved off the blankets over onto the grass. They sat cross-legged, facing each other. Hud had produced a penknife and they were playing mumblety-peg. As he took a tray to them, he heard Laura say firmly. "You missed. That's three you owe me."

When he took the tray to Martha she did not see him for a moment. She was looking at her husband and the girl in the bandannas. There was an expression of black fury in her eyes. She smiled absently up at Fletch and selected a round piece of bread with a sardine dead across it.

Chapter Twelve

Some of it, he guessed, was due to the heat, and some of it to the odd strain Laura had contributed. Everybody seemed to drink much too much. All except Dick and Sue, and they had gone home early. The rest of them had made a spectacular hole in the liquor supply, and he knew, fuzzily, that he'd done more than his fair share. The kids had come home from the movies and feasted off the surplus snacks and gone down the street to watch the Sunday night programs on a TV set that had a bigger screen than theirs.

When the sun had at last faded, leaving the day stickier and hotter than ever, the women had gone in to shower and change back to the clothes they had come in.

Now dusk was blue on the hill and it was already night down in the city. The lights down there were beginning to show brightly. He felt unsteady on his feet, and he had begun to lose track of people.

Midge came up in the darkness. "Fletch, is that you? Harry got taken drunk, dear. He told me to tell you he's lying down inside and we're supposed to wake him up in an hour. If possible. You may have a house guest on your hands."

"Always plenny a room for you and Harry, darling."

"Fletch! God, you better go in and lie down beside him. You're boiled."

He spread his lips in a stiff grin. "Not that bad. Got my sea legs now. What else you going to do on a bitch day like this? Old climate control. Drink and forget the temperature. Yessir, the best climate control in the world. Hey!"

He turned to stare at her and she was gone and he had the feeling she'd been gone for a long time. This was a night for losing track of people. He walked over and saw cigarette ends in the night. Two people were sitting in chairs.

"Who're you?" he demanded. "Thirsty people?"

"Nobody here but us chickens." He recognized Martha's voice.

"That you, Hud?"

"It's me, you big clown," Jane said, her voice a bit slurred, but icy. "You've had enough to drink."

"Darling, every time you tell me that, I have to go make myself another one just to 'xert my independence. You better cut it out or you'll get me drunk."

"Okay, darling. Then *please* have another drink. I insist."

"Better psychology," he said and sat down heavily on the grass. "Now I'm released from the . . . from the obligation."

"Then go make us one, dear."

"Just this minute sat down. Can't you wait? Anyway, you sound just a wee bit drunky yourself."

"And I'm going to get very drunky, darling. I'm going to hoot like owls before I'm through. Martha too. We made a pledge. She's the best friend I've got in the wide world."

"No," said Martha firmly. "You're a better friend than I am."

"Stop the love feast and tell me why the pledge, women. What is driving you to drink?"

"Offhand, you could say husbands," Martha said.

"And Bikini suits," Jane added.

"And the futility of life, maybe. We girls are hep to futility."

Fletcher got up ponderously. "Then you shall have drinks. Let's see. Something with gin for the Rogers woman. Something with rum for my lady." He walked off into the night and veered toward the bar. He could barely see the mixings, and knew it was time to move the show indoors. He made three drinks, opening the last fresh bottle of vodka to fix his own. The ginger beer was gone, so he used ginger ale. Seemed to taste just about the same, he decided. Just another splash of vodka. No wonder those

145

characters could do that dance sitting on their heels. He took the girls their drinks, cadged one of Jane's cigarettes, then carried his drink out into the front yard. He stood with his feet braced and looked off into the valley toward the city. They'd be sleeping in the parks down there tonight. And on roofs.

Someone suddenly linked an arm in his. He peered down at the pale oval of the upturned face and recognized Laura Corban.

"I seem to keep losing track of people, dear," he said. "Where is Ellis?"

"There's a news roundup he listens to every Sunday at this time. So he's out there in the car listening. Is that a copper mug? Spare any?"

"Sure." She took the mug in both hands, drinking from it like a child.

"It's a little nasty, isn't it?"

"No more ginger beer."

"Nasty but nice."

"And where would Hud be?" he asked, taking the mug back, taking a long drink from it.

"Oh, he's fun in small doses. He got a little too funny though, and I tripped him into some bushes at the back end of the yard. What a crash he made! I asked him if he was hurt and he said he was quite comfortable, thank you, and he planned to stay right there indefinitely."

"Usual shambles, this party. Worse, I guess. Harry passed out. Oh, Christ!"

"I think I know what you mean, Fletch."

"You do, eh. Smart as whisp . . . whips, aren't you?"

"Now you resent me. All I mean is we don't seem to be able to have any fun any more. The world has changed, or something. It's like that circus candy. Big and lovely and pink on a stick and you bite and it's gone and just a little sick taste in your mouth, too sweet and too little of it."

"You seem to have your fun," he said stiffly.

"I'm a boat rocker by nature. I like to see the other passengers look alarmed. But if I thought it was really going to tip over, I guess I'd stop and sit down, meek as a bunny. I thought about us Friday night."

"Us? How so?"

146

"Is there a sip left? Gimme. Yes, us, Fletch. And so have you thought about me so let's not kid the troops. I didn't sleep. I walked and sat on one of your silly bridges and looked at your meek little river until the police got nervous about me and brought me home at dawn."

"This is no town to wander around in at night, stupid. Our rape statistics are just as impressive as anybody's."

"Don't change the subject. Us. I'm a little high, I guess. What do you think about us?"

"We're lovely people."

"We're lost people. Remember what we found out? About each other? That funny feeling of not belonging anyplace."

"We belong right here, baby. Drunk and philosophical. What's the pitch? You want we should have a quick roll in the hay?"

"Oh, fine! There are more direct old Anglo-Saxon words. Why don't you use those? Like a nasty little boy writing on the men's room wall."

"You're an infernal machine set to explode in my face. And here I am without my Bandaids."

She laughed softly. "I seem to catch on. You're scared, aren't you?"

The copper mug was empty. He tossed it over his shoulder and heard it fall into the bushes in front of the house. "I guess so. I guess I'm drunk enough to be honest. I haven't run into anybody like you before. I don't know how to handle it. What are you after, anyway?"

"Maybe . . . I want to feel alive once."

"Right here in my front yard?"

"Don't be such a fool! Don't be purposely dense. Arrange things. Send Ellis on a trip or something."

"Then come to the side door and knock twice."

"Fletcher, don't you understand what I'm trying to tell you? Why are you trying to make it as tough for me as you can? I *do* have a little pride left. Not much. I'll grant that. But a little. And I'm fighting for . . . self-preservation or self-identification. I don't know which. It's time I found out something about myself. Through you, Fletch. Because you're . . . sensitive and understanding and aware of me."

"Who isn't?"

"You're running like a rabbit."

He took a deep breath of the warm night air. "If I was more sober, baby, I could say this better. Look, I'm fine. I'm a little twitchy this year. But I'm fine. I want to keep playing with my own dice on my own table. Believe me, it's an effort to be so . . . hell, austere. I look at you and you give me the jumps. I get crazy ideas. I've had them since Friday night. We run the hell out of here, you and me. Way away from the whole damn thing for keeps. So how many people are involved? Eight of us, baby. Four adults, four kids. So I'm scared. I don't want a sample, Laura. I'm afraid if I get a sample, I want to take over all the merchandise, because as I said, I have a slight twitch this year. But I'll get over it. So don't ask me again, please."

She was very still for a long time. At last she said in a low tone, "I'm damn selfish, Fletcher."

"Me too."

"It might be too right? Can anything be too right?"

"Sure. Alcohol is too right for an alcoholic."

She touched his cheek suddenly with her fingertips. "You're quite a guy, Fletcher," she said. And she was gone into the night. He ran his tongue along his lips. He knew he was still drunk, but the hard core of sobriety in the middle of his brain had expanded. He was full of a nagging disgust at the way the day had turned out. Laura was right. Nobody talked any more. Nobody had fun any more. There didn't seem to be any more people in the world like Dr. Tom Marsan. Haven't thought of him for years. God, I wonder if the old guy is still alive. He must be. Jane would have told me if he died. Bull sessions with him when I was a kid. He was Dad's best friend. He always treated me like an adult, talked to me like an adult. Too old-fashioned for Jane, though. She goes for the brisk young doctors. I guess on account of old Dr. Tibault being an unsuccessful, old-fashioned GP. Damn shame I dropped him. A rare guy.

And he suddenly had a strong desire to go and see Dr. Tom Marsan and spread his life out in front of the doctor and ask for some reasons, and some explanations. Go like

a kid in need. Funny, you could be grown up, with responsibilities and a family, and still there was one place in you
that was still a kid, still uncertain, aware of the need of
guidance.

He walked around the house, deep in thought. And as
he got out on the terrace, he heard the shrill ugly voice of
Martha Rogers, loud in anger. She was down beyond the
terrace, and he knew at once that it was a particularly ugly
and vicious scene in the making. He lengthened his stride.

". . . you dirty little bitch! Let go of me, Hud! I'll
scratch her goddamn eyes out."

In the moonlight he saw Hud holding Martha's wrists.
He was having trouble holding onto her. She was trying to
yank away, and kicking at his legs. Laura stood six feet
away, unmoving, not even looking toward them.

Hud was trying to be calm. "Now, Martha. Now,
Martha honey."

She was panting and grunting with her efforts to get
free. "Don't Martha me, you damn old goat. Think you
can get away with it and me fifty feet away from you. Just
what the hell do you think I am?"

Jane came running over. "What is it? What is it? I
heard you yelling from way in the house. Darn it, Martha,
we have got neighbors."

Martha suddenly went limp. She dropped onto her
knees, sitting back on her heels. Hud tentatively released
her wrists. Martha immediately put her hands flat against
her face and began to moan pitifully.

"What is it, Fletch?" Jane demanded.

"I don't know. She wants to beat up on Laura."

Laura said coldly, "Mr. Rogers pulled me down onto
the grass. I was trying to get away from him without making a scene when she came along. She kicked at us and
started screaming. She kicked me in the back and it
hurts."

"You were trying to get away. Yes, you were trying to
get away," Martha said bitterly. "I can just imagine that,
you little tramp."

"You better keep him on a leash, Mrs. Rogers."

Martha scrambled up again and this time Fletcher
grabbed her. She twisted in his grasp and raked his face

before he pinned her arms. "Damn it, settle down!" he yelled at her.

Hud said, "I was out of line, Martha. It wasn't Mrs. Corban's fault. I was just horsing around."

"Sure. You'd cover for her, wouldn't you?" Martha said hotly.

Laura walked over to Jane and held her hand out. "Thanks for a lovely party, Jane. I really enjoyed it. I'll thank you and Fletcher for Ellis too. I think he's still out in the car." She walked off without haste, her shoulders straight and her head high.

"You try that again," Martha shouted after her, "and I'll fix your wagon for good."

"Oh, hush!" Jane said. "Don't make more of a darn fool of yourself than you can help, Martha."

By the way Martha tensed and spun out of his grasp, Fletcher knew that Jane had said precisely the wrong thing. Martha's virulent temper was well known throughout Minidoka.

"What am I supposed to do? Stand there and cheer? Kibitz, for God's sake? I don't blame Hud too much. She's been waving it around all afternoon. She's been wearing the invite like a sandwich sign. I'm not going to let her work it off on *my* husband. I don't care what you do."

"Lower your voice!" Jane hissed at her. "Can't you act like a civilized human being? Can't you see what a spot you're putting me in? Ellis works for Fletcher. We have to be nice to them. Can't you control yourself?"

"I can control myself one hell of a lot better than you can, Jane," Martha suddenly said in a dead level voice.

"What do you mean by that?" Jane asked furiously.

Martha took a step toward her, still using that same dead tone. "Dolly thought we might try bridge for a change. I came out to get you and that Rice boy. I guess you were too busy. Down there in that rubber raft. Don't give me . . ."

"Martha! Stop!"

She took another step toward Jane. "I won't stop. Don't give me that virtuous act. You had me fooled good. You're as much bitch as that Corban wench. You and a college

150

kid in that rubber raft. I couldn't believe it and I couldn't be sure. And then I saw him get up and then I saw you get up and pull your swimming suit back on, and you showed up good in the moonlight, honey. So I went back in and I tell you it made me feel sick, and I told Dolly I could hear you way out in the lake swimming around, so we started another game of Canasta. Then Fletch came and sure you two came in looking like butter wouldn't melt. I'm just sick and tired of . . . of your kind of morals, and this whole stinking group and I don't care if I never set eyes on you again. Take me home, Hud. Right now. This minute. I want to go home and take a bath and see if I can get clean."

"Martha," Jane said in almost a whisper. "Oh my God, Martha!"

And Fletcher, walking away from them, walking blindly across the dark lawn, heard the way her voice sounded and he knew that it was true, and he could see how it was with them there in the darkness, and see her getting up in the moonlight, and see them having a cigarette together as a chaser and hear them talking in low tones and maybe laughing together and planning the next time.

He walked up to the side of the house and put his fists against the house and leaned his forehead against the house. Sure, it was a game you played sometimes, to tantalize yourself, to conjecture about her committing an infidelity, playing with the sense of outrage that flooded through you. But this was real. This had happened. This was indelibly, incredibly, sickeningly true. A big bronze kid with shoulders, and she had to take him, take the eager maleness, doing for another those things they had learned together, saying to another those words which belonged to marriage.

He sobbed aloud, his lips close to the side of the building. What was his name? Rice. Sam Rice, a pleasant guy with an open face and a good smile. And how many others? How many dozen times? How many hundred times? How many back seats of strange cars, and how many sleazy afternoon hotel rooms when the shopping trip took longer than she had thought it would, and how much foulness and how much pretense, and how much silent indulgent laughter at his expense, and how many alien hands on flanks and breasts and thighs he had thought were his alone? Sure she had acted strange last night. Why not? And it had taken longer to arouse her because she'd already had all she wanted, and then had to go through it one more time just to keep the dull husband happy and unsuspicious. And she'd come directly from the Rice boy into his bed, with a whore's conscience, with a whore's innate dexterity. How many people had been snickering at him behind his back for years? Had Hud ever gotten any? Probably. Whenever there was any around, Hud seemed to get his share in spite of his farmer-boy manner.

He heard a car door slam and heard the car drive away. He heard Harry Van Wirt's heavy husky voice, sleepy on the night air, and then heard them go too. Now the party was over. The last party.

He heard the whisper of her step in the grass, and she came up behind him and he felt her hand on his shoulder. "Ah, Fletch. Fletcher, darling." Her voice was thick and she was crying. Whore hand on his shoulder.

He spun and struck blindly at her with all his strength, struck with his open hand, not saying a word or making a sound. The hard slap rang loud in the night. His palm and fingers stung. It knocked her down and she sprawled back onto her shoulders, her skirt going up, her long legs scissoring in the moonlight, and he thought that her legs had looked like that to the Rice boy. He leaned his shoulders against the side of the house, holding his stinging fingers tightly.

She lay still on the grass on her back for a moment and then pushed herself up into a sitting position and leaned over to one side and spat, and he knew that he had cut her mouth.

"Fletch, darling. Darling, you've got to listen to . . ."

"There's not one damn word you can say. Not one."

"But I can't let you think that I . . . that I . . ."

"Did you let him? Did it happen? Isn't that the only thing you can say?"

"Yes, but . . ."

"Yes, but it only took thirty seconds, darling, so it real-

152

ly doesn't count," he said in a mincing imitation of her voice.

"But you don't understand. You don't understand!"

"What the hell is there to understand? For Christ' sake, are there degrees? Middle-aged bitch getting her thrills from school kids. You're a prize, you are! How did you get him to do it? A little cash on the line, maybe?"

"Don't," she moaned softly. "Oh, don't!" She spat awkwardly again, and gagged.

"Don't soil our lovely marriage with my nasty words? This is what gets me. You did it with my kids about sixty feet away from you. That's fine. Educational for the little rascals. We're done, Jane. Completely and utterly and finally done."

He watched her get awkwardly to her feet. The fine clear co-ordination of her body seemed to have deserted her utterly. "You've got to listen to me."

"That's where you're wrong, Jane. I haven't got to listen to you. I haven't got to do a damn thing to you or for you or with you. I haven't a single obligation left, as far as you are concerned. My obligation is to the kids. Are they home?"

"I turned out their lights and I was walking out when I heard Martha screaming."

"It's a good thing. Now listen to me. I don't want them to know or suspect what their mother has done. You understand that?"

"Of course, but . . ."

"Shut up and listen. I'll move my stuff into the study. We'll try to act normal until I decide exactly what can be done. I'm going to get custody of them. You aren't fit, and any court will tell you that. I'm making that kid correspondent, and I'm going to make damn sure that if you try to fight it, Martha will testify. The best thing you can do is accept it as quietly as possible."

"Fletcher!"

"Shut up! I've never felt so damn dirty in my life."

He walked away from her and into the house and went directly into the bedroom. He decided it would be easier to carry his clothing to the study-guest room in a suitcase. He took the suitcase off the closet shelf as she came in.

Her face was chalky and expressionless. The left side of her mouth was puffed where the lips were split and his fingers had left raised red stripes on her cheek.

He opened the suitcase on a chair and pulled out the top dresser drawer. He heard the creak as she sat on his bed.

"I just want you to hear how it happened. At first he was fresh. And then he apologized and I thought we were friends. I was lonesome for you. I drank too much and I was getting sick and he came out and said I should swim. The world was going around and around."

"At least spare me the details. I don't want a play by play."

She made no sign that she had heard him. "He swam out into the lake with me. I felt all funny and dreamy and apart from everything, like I didn't exist. He kissed me. I let him do it because I didn't think there would be any harm in that, and I was drunk and I was mad at you and I thought by kissing the boy I was getting even with you. But I couldn't think clearly."

"Will you, for God's sake, shut up!" he said, feeling a crazy anger. He slammed a stack of shirts into the suitcase and saw, under where they had been, in the drawer, the cracked leather of the holster and the blue oiled steel of the ugly and deadly-looking nine millimeter Mauser he had bought from a GI in Antwerp. The two clips lay beside the holster. He stood in a moment frozen in time.

"He kissed me again and again and he got the top of my suit down around my waist. He had his hands on me and I was scared and in a funny way it made me helpless to have him touching me, and in some funny way in my mind it seemed like it was you, so that I was half scared and half thinking it was all right because I was drunk, very drunk and floaty."

The dreadful words and the dreadful flat voice went on and on. He watched his hands slide the automatic out of the holster and take a clip and slip it up until it clicked in place, with a small, evil, oiled sound. He remembered that it was double action and you did not have to work the slide like on the forty-five, but merely pull the trigger. He turned and aimed it at her where she sat there, misty on the bed, hazy in his vision. And he noted with mild wonder that the barrel of the automatic was as steady as if it rested on rock.

She looked at the gun and looked at him. He knew that she was terrified of guns. It was perhaps the only thing in the world that scared her.

She looked back at the gun and she licked her lips and said, "Maybe you have to do it. I don't know. Maybe it is something you have to do and should do, but I'm going to go right on talking until you pull the trigger, Fletcher. Because the only thing I have left is to tell you what happened."

"If you keep talking you'll force me to do it."

She looked into his eyes, ignoring the gun. "You have to understand about my having the crazy idea that it was you. Because, you see, nobody else has ever had me but you. You know I was a virgin when we were married. And in fifteen years there was never anybody else but you, which I think you know in your heart if you think for a minute. So, being drunk, I guess that was why anybody touching me had to be you. And yet I had that crazy fear. But I couldn't do anything. He got my suit all the way off out there in the lake."

He knew he was breathing through his open mouth. He could hear the harsh quick sound of it. Everything in the world was blurred but her eyes.

"He towed me in, swimming along, and he kept his hands on me and it kept me in that funny helpless floaty feeling. If he'd let me alone for a minute I would have come out of it. And in the shallow water he picked me up and took me over to the raft. Then we were in darkness and, oh, my darling, I knew then that it was you as he was against me, and then I touched the back of his head and the hair was all wrong and it brought me out of it. I fought him, Fletcher. He's terribly strong. I fought hard and I found a heavy glass tumbler I'd dropped off the dock and I hit him with it as hard as I could, twice, and then he threw it away after he twisted it out of my hand. He had my arm pulled across me like this and I hit him with my free hand and he pinned that too, and pinned me with his weight so I couldn't move. While I was fastened down

155

there, and it was horrible, like animals fighting in the dark, he moved and . . . I felt it happen. It was a hard pain, and he had done it and I couldn't fight any more. I lay there like I was dead and he did what he wanted to do to me and went away from me. I wanted to die. I wished I was dead. It was like my whole world had ended. It wasn't his fault, any more than mine. He thought I . . . was a different sort of person. And then he was ashamed of doing it. I had to face you and come home with you. And afterward I cried, you remember, and if you had asked me why I was crying then, I would have had to tell you. And this morning I knew that I couldn't ever tell you, and I knew a thing like that would never happen again, and so I thought I would make it up to you for all the rest of your life. Doing little things for you. And maybe tell you when we were both old. Now I've said all of it, and I guess if you have to . . . do it you better do it quick because I don't think I can sit here any more without crying again, and I don't want to be crying when you . . . do it to me."

She looked at him steadily and gravely. He looked down at the gun, turned and released the clip and dropped it in the drawer, put the gun back in the holster and snapped the strap.

He finished packing the suitcase, closed it and snapped the locks. She was lying back across the bed, looking up at the ceiling.

"Are . . . you still going to . . . divorce me, Fletch?"

He paused in the doorway. "What else can I do? I can't live with you. I can't look at you without remembering that little scene. I can't ever touch you again. I get sick at the idea."

She neither looked at him nor answered. He went into the study and stripped the cover off the studio couch and made it up. There was no need of a blanket. The still night had folded warmly and wetly around the house. He undressed and went to bed with the study door closed. The moon made a pattern on the rug. She could have screamed, couldn't she? No, that story was full of holes. She'd wanted it, and maybe she'd put up a little scrap for the sake of appearances. But not much of a scrap. Roosters chase chickens who never seem to be running as fast as they can. Once rape is inevitable, relax and enjoy it. Hell, she knew which side of the bread they put the butter on. Make him think it was a form of rape, and you can go right on having your cake and eating it too. Take your pick of all the strong, eager young men. And let the gullible husband keep you in pretty clothes and pay for your nice house. What kind of a fool was he supposed to be?

The liquor surged around in his head. Oh, a dandy party! The finest of the social season. Sunday afternoon the Wyants entertained a small group at their new home on Coffeepot Road. During the evening the Wyants made plans for their pending divorce.

The memory of the Chicago redhead drifted back across his mind. He forced it away quickly. Not the same sort of thing at all.

Chapter Thirteen

Fletcher drove to the office through the first glaring, blinding heat of a new day. This heat wave was never going to break. The world was going to be like this from now on.

Breakfast had been particularly hideous. Awakening to the realization of what had happened the night before had been bad enough. But breakfast had been enormously worse. She had tried to cover the discoloration of her face with powder. When he had come out to breakfast she had said, "Good morning."

He had merely glanced at her, making no response, feeling a vague shame not only for his own reluctance to respond, but also because of the memory of melodrama, that incredible scene, both passionate and ridiculous. And he knew that he had come perilously close, in his hurt and disappointment, to pulling the trigger. Had he done it, it would have been in the spirit of a child smashing a favorite toy because it had pinched his finger.

The half-drunk melodrama of the night before now seemed ludicrous in the hot bright light of the new morning. He had no idea of what to say to her, and so he said nothing. When her back was turned he looked cautiously at her. She wore a faded cotton dress and her hair was not as neat as it usually was in the morning. As she took the few steps between stove and sink she moved heavily. Watching her, he had the weird feeling that there were two women involved, two Janes. And he should hold this one close and they could comfort each other, and both despise the evil the other one had done.

When Judge and Dink came to breakfast he tried to simulate a touch of morning cheer. He saw that Jane was doing the same thing, and from the reaction of the children, their quick puzzled glances, he knew that they were both overdoing it.

"Gee, what happened to your face, Mom?" Judge asked.

"I tripped over one of the deck chairs in the dark last night, dear." Her voice was quick and gay and her eyes were dead.

"What was all that yelling?" Dink demanded. "You and those people were making an awful lot of noise."

"I guess everybody was just having a good time," Fletcher said.

Dink gave him a quick sharp look. "They sounded mad to me."

The children ate with unfamiliar solemnity. Whenever Fletcher was looking down at his plate, he could feel them looking at him. When he looked up, though, they would be busy with their food.

When he got up to go the children were still there, so he went around to Jane's chair, bent and kissed her cheek and said, "Good-by, dear. 'By, kids."

Jane got up quickly and almost ran out of the kitchen, making a thick strangled noise in her throat as she left the room. It reminded him of Dink on Saturday morning.

"What's wrong with Mom?" Judge demanded.

"She . . . just doesn't feel very good today. I want you both to be good. Be quiet and don't nag her. It won't hurt you to spend a quiet day, both of you."

Strangely, there was no objection. He kissed Dink, rumpled Judge's hair and glanced back at them as he left the kitchen. They both sat there looking at him, and he thought he saw the light of accusation in their eyes.

He was enormously relieved to get out of the house. There had been other mornings, other hangovers, other stirrings of shame and remorse. You waited and it all went away. But not this time. It wasn't going to go away. In the back of his mind was a tiny cardboard stage bathed in moonlight where the doll figures of Jane and Sam Rice moved endlessly. No matter where he looked or what he thought of, he was aware of the doll figures back there, aware of their endless, blinded spasm.

He was aware of parking the car, and then he was suddenly aware of being in the office, behind his desk, with the squat, blushing Marcia Trevin standing in front of him. He had no memory of the walk from car to office, or of the usual morning greetings to the people he had seen.

"I'm sorry, Miss Trevin. I was thinking of something else. What did you say?"

"Mr. Forman's secretary just phoned and said the meeting would be at ten instead of nine thirty. Maybe you'd like me to type your notes."

"That would be nice, if you can read them."

"Oh, I'm used to your writing, Mr. Wyant. Mr. Wyant . . ."

"Yes, what is it?"

"Mr. Wyant, do you feel all right? I mean . . . you don't look as if you felt very good this morning." She was blushing furiously.

"Just type the notes, will you? I'm perfectly all right."

He saw the quick suggestion of tears in her eyes as she turned and fled to her desk. It was a tone of voice he had never used with her before. He turned and looked out across the landscaped lawn toward the low modern plant buildings, and the glint and flicker of the neat lines of cars in the plant parking lot. Beyond the parking lot he saw the tiny doll figures, straining in the moonlight. He pushed his knuckles hard against his eyes and still saw them, beyond the darting colored spots that pressure made. And then they had walked in, and in the Dimbrough living room she had been sweetly casual, and the boy had been smiling and deferential.

The muted thump and murmur of the production floors came into the office building, providing a bass background for the thinner, sharper noises of administration. Thin clack of Miss Trevin's electric typewriter. Distant obbligato on a calculator. A girl's sharp heels ticking down the corridor.

Marcia Trevin came in and mutely laid the typed notes on the edge of his desk and turned, not looking at him, to leave.

"Miss Trevin."

"Yes sir?" Poised, still not turning.

"I'm sorry I snarled. Maybe I am a little . . . out of sorts."

He saw then the blushing, sunrise smile. "That's all right, Mr. Wyant. Which do you want me to do first? That cost of sales analysis or the inventory level thing?"

"Use your own judgment."

"Well . . ." she said uncertainly, "I guess I can finish the sales one today. Mr. Corban said maybe there was one part of it you wanted to change, though."

"I haven't heard anything about that. Type it up the way I prepared it. If Mr. Corban wants it changed, he can make out his own report."

"Yes sir. Uh . . . Mr. Wyant . . ."

"What is it, Miss Trevin?"

"Mr. Corban is . . . very clever, isn't he?"

"A very bright young man I should say."

"When he mentions you to anybody, Mr. Wyant, he sounds funny."

"What do you mean?"

"I shouldn't say it. I don't know how to say it, I guess. As though you were, well, sort of old-fashioned in your ideas. He's sort of . . . patronizing. It makes me wonder if . . . he's really your friend, Mr. Wyant."

He was tempted to tell her to keep her nose at her typewriter and stop indulging her taste for intrigue. But she had such a serious, eager, adoring look. And she had let him know of other things which had been shaping up to his disadvantage, so that he had been able to prepare himself in time.

He made himself say, smiling, "I think we better both keep a weather eye on our bright young friend, Marcia."

"It's three minutes of ten, Mr. Wyant."

He stood up and started to head for the door. "Thanks, Miss Trevin."

"Mr. Wyant! Your notes!"

"Oh . . . thanks. That was stupid, wasn't it?"

He walked through her small office to the corridor door, aware that she was looking at him with puzzled concern. His mind veered back to Jane and suddenly he found himself in the small conference room without any memory of

161

walking there. Stanley Forman was at the head of the table, carefully cutting the end from a cigar.

"'Morning, Fletch. All present and accounted for. This time, Miss Townsend, see if you can keep track of who said what. All right, Harry. This morning we're discussing whether we can take on the big subcontract, or whether, in fact, we can afford not to. Let's hear the production angle."

Morose Harry Bailey began to read his notes in a dead flat monotone. Fletcher made himself listen for a time and then his thoughts drifted away, drifted back to the self-torture of his imaginings of Jane and Sam Rice and how they had been together. Harry's voice droned on about percentages of capacity, and increased maintenance staff for two-shift operation and extension of gravity conveyors.

Fletcher saw Ellis Corban sitting on the far side of the table, several places away. His face was a model of junior executive attention.

Harry finished and Stanley Forman said, "To sum up then, this stuff is enough like our usual line so that we can take it on without too much expense in tooling and rear-rangement of floor space. Vogaler, what's the purchasing picture?"

Vogaler gave a brief crisp analysis of the tightening materials situation and how their normal line would inevitably be cramped.

There was a report from personnel on the labor supply picture. Fletcher was once again lost in his self-torment.

He woke up suddenly. "What?"

Stanley frowned at him. "If it isn't too much trouble, Fletch, give us the financial picture."

It was a bad start. He began to improvise from his notes, read the wrong figures twice and finally, ineptly, managed to get it straightened out. He leaned back with a sigh. They were all looking at him and the room was silent. He had the idea that they all knew about Jane. The idea was absurd, but he couldn't get it out of his head.

"That isn't as bright a picture as I'd hoped," Stanley said. "Any comments."

Ellis Corban coughed politely. "Mr. Forman, I shouldn't bring this up because I haven't had an opportunity to discuss it with Mr. Wyant. In fact, the idea came to me just as the meeting was getting under way, and I don't feel I have it very well organized, but I think it might be worked out if we . . . ah . . . kick it around here a bit."

Fletcher stared down the table at Ellis. The man was doing it just right. With the proper mixture of humility and concern. Fletcher thought hard, trying to imagine what Ellis had dreamed up. And he knew it hadn't been anything evolved in the last few minutes.

"Let's hear it, Corban," Stanley said quietly.

"I guess you could say my plan has two phases. As to the first phase, it is costing us money to warehouse our trade units pending the availability of the thermostats. There is, of course, not only the cost of the floor space involved, but also the interest on the money involved. Why couldn't we do this? Contact the largest dealers. Offer them the units at a price a bit lower than our usual price provided they will accept immediate delivery and hold the units in stock until we can ship the thermostats. Every big dealer has a repair department capable of assembling the thermostats to the units. There is no good reason why that has to be done here. And we can make the price attractive without hurting ourselves because the cost of maintaining the inventory will be as great as the discount, and we can get immediate use of the funds. That, of course, would be subject to approval of Sales."

They all looked at Homer Hatton. He took a tug at his underlip, frowning. Finally he said, "In normal times they wouldn't stand still for it. But there isn't enough floor stock to keep up with new construction. So I think it will be okay. But the discount shouldn't be big enough to make the smaller dealers yammer about preferential treatment."

Fletcher said, "I confess I didn't think of that. It will be a help, of course, but I don't think it will keep us from going into the money market to tide us over."

"That's where the second phase of my plan comes in," Ellis said a bit blandly, and Fletcher cursed himself for not keeping his mouth shut, for forgetting that Ellis had mentioned two phases. "I was trying to think of all this," Ellis continued, "from the point of view of K.C.I., who has the prime contract with the Quartermaster General. I can't help but think that they're anxious for Forman to take on this job. They know we have the plant, the personnel and the know-how to fulfill a subcontract that large on time, and up to specifications. I would say that they are anxious to have us take it on. Wouldn't you say that, Mr. Forman?"

"From what I've seen the last few weeks, I'd say you're right, Corban."

"I've read of quite a few instances during the past year or so, Mr. Forman, where a prime contractor would arrange for an advance payment on the prime contract before deliveries had started, with it clearly understood that the advance payment would be passed along, in part, to a critical subcontractor. I believe that if we approached K.C.I. properly and perhaps arranged a conference with the Contracting Officer involved, such a deal could be worked out. It would give us an interest-free loan, in effect, and that, combined with unloading our stock of completed units, would give us enough so that I believe we could get by without having to arrange any short-term working capital loans, as outlined in Mr. Wyant's report."

The room was silent. Fletcher wondered if Stanley Forman was aware of how neatly and cleverly Ellis Corban had knifed him. He knew that Corban's plan would work out. It solved a rather unpleasant little problem. And Ellis had made certain that there would never be any misunderstanding about the authorship of the plan. Let the man do that a few more times and Forman would wonder why he should keep deadwood at the top while Corban did all the creative brainwork.

Fletcher said, "I'm willing to say that if Mr. Corban had had enough time to discuss this with me, I would have insisted that he bring it up at this meeting. That's the sort of thinking which has kept us in such good shape since the war."

It was, at least, an attempt, but Fletcher was aware that it had gone over a bit flatly. And, he realized to his dull surprise, it did not seem to matter very much. It didn't matter now if Elllis moved in on him and took the whole thing over. Funny how I always imagined this work was aside and apart from my marriage, that the satisfaction I took in it would continue no matter what. Now I can see how closely they were interwoven, how one cannot truly exist without the other.

"For God's sake, Fletch! Are you asleep?"

He stared at Stanley's frowning face. "I'm sorry."

"I asked you for your opinion. As long as this was Corban's plan, will you go along with sending him out to K.C.I. to see what he can swing?"

"Shouldn't Mr. Wyant go?" Ellis asked quickly.

"I think it would be only fair, Stanley, to send him out there."

"Done, then. Get off today if you can, Corban. Harry, you and Homer co-ordinate on getting those units out of here. Meeting dismissed."

"Do you want that in the notes, Mr. Forman," Miss Townsend asked plaintively, "about you asking Mr. Wyant if he was asleep?"

"No, for God's sake!" Stanley exploded. The meeting broke up. Fletcher stopped for a drink of water. When he went through Miss Trevin's office she said, "Mr. Corban is in there waiting for you, sir. And your wife wants you to call her."

"Put in the call when Mr. Corban leaves, please."

He shut the door behind him as he went into his office. He made himself smile, and he knew that this was precisely the right time to let Ellis know that one Fletcher Wyant was perfectly aware of the facts of life.

"Gosh, Fletch," Ellis said, getting up quickly, "that was a tactical error and I realize it now. I should have kept my big mouth shut and talked it over with you after the meeting. It would have been simple enough to ask Mr. Forman to call another meeting after the two of us had kicked it around."

Fletcher sat down behind his desk and leaned back, balancing his ankle on his knee. "Sometimes an idea is so hot you can't keep still. Lucky you thought of it in time to present it at the meeting."

"Yes, I guess it was. But, hell, you brought me in here. The last thing I'd want to do is make it look as though I was trying to go over your head and impress the boss."

"I don't think you have to worry, Ellis. I'll tell Stanley

that you thought better of opening your mouth after you started to speak."

"Well . . ." Ellis said uncertainly, "I guess the harm is done, if any."

"I don't think any harm has been done. You worry too much, Ellis."

"That's damn white of you, Fletch. To take it like this, I mean."

"Take what? If my department comes up with a bright idea, it's to my credit, isn't it? I mean you *are* working for me, aren't you?"

"Oh, certainly. But you know . . . I mean the way most companies are . . . I'd hate to have you think I've got any disloyalty in my system."

"Now you're joking, of course," Fletcher said evenly.

Ellis looked faintly uncomfortable. "Uh . . . I don't see what you mean."

"Just that if I should think for one minute that you're trying to cut the ground out from under me, I'd have you fired before you could get strong enough to make a fight of it."

The two men faced each other. Fletcher stood up slowly. Now they knew precisely where they stood. It was fair warning to Ellis. A warning he couldn't very well disregard.

"I guess I can get off today all right," Ellis said. "Any special instructions?"

"I think you're capable of handling it. Just one thing, though."

"Yes?"

"Don't try to move too fast. Don't be too eager. Take a few days over there. Give the impression we're not too terribly anxious to land the subcontract." He allowed himself a smile. "That's why I insisted you go, Ellis. If I'd gone, they might think we are placing too much importance on it."

Ellis flushed. "I see what you mean. I'll get in there tonight and go over to their offices first thing in the morning. I won't rush it."

"If you get back Thursday, that's soon enough. Friday is the Fourth of July."

166

They shook hands and Fletcher wished him luck. Ellis turned with his hand on the doorknob. "By the way, will this be all right with you? My car needs a lot of work, so I think I'll put it in the garage. I'd like to tell Laura that if she needs anything, she can call you. Okay?"

"Certainly."

"That was quite a party yesterday."

"Wasn't it."

"Glad you asked us, Fletch. Laura will probably give Jane a ring sometime today."

He sat at his desk after Ellis had gone. Miss Trevin told him Jane was on the line. "Hello?"

"Fletch? I tried to get you before when you were in the meeting." Her voice was crisp and formal. "It's about the children."

"What about them?"

"I don't think it would hurt if they were away for a few days. Say until the Fourth. We promised them we'd take them to the fireworks at the club Friday night, you know. I could take them."

"I'll be glad to. It would be good for them to . . . get out of the heat for a few days, I guess. But the camp doesn't start until . . ."

"I realize that. The Trumbulls asked me over a week ago if Judge and Dink could visit them at their camp at Lake Harrison. Their boy and girl are almost exactly the same age you know, and Madge said they had no one to play with up there, and she has help this year, and she'd be glad to have them. I said no at the time because of them going away to camp so soon. She said if I changed my mind, to bring them up any time."

"I guess that would be okay. What do the kids think?"

"They liked the idea, I guess. They seem . . . a little odd today. It's hard to tell what they're thinking."

"It's fine with me. I think it's a good idea, in fact."

"We can leave here right after lunch. I have my keys. I thought we could taxi down and take the car, if that's all right with you."

"Fine."

"It's not a good road and traffic is usually heavy and it's

167

a hundred miles, so I thought if she asks me, I'll stay over tonight."

"Do as you please."

"If I'm not home by nine, then I'm staying over. I've told Anise not to come this week."

"I don't plan to get home before then anyway."

"Oh, I see."

He held the line for a few seconds and said, "Well, is that all?"

He heard the soft click as she hung up. He shut his hands so hard his knuckles hurt. He wanted to smash things, overturn the desk, kick out the window. Instead he waited until his breathing was normal, and then tried to lose himself in his work. It was a formula that seldom failed. On this day the effort was useless. Evil figures crawled through his brain. He kept thinking of the good days, and he wanted to cry like a child. He remembered the days when Dink was one and Judge was three, and they were nearly driving Jane mad. And he had had to leave her for the crazy months overseas. Her letters had always been a declaration of love and faith, strengthening him, and making him feel soiled and guilty in the arms of Beatrice and the abundant Hannah. He thought of all the nights of love with Jane, of how it always varied. Sometimes warm and slow and sleepy, and sometimes wildly inventive, and sometimes pure magic that took you away from yourself, away from a known world. Had any man ever lost more, and lost it more brutally? He wished with all his heart that she had denied the incident flatly and calmly and decisively, and that he could have learned to live with the lie—rather than having it this way, where there seemed to be nothing left.

Chapter Fourteen

At ten o'clock on Monday evening the city stewed like a pot over a slow fire. The overworked police began to have the feeling that some vast lid was about to blow off. There was a thread of fear in them, and even the milder members of the force used quick brutality as the solution to most problems.

An interne carefully counted twenty-three stab wounds in a stocky Italian body and marveled that the man had lived long enough to die as they were wheeling him into the emergency operating room. Somebody found a starving dog under the Town Street bridge. A person unknown had carefully sewed its festering mouth shut with heavy cord. Three young girls of decent family were picked up naked in a sedan parked on a downtown street. It was discovered that all three were full of heroin, and that two of the three were diseased. A pulpy bloated body was fished out of the river by four small boys. An elderly man was nabbed in the park for indecent exposure and on the way to headquarters he managed to dive out of the open window of the prowl car to die under the wheels of a city bus. A hysterical girl was found wandering on the highway near lover's lane. They found the body of her escort ten feet from the parked car. The four men who had raped her had hit the young man a bit too hard.

The night heat was like the string of a bass fiddle, a string which had been plucked and now vibrated in a tone just below the ability of the human ear to hear it. A man sat in a small dirty apartment near the river. There was a boy scout hatchet near his feet. Those who had heard the screams called the police. They broke the door down and the youngest cop was sick in the hall. The man sat there, studying first his palms, and then the backs of his hands, over and over, as though there were something there he would understand if he looked long enough and thought hard enough. A small boy toddled into a doorway, fingers in his mouth, and stared mildly at his teen-age sitter and her boyfriend on the dark couch. The boyfriend cursed. The sitter snatched up the boy so violently that he howled with fright and pain. She thrust him back in his crib. If he kept crying, the boy would go. If she didn't come back soon, the boy would go. She held the pillow down tightly with both hands for a long time and then went back to the living room, heard herself say faintly, "He went to sleep," as she slipped back into the boy's rough impatient arms.

The police cursed the night and the heat and the animal city as they built up long weary hours in future courtrooms. The city lay on a hundred thousand sticky beds and fought for air.

At ten o'clock Fletcher had known for some time that he was going to phone. He had known in the meeting that he was going to phone, as soon as it had been decided that Ellis would be sent to K.C.I. She had been in his mind ever since. Yet, somehow, he had fought against it, fought to the very limit of his strength.

He had wandered through the areas of the cheapest bars, collar open, sleeves rolled up, coat over his arm. He'd lost his hat someplace, and he couldn't remember where, or how. He'd sat in one dim bar and a tawny, hardmouthed girl had sung one of the old songs and it had made him cry, silently there, in the dimness, with the glass cold against his hand. That was many bars ago, and he was beyond tears.

He saw the booths in the back of the drugstore and he went in. Ceiling fans stirred the air, and there was an indefinable smell of garbage. He had two dimes, and first he called his home and counted the rings for a time, and then forgot to count and finally hung up. He stood heavily in the booth, and then remembered he had to look up the number. He got the number and started to dial and forgot it, and had to go back to the book and look again.

She answered on the third ring. "Hello?" She sounded far away.

"This is Fletch."

"Oh! What do you want, Fletcher?"

"That's a good question. A very good question."

"You're drunk."

"Oh, a little. Not *too* drunk, if you know what I mean, honey."

"I'm afraid I do. You better go take a cold shower, Fletcher."

"Let's both take one. Little co-operative shower. Very brisk."

"This is a party line, you know."

"Good thing. Wake them up. Give 'em something to talk about. Ellis go bounding off okay?"

"Yes. He took a three o'clock flight. I drove him out."

"Kiss him good-by?"

"I believe so." She sounded irritated.

"Jane's away. Up at a lake. She likes lakes. Got to tell you about that sometime. She's nuts about lakes."

"I was reading, Fletcher, and enjoying it. Do you have anything at all to say?"

"Last night. Didn't I turn down a deal?"

"I got that impression."

"Changed my mind, baby. Quick-like. Right after you left."

"Think it over some more and call me in the morning."

"I tell you I'm fine! Sober as a damn judge."

"Frankly you sound sloppy and messy and I don't want you barging around here tonight. Is that clear?"

"Ellis said you'd phone me up, you want anything. No car, he said."

"The garage was too busy. They couldn't take the car. Good night, Fletcher."

"Wait a minute!"

"Go to bed, Fletcher. Good night."

There was a sharp, decisive click. He fished in his pocket and found another dime. Then he went out and asked the address of the drugstore. He went back into the booth and phoned a cab. When it came he was waiting out on the corner, feeling faintly queasy. He gave Laura's address. On the dark street the houses looked all alike, back in the elm shadows.

He paid off the cab and stood in the shadows for a time, and then walked up to the porch steps with an attempt at briskness and decision. But he stumbled on the steps and caught himself with his hands, hurting his wrist.

He pounded on the door, calling, "Laura! Laura!"

He looked through the glass. The hall light clicked on and he saw her stride quickly down the hall toward the door. She wore a dark blue robe and her face was set and angry. She fiddled with the door and then opened it. It opened about five inches before the night chain snubbed it.

"Really!" she said. "I *do* have to live here."

"Take that silly chain off, or I'll huff and I'll puff and I'll blow your house down."

"Listen to me! Can you understand what I'm saying?"

"Sure. Anybody'd think I was drunk, the way you talk."

"I don't want you in this house . . . in your present condition or any other condition. This house is out of bounds. Can you understand that?"

"Come on. Get the car keys and we'll go to my house."

"I'll phone a cab. It will be here in five minutes and take you home."

"Just got rid of a cab. Sick of cabs. Gets monotonous. Be a good kid and let me in."

"No!"

"LAURA, LET ME IN!"

"Will you shut up! Please!"

"LAURA!"

She fumbled with the chain and swung the door open. He walked through, reaching for her. She twisted out of his arms and turned off the hall light. He reached for her again and she hit him sharply across the mouth. The shock silenced him.

She said, "Get back away from the door. I think somebody called the police."

The pale car drifted down the street. It stopped in front. A uniformed man got out and came up the walk. She pushed at Fletcher. "Get in the other room. Sit down on the floor before you knock something over."

He went into the other room, found a chair and sank gratefully into it. He heard a heavy voice, heard her calm

172

answering tone. "It didn't come from here, officer. Further up the street I think. I heard it too. A man shouting."

The door closed and he could vaguely see her as she came toward him. She stopped a careful distance away. "Really!" she whispered.

"Sorry," he mumbled. "Drunker than I thought I guess. Hell of a note."

"I don't want you here."

"See what you mean."

"I've got to get you home somehow. Is your wife really out of town?"

"Yes. I wasn't kidding. Look . . . maybe some black coffee and then call a cab . . ."

She stood in silent thought. "All right. Don't come out into the kitchen until I get the shades down."

He sat until he saw the bright kitchen lights go on. He stood up and felt his way toward the kitchen. He lurched alarmingly and hit something. It went over with a loud crash. She came running. "Oh, God! The lamp."

She helped him, got him safely into the kitchen and in a chair at the kitchen table. She said, "I make lousy coffee."

"Just hot and black. All I need."

When it was on the stove she came and sat opposite him. "This doesn't seem like you, Fletcher. Like what I thought you were."

He felt that his grin was idiotic. "Long story. Remember the scrap las' night?"

"I remember that silly woman yelling at me."

"You left," he said heavily. "She was still yelling. Jane told her to shut up. She turned on Jane. I was standing there. Standing right there. Told Jane about seeing her Saturday night at the lake. Seeing her in the moonlight with a college boy in a rubber raft. Getting up, putting her suit back on, for God's sake."

He wanted to giggle at the startled look on Laura's face. "What!"

"Just that. Just like I said. And Jane confessed. Told me flat she'd done it. Bitch. Dirty sneaky bitch. Never knew she was like that. Almost killed her. Had the gun on her. Finger on the trigger. She tells me go ahead. And I can't do it. The kids in the house, I guess. Stopped me. Something stopped me. All mixed up today. Ellis sticks a knife in my back in the meeting. Sent him away. Got a little drunk. Thinking all night about you. Me being damn prude. Loyal husband or something. No future in that noise. Wanted you and came here. Too . . . drunk. . . ."

And then she was shaking him and the coffee was steaming hot in front of him. He managed to get it to his lips. He burned his mouth. It burned its way down into his stomach. She sat opposite him again. Her face was blurred. He tried to smile at her. And then it was tremendously important to let her know how good the good years had been—how perfect and how precious.

He talked and sometimes his words would seem to fade away as though someone else were saying them in the next room, and then they would be loud and she would shush him. He knew he was being incoherent, but it was very necessary that she should know.

She had him by the arm with surprising strength and he was out in the night again. "What's . . . what's going on?"

"I'm going to drive you home. Come on now. Here's the car. Up you go."

He sprawled in on the seat. She slammed the door and he pulled himself erect. He sat, waiting for her to start the car, and then the door was open again and she was pulling at him.

"You change your mind, baby?" he asked thickly.

"About what? Come on. Get out. You're home. Careful, now."

He peered around and saw that she had indeed driven into his driveway. The house was dark. He remembered that Jane was at that lake. Kids were away. At her command, when they reached the front door, he dug laboriously for his keys. She unlocked the door and swung it open. He couldn't find the light switch. Somebody had moved it. Wrong house, maybe. She found it. He banged into the doorframe, found the hall, and walked down to his room. The hall kept tilting and bumping his shoulder. He sat down on the bed and saw her go to the closet, get a hanger, hang his coat on it. With the bedroom light on he saw for the first time that she had changed to crisp tailored slacks and a white shirt cut like a man's.

"Look . . . wonnerful in that outfit, Laura, honey."

"Lift your foot. Okay, the other one. No, don't fall over until I get that shirt off."

She unbuttoned his shirt deftly and pulled it off. "Say, you're pretty good at this. Old Ellis come home stinky?"

"My father used to take a night off once in a while. Lie back now. Up further. That's it. Brother, you really took on a load."

She undid his belt, unzipped his trousers while he tried, fumblingly, to help. She went to the foot of the bed, took the cuffs of his trousers and with small hard jerks pulled them out from under him until they were free and she could draw them off over his bare feet. She found a pants hanger and hung those up too. She turned out the light and then pulled the sheet up over him.

He reached blindly in the darkness and caught her wrist, pulled her awkwardly down onto him.

"No, Fletcher. Not here. And not the way you are."

"I know that," he said, his mind momentarily clear. "Let me hold you. Just one minute."

She relaxed and stretched out beside him, on top of the sheet. He held her. He said, "Big damn fool, eh?"

"Not all the way, darling. Just a bit foolish tonight."

"Thanks. You pick up stray dogs too?"

"Not often."

"Look, tomorrow? Want to see you tomorrow, honey."

"Tomorrow and sober. And not at my house and not here."

"Where?"

"Somewhere in the hills, darling. Somewhere outdoors."

"Hey, how about a picnic?"

She laughed softly. "A picnic, then. Phone me." She kissed him lightly on the ear and left. He listened but he did not hear the front door close. He did hear her car door, and heard her drive away. The headlights swept into the room and then left it in a darkness that seemed deeper than before. Thinking about her seemed to be the only thing in the world that would drive the small obscene cavorting little doll figures out of his mind. And he thought about Laura and how she would be, and soon he went to sleep.

He woke up with a blinding, crashing hangover that effectively blocked out any consecutive thought. The only reality was the pain and dry thirst and quivering nausea, and until they were relieved, he could think of nothing except ways and means. He had a vague memory of himself as a hooting, wavering figure, stomping through the thick night of the city, but he had no room in his head for remorse or guilt. He managed to sit up by degrees. His watched had stopped. The bedroom clock had stopped. He guessed it was late. Let it be late.

After he worked his way out of bed by degrees, he padded miserably into the bathroom. He held onto the sink and drew a glass of water. It went down and came right back up. He retched miserably for a long time. The next glass stayed down and he followed it with three more, then got into the shower. He stood under the spray, mechanically changing the temperature to hot, then cold, then hot again, over and over, while he wondered if this business of Jane was going to turn him into a prime alcoholic. They always said the problem drinkers drank because of some basic inadequacy. Jane had neatly proved him inadequate. Insufficient.

Suddenly he remembered Laura. He stood very still under the cold spray. Good Lord! Very dignified little routine, that was. Sloppy drunk and on the make. She'd brought him home. Undressed him, even. All very brisk and efficient, and you wouldn't think she could cope in exactly that way.

He felt a little better. He toweled himself harshly, drank some more water. It didn't help the thirst, just made him feel bloated. He put on fresh shorts and socks and went to the phone, dialed the time number first.

"The time is now sixteen minutes of ten," the metallic voice said. "The time is now sixteen minutes of ten. The time is now fifteen . . ." He hung up, fighting, as always, against the urge to thank the mechanical recording.

176

He dialed the plant number, asked for himself. Miss Trevin said, "Good morning, Mr. Wyant's office."

"Miss Trevin, I'm a little under the weather this morning."

"Oh, I was so worried. I called you a little while ago. There wasn't any answer. Is it serious, Mr. Wyant?"

"No. A little touch of heat exhaustion I think. I might try to get in later in the day. Anything cooking?"

"Mr. Forman stuck his head in the office about nine thirty, and then he went away without saying a word when he saw you weren't at your desk. And there was a person to person call from Mr. Corban. What will I do if it comes in again?"

"Tell the operator I'll phone Mr. Corban tomorrow morning at ten o'clock at K.C.I."

"I think when he couldn't get you, he talked to Mr. Forman."

"Oh. Well, in that case, maybe the call won't come in again."

"Should I tell Mr. Forman you're ill?"

"You might do that please."

"If you don't feel right, Mr. Wyant, you shouldn't try to come in today. There isn't anything terribly important lined up that I know of. Mr. Fedder has an appointment for ten thirty tomorrow morning."

"Hold the fort, Miss Trevin."

"Yes sir. I certainly will. I hope you feel better."

He hung up. Jane had stayed over. She probably wouldn't be in any great rush to get back. He put his hand on the phone to lift it and call Laura, then changed his mind. He went into the kitchen, put coffee on, went to the front door and got the morning paper. He remembered the milk and got it out of the box. It felt a little warm, but he put it away in the refrigerator. There was a hard throb in his head that felt as though it bulged the bone over his right eye with each pulsation. Lord, two rough nights in a row. If the geometric progression continued, tonight was going to kill him for sure. Laura. A vague memory of holding her slimness beside him, of lips touching his ear in a good night kiss. "Phone me."

He went back in to the phone. She answered before it seemed to have a chance to ring at all. "Hello?"

"Laura?"

"That wasn't shrewd of me, was it? Snatching the phone. Now you know I was sitting here waiting. How are you? Bleeding from the eyes, darling?"

"I'm sorry, officer. I didn't get the license number of that truck."

"Hmmm."

"Very messy, Laura. Very sad. You're a patient type. You listened to all my drunken woes."

"I take it . . . she isn't back yet."

"No."

"Do you remember about our picnic?"

"You mean leave the office?"

"You're too smart to talk like this from the office, dear."

"Right. I begged off today. And I was trying to remember something. I knew it was a good something, but I couldn't quite catch hold of it."

"From where I sit I can see a very tricky item. Ellis' people gave it to us. Red leather, with thermos bottles and dishes and things. Guaranteed to collect ants."

"It might be a shade cooler in the hills."

"It might, darling. It just might."

"I'm without vehicle."

"I was supposed to take ours in this morning. But I didn't. The end of that road of yours with the elfin name? In . . . oh . . . fifteen minutes?"

"Don't expect me to scintillate. I'm still hurting."

"Fletcher, my silly heart is going boom, boom, boom. Like drums."

"Here too."

"Hang up, darling. I can't. And time is going by."

He hung up gently, winced as he stood up too quickly. He shaved in frantic haste, promising to clean the razor later. He looked at his sports shirts, selected one, then stood for a moment, feeling an odd sharp pain. The shirt was a soft shade of grey, very lightweight. Jane had bought it for him and it was of imported Egyptian cotton. She had paid far more for it than he ever would have paid for a shirt. It had not been any sort of occasion. She had seen it and liked it and bought it. He put on the new grey dacron slacks, the comfortable moccasin-type shoes. He made a quick survey in Jane's full-length mirror. Okay. Just a shade pasty and a bit puffy around the eyes. He held his hands out and his fingers trembled, but not too badly. He cooled the steaming coffee with faucet water and drank it at the sink, using it to wash down three aspirin.

When he went out the front door, testing the snap lock after he pulled it shut, the full heat of midmorning struck him, and he realized that the house had retained some of the deceptive coolness of early morning.

He had not thought of the walk to the corner as being strange and difficult, and yet it was. Children played with a black cocker spaniel in a neighboring yard, and they stopped their play to stare curiously at him. He saw through a picture window, saw a vaguely familiar woman straighten up, a dust cloth in her hand, and stare out at him. It was the same sort of feeling as skipping school. Guilt and recklessness. The sun was a tangible weight against the nape of his neck and against his shoulders through the thin shirt. He glanced back at the house and saw the hills beyond it and saw, high and far away in the morning sun, the red barn. Somehow the crazy week had started with the red barn. Started with that feeling of drifting discontent. He knew that there was an unpleasant enchantment, a spell about the place. Perhaps going there with Laura might exorcise that particular spirit.

When he got to the corner he crossed to the other side of the drive and stood in the shade of a red maple to wait for her. Traffic was fast on the drive. Gasoline stink lingered in the air. The tires made sleek ripping noises and down toward the city, in the distance, the cars disappeared into heat shimmer, with chrome glinting, and a look of wetness on the wide asphalt with its sharp yellow lines.

He waited for five minutes and then the Corbans' green sedan came up out of the heat haze, slowing to stop beside him, and he saw Laura's smile as he opened the door and got in beside her. She drew away from the curb without looking behind her, and a car blatted angrily at them.

"Where to, darling?" she asked. "Any ideas?"

"There's a red barn I can see from my bedroom window. It is a long way away, and quite high, and it looks pleasant up there, somehow. Whenever I look at it, it makes me feel restless. I've never seen it close by, but it looks abandoned. And we'll be able to see the city from there, I think, and look down at the river."

"How do we get there?"

"It will have to be trial and error, Laura. Turn left at the next light."

He turned and looked at her. She wore a white, off-the-shoulder blouse, a lurid peasant skirt, flat gold sandals with long thongs wound and tied around her ankles. The car seemed too big, the wheel too high for her. She wore a small intent frown as she drove. After they made the corner, he took the wheel. She sat curled beside him and he could feel her eyes on him. He remembered the look of her body at the Sunday party and it gave him a breathless empty feeling.

Chapter Fifteen

After Jane fled from the breakfast table and shut herself in the bedroom Monday morning, shut herself in the room where for the first time, with Fletcher in the house, she had slept alone, she lay across her bed and waited for tears but they did not come. There had been too many tears in the night.

Fletcher had driven away, and she heard the muted sound of the children talking. She sat up on the edge of the bed and told herself that she couldn't sit like a lump for the rest of her life, grieving over a fact that couldn't be changed.

There had never been any horror like that of hearing Martha talking in that deadly tone and knowing that she couldn't be stopped, knowing that Fletcher was standing there, listening, knowing that it was killing something inside of him.

She knew that there was one thing in life that was absolutely certain. You pay, in some way, for everything you do. There is no mercy in the court. And it had been absurd to think for one moment that there would be no payment for that nightmare at the lake. She had known that in the shocking instant that it was happening.

There had been a strange pleasure in feeling the hard smash of his open hand against her face. And there would have been more of the same feeling in the hot smash of the bullet. But that was last night. And this was today. And you kept living. You didn't die because you willed it when you lay there alone in that rubber raft, watching the tremble of his hands as he lit a cigarette. No matter what, you went on living, and if life became pointless then it was something to be endured, and it could best be endured by

181

rising to it, not sitting like a fat lump on a bed and wailing for what had been, but could never be again.

It was easy enough to say that he was unfair. One slip in fifteen years, and then a very unwilling slip, a slip against which you had fought like an animal. But the real fault had been out there in the lake, just before that. When he had pulled the suit off over your unprotesting legs. So you pay for that.

She remembered the Chicago business. The way her mind had crawled with all sorts of imaginings. His mind, with that special sickness of jealousy, would be doing that now. There was one vague chance, she knew. He might, for the sake of the children, give up the idea of divorce. They would live together like strangers, and that, perhaps, might be worse for the children than any divorce. If he decided that, it would be her chance. And she knew, coldly, how she would handle it. She would determinedly set out to seduce him. If she could manage it, perhaps they might get back a fraction of what they had once had. The magic might be gone forever, but a new relationship of comfortable mutual need would be better than nothing.

She straightened her shoulders. Confession had been made. And she was *not* going to become a mealy thing, whining around for forgiveness. If there could be any forgiveness in his heart, he would forgive a calm woman with some pride left, not a groveling thing. She briskly changed to the most attractive clothes she could think of. She took a lot of time with her hair and with her make-up. She cleaned off her nail polish and replaced it with fresh.

And then she walked out with her head up. The children shouldn't be around during this, the worst time. She remembered Madge Trumbull's invitation. Madge had left it open. She asked the children what they thought. It was obvious that Judge and Dink knew something was up. Something that threatened their emotional security. Yet, in the canny way of children, they did not try to find out what it was. The children took their cue from her, and drummed up a proper amount of enthusiasm, and trotted off to pack. She phoned Fletcher and he was in conference and she asked Miss Trevin to tell him to phone her back.

On the phone she managed to keep her voice cool and

polite and formal, though she was perilously close to tears.

After lunch they taxied, with luggage, down to the Forman parking lot and took the Pontiac and headed for the lake a hundred miles away.

Madge Trumbull was alone at the lake with her two kids, and she was delighted that Jane had changed her mind. She said Judge and Dink were most welcome and couldn't they stay longer than Thursday. She said they were never any trouble, and she would even like to keep them all summer. But Jane explained how excited they were over going to the summer camps that had been picked out way before Christmas. They all swam in the late afternoon, Jane in her old suit, knowing that she would never again be able to wear the new one. It was a much bigger lake than Lake Vernon, and the water was colder. She swam hard, trying to tire herself. Afterward, she and Madge sat on the big porch while the combination maid and cook prepared the dinner. They drank cocktails and talked and once Jane was on the verge of telling Madge the whole thing, and then quickly changed her mind. It wouldn't do any good. And, if she and Fletcher managed to heal, partially, this most serious of all rifts, it might do harm, as Madge was definitely not noted for her ability to keep secrets.

So she talked and twice she forgot the whole horror for a few minutes at a time, only to have it come flooding in on her, worse than ever.

They stayed up far too late after all the kids were in bed, and after Jane had at last gone to bed she knew that a fresh supply of tears had filled the well, so she turned her face into the pillow and bunched it against her mouth and cried until there was a large damp patch under her eyes. Then, drained and exhausted, she turned the pillow over and tried to pray. It had been too long since she had prayed. It made her feel self-conscious and awkward. She and Fletcher had both drifted away from church, except for Easter and Christmas visits. And lately the children had been permitted to get away with not attending Sunday school.

There was a pine smell in the night air and she lay on

her back and tried to pray. And then, returning to childhood, returning to a ceremony that she had not used since long before her marriage, she got out of bed and knelt on the rag rug by the bed with the cool night breeze against her body. She folded her hands and knew that it would have to be in words she could say aloud, as in childhood.

"God, I . . . I have committed a sin of the flesh. I was . . . weak, and maybe weakness is evil, but it was not . . . deliberate evil. I don't think I am a bad woman. I have been . . . a foolish woman. Maybe we don't live the way we should. But I have no excuse. I beg Your forgiveness, and I beg of You to return to me the . . . love and respect of my husband. Amen."

She climbed back into the bed and pulled the blanket up and shivered for a time until she was warm again. The prayer had left her with a feeling of futility. It had been an empty, theatrical gesture, she felt, and if there was a God, He surely had long since given up listening to the Godless people of Minidoka.

She left the lake a bit later than she had anticipated. She said good-by to the children and hoped that they had not noticed that her farewell had been a bit more fervent than the situation demanded. All the way to Minidoka, down the road that wound down through the hills, she planned the talk she would have to have with Fletcher.

Jane sensed that Fletcher had spent a night as miserable as hers, and perhaps worse. Emotional exhaustion made it impossible to maintain that hard edge of anger. Fletcher would be drained, numb and miserable. Perhaps, after all, this would be the best time to talk, before either of them had achieved any set pattern, any blind spot too pervasive.

She knew what she had to say. I want to be taken back, on your terms. If we can keep just a little of what we had, I want it kept at all costs. I'm no good without you. The thing that hurts the worst is your pride, and your self-respect. But I told you the truth of how it was. Suppose when I was alone, somebody broke into the house and raped me. What would be your reaction to that? Divorce me as unclean? Suppose the man didn't break in. Suppose I unlocked the door for him, knowing that I was being foolish, but thinking that nothing would happen. Where does guilt start, Fletcher? If you can think of my reluctance, think that I fought, then can't you start believing again that this body is yours? I've tried to keep myself young for you. And, Fletcher, look into your own heart and see if you can find a memory of a time when you were at fault, and much more willingly, much more the aggressor than I was.

There could not be a calm talk, she knew. There would have to be a scene. But perhaps the scene could end in calmness.

She went slowly down the drive. After the light she had to turn right in the third block, onto Coffeepot Road. Two cars were waiting to turn left on green across the traffic. She went by and caught a glimpse of a green car, a slim arm outstretched in signal, Laura with Fletcher beside her. She drove on and traffic was too heavy for her to look back. She tried to laugh at herself. Diseased imagination. Such a coincidence was just a little too much to expect. The Corbans' car was green. Of course, but Fletcher would be in the office, and so would Ellis, and if Laura was riding around with a man, which was likely, it could hardly be Fletcher.

She turned up the road and into the drive and parked in front of the garage doors. She took out her small overnight bag and unlocked the front door and went into the house. She smelled coffee at once and went to the kitchen, still carrying her bag. She touched the side of the pot. The gas flame was out, but the pot was very hot, almost hot enough to burn her.

She put the bag down and walked frowning through the house. She knew enough about him and his habits so that she soon found out he had come home drunk. He had slept in his shorts. His pajamas were still neatly folded. She examined the bathroom. He had cleaned up pretty well, but there was still evidence that he had been sick. The clock had stopped. The alarm was still wound tight, so it hadn't gone off. The hot coffeepot meant he had overslept, and he had not put the aspirin bottle back in the cabinet near the sink. It was still on the linoleum counter top. She began to wonder what clothes he had worn to the office. She went through his wardrobe and could not find anything missing that he might have worn. The new dacron slacks were gone. She checked his shirts. Suddenly she realized the grey Egyptian cotton shirt was gone. It was hardly an office costume. And didn't she have the vague impression that the man beside Laura had been dressed in grey? She looked at her watch, the small gold watch he had given her on their tenth wedding anniversary. Twenty-five after ten.

She sat by the phone for a time. Miss Trevin would know her voice. She remembered something she had read, and took a Kleenex and put it over the mouthpiece. She consciously made her voice more nasal and faster.

"Good morning, Mr. Wyant's office."

"Can I speak to him please?"

"Who is calling, please?"

"Miss Reilly. It's a personal matter. I'd like to talk to him."

"I'm sorry, Miss Reilly, but Mr. Wyant is out sick today. Perhaps you could reach him at his home if it's important enough to disturb him." Trevin gave her the number and Jane thanked her and hung up. She phoned the plant number again and asked for Mr. Corban. Sorry, but Mr. Corban is out of town. He isn't expected back until late Thursday.

She made one more call, to the Corbans' house. She sat and listened to the long ringing of the phone in the empty house. After a while she replaced the phone on the cradle.

He certainly had wasted no time. The minute he got a ready-made excuse he went snuffling off on the hot trail of that little piece. So her self-advertising campaign on Sunday had borne fruit already. Wave it a couple of times and watch the men flock around. With Fletcher at the head of the line. Pack of dogs trotting amiably after a bitch, tongues lolling.

She was vastly and enormously angry. She took her overnight bag and flung it on her bed. He'd been too drunk to remember he was supposed to be sleeping in the study. She used some of the surplus energy of anger to rip the sheets from his bed and make it up fresh. Suddenly, as she was balling up the sheets, she stopped and stared hard

186

at a small dark red smudge. She smelled it, and caught the faint perfume of lipstick. Not her shade. With her coloring she had to wear something with a good deal of orange in it, or else look like death itself.

Indeed he had wasted no time smuggling the little bitch into my house, into my bedroom to smear her dirty mouth on my sheets. She hasn't got the moral sense of a mink. Little mare, all aquiver for the stallion. Any stallion. This makes what happened to me look like a Presbyterian kiss. This is revolting. This smells to high heaven.

She marched to the phone, suddenly aware of exactly what she would do. She phoned the Dimbrough camp at Lake Vernon and once again held the Kleenex over the mouthpiece. She heard Dolly answer the phone. "Hello?"

"Say," she said nasally, "could I talk to Sam Rice. Is he around?"

"Just a moment, please."

It was a long time before she heard the thump as he picked the phone off the hall table. "Hello?"

"Don't say my name, Sam. It's Jane. Jane Wyant."

"They're all out on the dock," he said, lowering his voice. "What's up, Jane?"

His voice somehow made him clear again in her mind. Her memory had been smudged. She could remember the tall hard body, and the strong slant of his shoulders, but until he spoke she could not remember his face clearly. A boyish face, and, of course, an evil face. Her resentment came back so strongly that she almost hung up, unable to go through with it.

"Sam," she said calmly, "things are in a bit of a mess."

"How so?" She heard the caution in his tone.

"It seems we were watched."

There was a silence and then he said, almost tenderly, "The hell you say! The hell you say!"

"Martha Rogers. She came out to enlist us for bridge or something. I guess she arrived at what you'd call a crucial moment."

"You sound calm as all hell, Janey."

She resisted the sharp impulse to tell him to stop calling her that. "Oh, I'm very calm. We had a party here Sunday.

Martha got tight. She got mad at me and made a scene in front of Fletch. She was . . . quite graphic about the whole thing."

"Jane . . . I'm terribly sorry. What can I do?"

"Everything has been blown sky-high. *Fini*, or something. So . . . I find that I'm a lady with a name. And . . . no game."

She heard his startled grunt. "I think I see what you mean, my lamb," he said intimately. His tone was coarser, more insinuating. "You *didn't* have much fun, did you?"

"Not very much." She felt quite frozen inside. Quite calm.

"Busy?"

"I thought I could drive up. But not all the way. You know what I mean?"

"Sure. Tell you what. I'll take a little stroll. Know the fork where you turn left to come to the camp, about a mile and a half from here ? Turn right. I'll be a couple of hundred yards up the road. Got any beer?"

"How utterly romantic! Yes, there's some cold. I'll bring it."

"And sandwiches too, if you want to go all out. One hour?"

"Let's see, that would make it quarter to twelve."

"Okay, Janey? Good."

She hung up. She did not let herself think. Assignations were supposed to be tender and haunting and mysterious. This one came with beer and sandwiches. What you might expect of Sam Rice. A casual animal arrogance. Come and get it, and you bring the beer. She worked quickly, and every time her mind veered dangerously away from the routine of getting ready to go, she focused it on the small red stain on the sheet and felt anew the rush of righteous anger. She half ran to the car after changing her clothes, packing the assignation lunch. She yanked the car door shut, backed out into the street too fast, wrenched the car around. On the way north she drove fast and hard, scaring herself on the corners, and then she slowed down to a crawl, realizing she was too early.

She parked by the turnoff onto the dirt road that led to the lake, and sat quite rigid, quite unthinking and unfeeling while the inevitable minutes went by. She started up again. The hardest part was when she came to the fork he had mentioned. This was the moment of decision, of final decision. It was possible to drive on down to the Dimbrough camp and make some excuse for dropping in. She slowed until the car was barely moving and made the turn to the right. It seemed to take every bit of strength in her arms and back to make the right turn.

He was where he said he would be, and he was sitting on a log on the far side of the ditch. He got up and came striding across the ditch, smiling into the car at her, and she liked no part of his smile or his manner. He was too wise, too knowing, too utterly practiced at all this.

He opened the door on her side and said, "Hi, beautiful lady. Shove over. I know a happy sylvan spot hereabouts." She moved over and he got in. He put his arm around her and she sat still and silent as he lightly kissed the tip of her nose and said, "You are cute as several bugs, my friend." She forced a smile.

Sam drove slowly and carefully, turning right onto a lumber road, a bare trace through the woods. Grass grew tall between the wheel marks and brushed the underside of the car. Branches scraped against the sides. The track climbed slowly for nearly a half mile, and ended at a clearing where the pines grew tall and the ground was soft with needles. Jane felt as if her teeth were about to start chattering. She remembered the prayer of the night before. And this was more than weakness; this was cold intent. She made herself think of Fletch, of his body, of the body of Laura Corban.

Sam got out and said, "Like it? Nobody within miles but us chipmunks. Just you and me and some beer and a lazy afternoon. Untense, will you?"

Again she pulled her lips back in a rigid smile. "I'll try."

"A blanket is indicated. Anything in the back?"

"I think so. Yes." Sam found the right key and unlocked the back. He pulled out a grey blanket with a blue stripe, a heavy Navy surplus blanket that Fletch had bought after the war. A picnic blanket that they had often used, the four of them, with the stain where Dink had tipped over the thermos of coffee.

He took the big brown paper bag of beer and sandwiches and stood with the blanket over his arm, looked around, and said, "Over there, I guess. Come on."

She followed him, rigidly expecting sacrifice. Maybe it would be easier, she thought, if he would at least pretend to tenderness. But he made it so . . . direct. She detested the young male arrogance of him, but more than that she resented the matter-of-factness of it all.

He handed her the bag and spread the blanket out neatly on the soft bed of pine needles. "The magic carpet, angel. Take a load off."

Jane sat down awkwardly. Sam sprawled quickly beside her, laced his long fingers across his stomach and squinted up through the pine branches at the sky.

"This," he said, "is a most pleasant and unexpected bonus. I don't feel like I want to ask too many questions."

"Then don't."

He glanced sidelong at her. "You've got one of those tumbril looks. A sort of head-in-the-basket look, dear."

"Have I? I'm terribly sorry."

"Or maybe a preoperative look."

"Do you have to talk, talk, talk, talk? God!"

She looked quickly away from him and set her teeth in her underlip, biting down until it hurt.

She gave a startled gasp as he grasped her shoulder, pulled her quickly down beside him, turned her into his arms. "Talk, talk, talk," he said huskily, then found her lips. She made herself put her arms around him. Her arms felt like heavy things filled with wet sand. His mouth worked at hers and she tried to respond, tried to summon up the fluid melting of desire. But it wouldn't come and she couldn't lose herself. No matter how she tried, she was Mrs. Fletcher Wyant lying a bit absurdly at noon on a blanket in the woods with a college boy. It was grotesque, undignified, and in poor taste. She tried to simulate excitement, and knew that she was doing it awkwardly. She shut her eyes as he fumbled with the fastenings of her clothing. He took off her blouse and unhooked her bra and slid it down off her arms. He held her tightly again, kissing her lips and her breasts, but she felt nothing but awkwardness and vague alarm. She could no longer pretend. She lay rigid with her eyes squeezed tightly shut and her hands clenched, and she wished he would just hurry. Just hurry and get it over with so she could know that she had done this to Fletcher coldly and purposefully. She wondered why he was touching her no longer. She warily opened her eyes. Sam was sitting up, looking down at her with a rather odd expression, and she instinctively folded her right arm across her breasts. Sam gave her a tired disgusted smile. He reached over and picked up her blouse and bra and tossed them onto her. "Okay. Cover up."

"Go ahead, Go ahead with it. What's wrong with you?"

"Put your clothes back on, Mrs. Wyant."

"It didn't seem to bother you the other night. This is your favorite sport, isn't it?"

He turned his back to her. She heard the snap of his lighter, saw a drift of blue smoke skid away in the warm gentle wind. She sat up at last, dressed quickly, tucking her blouse awkwardly into her skirt.

Sam dug into the bag, took out two cans of beer, found the opener. She heard the beer hiss as he levered holes into the cans. He turned and handed her one can. His expression had changed. He looked amused.

"Skoal, sugar."

The beer can was chill in her hand. "Why did you stop?" she demanded.

"I didn't want you to strain yourself."

"How do you mean?"

"I'm stupid, maybe, but not that supid. The other night I was a symbol of . . . oh, blind fate or something. I was something that happened to you and you didn't like it, and you weren't willing to admit it was partly your fault. My name is Sam Rice. I brush my teeth every day. I'm kind to small children and dogs. I'm not some kind of machine you're going to use to get even with your husband. See?"

She took long swallows of the beer. "You don't make sense, Sam."

"Not the kind of sense you want me to make. You've got me all established. A rapist of the second degree or something. So you can blame me, not yourself. But it happens I'm not. As I said, I'm Sam Rice, a human being. Sorry to disappoint you, my friend. If you were a pig, fine.

We'd have a nice little picnic. Trouble is, I believed you the other night, afterward. You're no pig. And I'm no instrument of vengeance, dear. I know how you work. You're a rarity. With you there has to be love, and with no love, it doesn't work. I mean, I'm not against it as an operating procedure. It is just a touch on the rare side."

"Sam, I . . ."

"Hush up. Not about me. About your guy. Because who else can you talk to?"

She could not look at him any longer. She looked away. The words came, slow, awkward, then faster, more fluently . . . all of it. The whole mess. The party, the sheet, the coffeepot, all of it right up until the moment of meeting him.

He put his hand on her shoulder. "I don't mind your being sore at me. I told you that before, Janey."

She let the can drop. It rolled off the end of the blanket, leaving a trail of wetness where the beer spilled. She hitched closer to him, turning her face against his chest, and it was a painful sort of crying. No gentleness in the tears. They burned. And the sobs hurt her throat. Through tears, as he held her with one big arm, she saw the brown hand close slowly on his empty beer can, flattening it, before he tossed it away to clink against a stone.

"I'm glad I stopped, Janey," he said. "That's no way to do. No way to get even with the guy."

She used a paper napkin from the lunch to dry her tears. She moved away from him, rolling onto her stomach, supporting herself on her elbows. What was left of the sobs made little holes in her sentences.

"Why can't I get even that way? Why not, Sam?"

"As I said before. You're not a pig. There has to be love. Emancipated womanhood is a farce, baby. We're still working on a double standard."

"He can and I can't?"

"If you can, it means you've stopped loving him. With him it doesn't mean that at all. That's where the double stuff comes in."

"Oh, sure."

"Try to reason it out, Janey. Evidently he took a quick hack at that Corban dish, and dish she must be, out of some idea of getting even with you. So you come roaring up here to get even with him for getting even with you. Offhand, it doesn't sound like there'd be much future in that sort of thing."

"How do you mean?"

"You're using the fidelity pitch to nibble holes in each other. Maybe fidelity is just some kind of symbol."

"Oh, it's a lot more than that. Sam. A lot more."

"You and this Fletch of yours are regally fouled up, no?"

She felt the tears starting to come back. "And there's no way out of it. That's the trouble. No way out at all."

"Hell, you're both too tense. Look. Let him have his little roll in the hay, or six. He'll think he's gotten even with you. It may make him a little ashamed. You say you gave him the straight story on our little fiasco. He'll start thinking about that, and because he's ashamed, he'll start making excuses for you. Maybe, he'll say, I was too hasty. Good Lord, fifteen years of learning to live with each other. A nice wife who doesn't leave hair in the sink, and who does the coffee right and cleans up after the brats. He isn't going to toss all that over when he gets over his mad."

"But just living together, Sam. That isn't enough. It never could be enough. It would be like . . . cellmates. You have to have magic, Sam."

"Are you saying that for your own self, you want all or nothing?"

"No. I want him. I want to live with him. I want him around. Where I can look at him. I don't care how. Just to have him there."

"Easy, easy. See, if you and I had gone through with this today, it wouldn't have been any use to you unless you could let him know. Maybe he'd get over that fiasco. Would he get over a deal like this?"

She lowered her head so that her forehead was braced against her fists. "No, Sam. He wouldn't. But the thought of him and . . . Laura. It makes me . . ."

"Okay, it makes you feel bad. Little penalty for shedding your suit the other night. Look at it that way."

"But if he does come back to me, every time I'll think of . . ."

"Why? God, she isn't going to mark him. A night's sleep and a hot shower."

"Don't be so damn casual!"

"Hell, unwrap the sandwiches. I'm fixing to starve."

They ate and they finished the beer, and as they ate he talked to her gently, casually, encouragingly. She found herself liking him. She couldn't help liking him. After he tossed the last can of beer away, he lay back and fell asleep with the astonishing quickness of any husky young animal. She watched the slowly changing patterns of the afternoon sun in the pine boughs. He breathed with the slowness of a trained athlete. Oddly, he looked older when he was asleep. A golden dollar of sunlight moved toward his eyes. When it touched his closed lids he grunted and turned away from it.

She watched him. She sat hugging her knees, watching him sleep, and slowly she forced herself to accept the horror of the realization that he was, after all, a nice person. And accepting that, she knew that she was far more to blame for what had happened between them than he. She relived that first moment he had touched her, after they had fallen from the skis. Perhaps that was the moment of decision, unknown to her at that time. Other men had tried that sort of thing and she had chilled them immediately and effectively. Yet somehow she had failed to do that with Sam.

Hating him, she saw, had been just a defense. The easiest way to keep from taking a slow calm look at herself. A way to keep from admitting that she had, in some obscure way, become restive, become curious.

She thought for a long time, and she began to realize what she must do, what she had to do to cleanse herself. It was nearly three by her watch. She stretched out gingerly beside him, moved her head into the angle of his neck and shoulder, and put one arm across his broad chest.

He awoke at once and said, "Well, hello!"

"Sam. Sam, I've been hideous to you. And you've been pretty wonderful."

"Wonderful Sam. They all call me that."

"Sam, it isn't love, but it's almost love. And it wouldn't be just to get even or anything. It wouldn't be . . . some-

thing I'd ever save up to taunt him with, or anything childish like that."

"Let me catch up. Go slower."

She turned so that she could speak in a barely audible
tone, directly into his ear. "If you'd be . . . very gentle . . .
and patient with me, Sam, I think that I could . . . that
maybe it would be . . . I mean, I've been so damned unfair
to you in every way. And if you still want me . . ."

He reached over and laid his hand against her cheek.
"You are a nice guy, Janey. But don't spoil my act. I'm
full of virtue and manly restraint. The offer is . . . understood and appreciated. But you'd regret it, and you know
it. Now let's get the hell out of here before it's too late."

He stood up lithely and held out his hand and pulled
her to her feet. He folded the blanket. They walked to the
car with his arm around her waist.

As he turned the key in the ignition she saw that his
hand was trembling. She understood. When she let him off
he walked away with his tall quick stride, not looking
back.

Chapter Sixteen

Fletcher drove up into the steepness of the dirt-road hills, knowing that he would find the red barn. Her vivid skirt was spread wide across her drawn-up legs. She seemed to sit beside him in some strange trance, her body responding slackly to the sudden lurches of the car over the potholed roads.

He took quick little glances toward her, seeing the small golden hand resting on her ankles, fingers against the gold thongs. The high world shimmered in heat and the insects sang like a million tiny electric motors, keening endlessly. The leaves beside the road were motionless, caked thick with the white dust. And behind them the dust rolled high and white.

"Not last night, Fletcher, my darling," she said softly.

"Eh? I know."

"Not that way. Not dulled and messy and habitual. Do you know what I mean?"

"I think so."

"It has to be like . . . a little death. Does that sound strange?"

"A little, I guess."

"Maybe I can teach you what I mean. A little death, and the cowards would go to it blindfolded, or drunk, or both. Have you ever fasted? I mean really."

"I guess not."

"We'll have to try that, Fletcher. After the first few days you aren't hungry any more. But everything gets brighter and sharper. Colors, taste, smell, touch. That's the way you ought to go to a little death. Go in such a way that everything is stamped deep and bright on your mind. Do I frighten you?"

"That's a funny thing to ask, isn't it?"

"I want you to be frightened. Because everything . . . so much of everything has been locked up so long. So damn endlessly long, Fletcher. And you're going to let it all out. All out at once."

"Isn't that what I want?"

"I don't know what you want. I don't know what you expect. I'm just grateful that . . . you've come to me, in spite of the reason. Because reasons don't matter any more. Not to us. Not after today."

There was an odd flat quality to her voice. As though she had stated some new immutable equation. Apparently, he thought, she was giving this a lot more weight and meaning that he had imagined she would.

"Sounds mystic," he said, with an attempt at lightness.

"Perhaps it is. You see, there's going to be no love, Fletcher. None."

He lifted his foot from the gas pedal involuntarily. "What?"

"Don't look so alarmed, darling. What we are going to have isn't going to be love. No vows about eternity. Nothing sweet and sticky, full of gasping sighs and odes to eyebrows. I've outlived love, Fletcher."

"What shall we call it?"

"A nice plain word, Fletcher. Very simple. Begins with the same letter and has the same number of letters. Lust. And the fulfillment of lust. And nothing less than that. A little death through lust, Fletcher. And the beginning of a lot of little deaths for us. We want it to be just as evil and animal and contrived as we can possibly make it. So we aren't people any more. That's what I want. To stop being anything but a she-thing. And you are the he-thing. I want you with cloven hooves, Fletcher. And we'll do everything we can think of to close ourselves off from a pretty little world of manners and customs and tenderness. We'll be in our own world, Fletcher. A world that we'll make for ourselves, where there's just color and sound and smell and feel. Things we can stamp deep. Pleasure and pain all twisted up together in crazy ways, and nothing at all we won't do, because there won't be any rightness and wrongness any more."

Her voice had a strange singsong quality and when he glanced at her it seemed to him that in spite of the glare of sun on white dust, the pupils of her eyes were enormous. The look of her made his throat thick and he reached one hand for her.

She pushed his hand away. "No, Fletcher. Nothing as traditional. Because this has to be new. Where we make our own customs. This time, this first time, it will be my turn to make our customs and make our rules and guide our actions, and next time it will be yours. Agreed?"

"Yes."

"A little death, Fletcher. And we'll come back from our little death and hate what we have to go back to. Because this will be our reality. And there won't be anything else."

"Yes."

"An endless experiment in evil, Fletcher. Because that's the only thing left in the world."

"Yes."

"You know what I am, I think. What would I have been ten thousand years ago, Fletcher?"

"I don't understand."

"After today you'll know."

He paused at a crossroads to get his bearings. He turned up a steeper rockier hill than any they had been over. The car labored and stones slid under the back wheels. A hundred yards beyond the crest of the hill he saw the barn. There had been a house once, but nothing was left but the tall naked stone chimney, a trace of where a wall had been, a rusty pump. He turned in and the tall grass scraped the underside of the car. He turned off the motor. The cooling engine made clicking sounds and it was so still that he could hear the sighing sound the grass made as it stood up again where the wheels had matted it down.

He got out and looked out over the city, miles away. She stood beside him.

"Did you say," she asked, "that you could lie on your bed and see this barn?"

"Yes."

"I like that. Look at it tomorrow, darling. Look at it and remember what today was like. Because this isn't one

198

of those country-club escapades. You know that, don't you?"

He looked down at her. Her face was tilted up, strange little face with its look of what he had thought of as a delicate strength. Now the arch of the brows, the set of the mouth, they had another meaning. He groped clumsily for her and she stepped back, laughing a little. "Remember? This is my day, Fletcher. Entirely mine."

"Unless I take over."

"But I won't let you. Get the red case and the blanket, darling."

He got them out of the back seat of the car. They walked through the tall grass. He held up the top strand of a rusty barbwire fence. She slid through gracefully and took the case from him. He stepped over the top strand.

The big door that had once rolled back and forth in its channel lay to one side, splintered and rotten. The barn was dim inside. Blue sky showed through the roof holes. Sun dotted the ancient matted debris on the floor. There were holes in the floor, and the boards cracked under his weight. The air smelled of dust and spiders and a lingering winter dampness in the hay.

Laura said softly, "It smells of decay."

"We could go out . . ."

"You *are* a fool, Fletcher. So much to learn about me. This is the right place because it is like this. Don't you see?"

And she walked quickly away from him into the barn, avoiding the holes in the floor, the vivid skirt swinging from her small round hips—a varicolored flame in the half-darkness of the barn.

"Here," she called. "Back here, Fletcher."

He followed her back. She had found a battered box stall with a foot or so of matted hay on the floor. He spread the blanket on the hay.

"Now sit there, Fletcher. Sit quite still. Lock your hands behind you, Fletcher."

He did as she said, feeling faintly ridiculous. She undressed very slowly. She never took her eyes from him. Each move was artifice, each gesture contrived, each posturing slow, provocative. Her body had a luminous, almost phosphorescent look in the gloom. Desire for her was, for a time, inhibited by the artificiality of the situation, the faint flavor of ludicrousness. And he knew that had her body been less than perfection, it would have been at best a banal charade, a coarse midway girl show. Slowly, slowly she became all of reality, moving there in the odd light, and the want of her affected his vision.

She knelt lightly by the red case and opened it, and a small dot of the golden sunlight touched her bent back, showing the sheen of it, the silk with its suggestion of faint down. There was nothing left in all the world but this woman.

She took a bottle of red wine from the case and her voice was far-off and strange in his ears, like the voices of people in an automobile as you are falling asleep. "Not much wine now, Fletcher. Just enough for us to taste it."

And she held a bit of bread over the matted hay and poured wine onto it, then holding the bread between her teeth, lips pulled back, crawled slowly to him. Her kiss was raw with the taste of wine and great lights pulsed inside him, breaking as his locked hands slipped, as he reached for her.

It was not love, and she had been right in saying that it would not be love. It was a twisted wrenching agony.

There was a time when he saw her eyes, and they were sightless, rolling. And her mouth was something broken. The sunlight was yellow metal at her throat. He had in that moment the feeling that he did not exist for her. There was no identity to him. He existed only as a part of her body, in the same way that the male spider even while being eaten, continues to perform its instinctual function. This was, he knew, as she had said, a little death.

He was in a long corridor, endless, black as womb. He ran as hard and fast as ultimate terror. There was no sound but the slapping of his bare feet against the smooth chill floor. The corridor walls were glass. Beyond the glass was a green luminescence. On either side of him a white horse ran, and because of the glass he could not hear the sound of hooves. He knew that he dreamed, and told himself that he dreamed, but he could not escape from the dream. The white horses ran with the absurd gait of a merry-go-round, a slow rocking gait. Laura rode each of the horses. She was on either side of him, riding naked, glazed eyes turned toward him, slim thighs clasping the muscle roll of the horses' flanks. On his right Laura was white as chalk. The Laura on his left was a deep blue-green, her body shining as if oiled, her hair trailing long behind her in the wind of passage. There was no sound but the hard fast slap of his feet, and the glazed eyes watched him.

He screamed and his cheek was against the damp smell of the hay. It tickled his upper lip and he moved heavily back onto the blanket. She spoke his name and curled against him, and he felt nothing but a vast sick weariness. But she was at him then, with cleverness of lips and fingers, and he saw that the sun was lower, that the round spot of sunshine was against the box stall wall.

He felt the slow return of wanting, a reluctant starting. And as he turned he saw the man standing there in the broken doorway of the box stall. A beefy, square-skulled man with nothing alive in his face but his eyes, and he was dressed in work clothes and his hands hung still and curled by his sides. For a time seeing the man there meant nothing to him. The man was a part of the new reality of the day, even a part of the dream of horses.

He felt Laura tauten and then heard her sound of dismay, felt her thrust away from him, moving toward her clothing. It was only then that Fletcher was able to understand fully that a man stood there, watching them.

Fletcher rocked up onto his knees and said, "Get out!" His voice sounded odd in his own ears, as though it had been years since he had used words.

The man took a slow step into the stall, his weight compressing the hay under the heavy shoe. "This is my place," the man said thickly. He spoke to Fletcher, but he did not take his eyes from Laura, from the sleekness of her in the barn gloom. And he took another slow step toward her. Laura crouched, quite still, her hands on her clothing. Fletcher was on his knees. The man balanced warily, nostrils spread, neck swollen. Fletcher looked at Laura's eyes, and saw the blindness in them, and he knew suddenly that this was, to her, after her initial surprise, another part of the same day, another part of the same death, and that she could accept this man, accept him in the same anonymity, in the same facelessness that she had accepted him. She seemed oddly like some silken machine which had rested idle for too long, and now, awakened, would continue to function without thought, without discrimination, almost without conscious wish.

Fletcher came up off his knees, lurching toward the man, his footing uncertain on the hay. And the hard hand swung at him, a casual backhand swipe that hit him like a club over his ear, so that he fell back, his elbow scraping the side of the stall as he fell. He rolled to his feet again and the man turned to face him, wearing an expression of annoyance rather than anger. Fletcher dodged the blow and grappled with the man and they fell, rolled on the slope of hay to the stall door. Fletcher felt the rough work clothing under his hands, felt the hard strength of the man, smelled the sharp acid of perspiration. The man bucked him off and Fletcher, trying to get to his feet, stepped on the edge of one of the holes, fell heavily on the barn floor, a pain like fire running through his ankle. He got up. The man had turned toward the stall door again. Fletcher made two soundless strides, and as his weight came on the wrenched ankle he nearly cried out. He pulled at the man's shoulder and hit him, the blow missing the bone of jaw, striking instead into the softness of throat under the jaw.

The man grunted and put both hands to his throat and coughed. He hit at Fletcher and the bad ankle kept Fletcher from dodging. The blow struck his chest, under his heart. He fell against the man and pulled him down and the man's head struck the stall door and he was suddenly slack. Fletcher saw the piece of chain near the stall wall. Four huge rusted links, each the size of a fist. The man was stirring weakly. Fletcher reached across him and grabbed the short length of chain. He held the link at one end and swung it back, knowing precisely how he should flail at the heavy face, knowing the ruin it would make.

He held the heavy chain poised, the end swinging a bit, rust harsh against his palm.

"Do it!" she said. "Do it!" Her voice was thin, and clear, and strong.

He turned his head slowly, the chain still poised, and looked at her. She stood in the stall door, her shoulders slumped, her hands spread against her belly, fingers faintly hooked so that each fingertip made a deep depression. She was not looking at him, but at the face of the man, and her eyes were narrowed, as though she looked into a strong light.

Fletcher felt as though he had dived from some high place, as though he coasted slowly up through the paling shades of green toward the surface. He broke through the surface into daylight and sanity. He threw the chain aside. It thudded and clinked against the floor, skidded, and slid slowly down through one of the holes in the floor to land against the earth underneath, clinking again.

He stood up slowly, aware of his own nakedness. She stood in the same position, and she made a small mewling sound. He slapped her hard. She turned toward him, eyes widening.

"Get your clothes on," he said.

He kept his back to her as he dressed. He could hear the soft sounds of her as she dressed, the whispering sound of fabric. He sat and tenderly pulled his sock on over the puffing ankle, worked it into the moccasin shoe, pulled the lace as tightly as he could.

The man was sitting up. He held his hand flat against the side of his head and squinched his face up. Fletcher looked at Laura. She zipped up the side of the gay skirt, settled it properly on her slim waist. She met his look and there was nothing in her face, nothing but a faintly puffed look, a sated, artificial calm. She folded the blanket with professional neatness after shaking the clinging bits of hay from it. She held it over her arm and picked up the red case.

Fletcher stood over the man. "You all right?"

The man glared up at him and stood up heavily. "This here is private property, mister. Take your tramp woman some other place." He was trying to bluster, but Fletcher sensed the uncertainty behind it. The man was only too aware of what he had tried to do, and he knew that they both knew it.

"If you're all right, we'll go," Fletcher said calmly.

"I got your license number and I'm going to report you," the man said.

Fletcher sensed that the man was regaining confidence, sensed that indeed he might make a report, motivated, perhaps, by his own awareness of guilt.

Fletcher looked in his wallet and counted what he had. Thirty-six dollars. He took it out, all of it, folded it twice, reached out and slid it into the pocket of the man's work shirt.

"Call it rent if you want to," he said.

"I can still report it," the man said truculently.

"And the lady and I will tell what we paid you."

The man knuckled his lips. "Get off the property," he said softly.

After they had passed the fence Fletcher looked back. The man stood in the doorway of the barn. He licked his thumb and began to count the money.

They got into the car and Fletcher backed it out of the dooryard onto the stony road. He went cautiously down the steep hill in second gear. Laura did not speak. A mile further he pulled in under the shade of a giant locust tree with its grooved prehistoric bark, grey as elephants.

"How is your ankle?" she asked tonelessly.

"Sprained, I guess. Not too bad though."

He sat, facing her, his crooked arm hooked over the back of the seat. She had the bright skirt pulled halfway up her thighs, her slim legs extended straight ahead. He remembered again the exquisite daintiness of the Hindu figurine.

The car was hot. Sweat trickled down his ribs. "Laura," he said.

"It wasn't supposed to be beautiful. It was supposed to be . . . what it was."

"Are you making that sound like an apology?"

She turned her head sharply to look at him. "No."

"Then why?"

"Because you act . . . I don't know. Ashamed."

"I don't know how I'm acting. I feel as if . . . I'd been taken apart and put back together in the wrong order."

"A little death?"

"Maybe."

She leaned her head back on the seat and closed her eyes. There were new dark patches under her eyes. "Soon again?" she said softly. "Soon?"

"I . . . I can't even answer that. It was two other people back there. I can't answer for him."

"I can answer for her. She says yes. Soon."

"I don't want it to happen again. Ever."

He expected protest. She turned her head slowly, opened her eyes and smiled. It was a very lazy, very enigmatic smile. "We can't keep it from happening again. Neither of us, Fletcher. No matter how hard we try."

"Because it was that good?"

"Don't try to simplify, dear. Not because it was that good. Because it was that evil. Something in both of us responds to that. Let's say it. You wanted to kill him. I wanted you to. Because we . . . had just finished opening doors that lets that sort of thing out. Now the doors are open. All the way."

"Doors can be closed."

She moistened her lips, yawned without covering her mouth, and he saw the pink tongue back-curled like a cat's. "Then try to close them, darling. Try hard. Now drive back. I want to sleep, deep and hard. All my springs are unwound."

He started the car and drove in silence. The white dust rose behind them. Cattle lay under the shade trees. A cat stalked in the dry grass beside the ditch.

He drove and his mind was full of a thousand pictures of her, of the oiled boneless strength of her. It made him remember a time long ago, a high-school night when the Kribe brothers had the tree house, and the Kribe family was away, and they had the half-simple Swedish maid up there, and they had taunted him and then left him alone with her up there, and the gas lantern made harsh blue-white light against the board walls of the tree house, and how it had been, and how she had laughed softly all the time deep in her throat. And now, riding with Laura, it was somehow like the next morning after being in the tree house, and it was a Sunday morning and he had come down to face his family at the breakfast table, knowing in desperation that in spite of the hot bath, the harsh brush, they would merely have to look at him and they would know. This was like that. This was a shamed panic in the back of the mind, and yet a panic diluted, as long ago, with the memory of a shrill delight.

Love, then, he thought, is something which makes a deep and almost solemn sweetness of the moment of union. And those others, without love, had been just uncomplicated physical release, as he had thought this would be. But in this a strange psychic pendulum swung to a place opposite love.

This was a moment of hate in union, a time of pain and disgust. A black mass spoken backwards to an alien goddess. As she said, it opened a door. And you found odd things behind that door. Odd, pitiless, insatiable things.

Love, perhaps, left you with a warmth, with a tenderness.

This left you with a feeling of chill. Of utter cold.

He turned onto the narrow asphalt that led down to the busy main highway. The red barn was behind him. He saw the speeding cars crossing the junction ahead, with flicker of chrome and whispering roar.

A short time before, he had been a part of all the bustle and motion and color of the world. It had all been a thing accepted, barely noticed.

Yet now, after Laura, he felt as though he crouched alone in some dark place and watched the outside world through some slit so cleverly camouflaged that no one could detect it, could come close and look in on him and see what he was.

He moved into the right-hand lane and slowed down as he came to his street. He pulled over to the curb, put the emergency brake on, left the motor running.

She stirred as though coming out of sleep. Her mouth looked bruised.

"Don't try to say anything, Fletcher."

He looked into her eyes and saw something very like amusement, or perhaps a faint scorn.

He got out and slammed the door. She slid over, released the brake and moved out into traffic without glancing back. She seemed small behind the wheel, and she sat with her chin high to see over the long hood.

Fletcher waited for traffic, then limped slowly across the road and up the quiet afternoon of Coffeepot Road.

Chapter Seventeen

Fletcher was shocked to discover, when he entered the silent house, that it was not much past three. The world had changed in a short time. The house looked different, as though someone else lived here. He looked at his right hand and saw the dull brown stain of rust. Rust on his hand, and the taste of her across his mouth, and a hundred places where her fingers had touched and brought deadness.

He limped into the bedroom and saw Jane's unopened overnight bag on the bed. There was no need to call her. There was a quality to the stillness that told him the house was empty. He took off the grey shirt, crumpled it and stuffed it into the laundry hamper. He took off his slacks. There was a shred of straw clinging to the cuff. He picked it off and rolled it into a ball between his fingers. He hung the slacks up with great and unusual care, and tossed his empty wallet onto the desk in the study. He sat down and pulled his shoes off, then gingerly peeled the sock from the bad ankle. It had a bloated, underwater look. When he poked it with his finger the dent took several seconds to fill up again. It hurt worse to walk on it without the support of the shoe.

He took a long shower and did not feel completely clean when he stepped out of it. He put on some old, paint-dotted khaki shorts and a T shirt and hunted for the adhesive tape. After ten minutes of futile search he decided that the kids had used it for something. In the chest in the utility room he found some old sheeting, tore off a long strip and bound his ankle clumsily but tightly. With an effort of will he could step on the foot without wincing. He iodined the scraped elbow. After digging through drawers, he found the pair of wool socks with the leather soles and he bit his lip as he eased one on over the bound ankle.

Though he was aware of massive hunger pangs, the desire for sleep was more pressing. He stretched out on the studio couch.

Somebody was shaking him and he growled and stared up at Jane standing over him in the dim room. Sleep had been so heavy that he could not figure out what time of day it was, or what he was doing asleep in the study.

He had sweat heavily in his sleep. The T shirt was sodden. As he peered uncertainly up at her, all the memories came back, memories of a luminescent tormenting body, and memories of the dust smell and the field insects.

"Are you all right?" Jane asked.

He sat up, rubbing his face. The memories had turned Jane into a calm-faced stranger. "What time is it?"

"Nearly five."

He scratched his chest, yawning. "I was dead."

"Do you want to eat here or what?"

". . . I don't know." He stood up and gave a sharp gasp of pain as his weight came on the forgotten ankle. He caught her shoulder for support.

"What's the matter?"

He took his hand away quickly, balancing most of his weight on his good ankle. "Wrenched my ankle."

"Have you done anything about it?"

"Tied it up tight. Couldn't find that wide tape anyplace. Used a piece of sheet from the chest in the utility room."

She snapped the blinds open and the late sunlight came in at an angle. She looked as crisp and confident as any office nurse. "Sit down. I want to take a look at it."

"It's fine. It's all right." She pushed at him gently and he sat down and held the bad foot out. She knelt on the floor and gently pulled the sock down and worked it off his toes. "Ow!" he said softly. She untied the fat knots and unwound the strip of sheet. The fabric had left its patterns on the puffed flesh. She touched it lightly. "A doctor ought to look at it. It's a bad sprain."

"I'm not going to bother any doctor with that."

She sat back on her heels. "Then you better do what I

tell you. We'll soak it in hot water and Epsom salts. After it gets a good soaking. I'll tape it."

"Why the Epsom salts?"

"It takes the soreness out and keeps it from stiffening. Come on now. I think you ought to be in the living room. Can you make it out there?"

He stood up and tried a tentative step, winced.

"Put your arm around my shoulders. Don't be afraid to lean."

She put her arm around his waist. He leaned on her heavily, barely touching his foot to the floor with each step. She walked him into the living room and over to his favorite chair. He lowered himself clumsily into it.

She walked quickly out of the room and came back in quite soon carefully carrying a big washbasin. It was steaming. She sat it down on the floor in front of the chair. "Put your foot in it."

He touched his heel to the surface of the water and jerked it out quickly, hurting his ankle. "Oh, sure! Burn it right off, I suppose."

"It *has* to be hot, or it won't do any good. Come on now. I had my hand in it. It isn't that hot."

"Your hands are used to hot water."

She went off and got the Epsom salts, dumped a lot of it out of the cardboard cylinder into the water. He shut his teeth hard and managed to hold his heel in the water. Then, a fraction of an inch at a time, he worked his foot down until at last it rested on the bottom of the basin. He let out his pent-up breath.

"That will take the soreness out. How did you . . . I'm sorry."

"I stepped on a stone and it rolled. I fell and skinned my elbow."

"Did you put anything on it?"

"Iodine."

"Let's see it. Well, that's just a scrape. Do you want to eat here? There's shrimp in the freezer. I could make a salad if you'd like that. And peas."

It made him feel uncomfortable. "That . . . that would be fine. I mean I wouldn't put you to the trouble, but I can't get very far on this ankle, I guess."

"It's no trouble." At the kitchen door she turned. "I could make you a drink if you want."

"Are you going to have one?"

"Yes, I thought I would. Gin and tonic. That's cool."

"Yes, I'd like that. This . . . is about the longest heat wave I can remember."

"Every day seems a little worse. We usually get them in August."

"Yes, this is early for it."

He could hear her getting the ice. He reached over and got a magazine off the tricky little wrought-iron rack on which you hung them across the iron bars. He opened it and tried to start an article on the army weather stations in Alaska, but he couldn't keep his mind on it. Yet he managed to appear absorbed in it when she came in with his drink.

"Oh! Thanks. That's fine."

She put her finger in the water in the basin. "I better add a little more hot. I've got a kettle on the stove."

She brought it in and he took his foot out while she poured the steaming water. After she left the room, it took him a long time to get his foot back into it. It didn't feel as sore. He sipped the drink slowly. Two drinks before dinner. Maybe three. But no more, and no drinking after dinner. No three bad evenings in a row.

Jane came through the living room on the way to the bedroom wing and glanced at him and said, "I planned to throw those shorts out."

"They've got all the pockets regular pants have. It's hard to find shorts with all the pockets."

"They've got all the pockets because they used to be pants until you cut them off."

"Say, that's right. I forgot that."

"I'll mix you a fresh drink later."

"No hurry."

When she came back he saw she had changed to a black dress with smart plain lines. He always liked her in black. Her hair wasn't tied back, and the long soft shining blonde waves fell to her shoulder. When she wanted to have it cut, he had said no. Flatly.

"Going someplace?" he said.

"I thought that after dinner I might go down to a movie or something. It isn't definite."

She picked up his empty glass and took it out to the kitchen. She was back with his refill in a few minutes. "Am I making them strong enough?"

"I'm in a weakened condition. These are just right."

The rolled paper thumped against the front door and she went and got it, unrolling it as she walked toward him. She looked at the headlines. "No break in sight in record heat. Oh, dear." She handed him the paper and went back to the kitchen. As he read the paper the house seemed oddly silent. At first he thought it was because of the children being away. And then he analyzed it and remembered that she had a very familiar habit of singing half under her breath while working. Tonight she was silent.

He read the news. Last night had been a night of violence in the city. Police answer record number of calls. He grimaced as he remembered one of their calls, while he sat in Laura's dark living room.

Jane came in with a big towel and the roll of tape. She knelt in front of him. "Lift out."

He lifted his foot out of the water. "Here, I can dry it."

"I can get at it easier." She rubbed it dry with the big towel, then clicked the spool of wide tape out of its container. She picked up the edge with her fingernail and ripped out a piece several feet long. "Now just hold it like that."

He looked down at her. She was biting her lip in concentration as she started the first wrapping around his ankle. A sheaf of the shining hair swung forward and she tossed it back with a quick movement of her head. He wanted to reach forward and put his hands on her shoulders. The impulse was so strong that he clamped his hands hard against the arms of the chair. He felt a stinging in his eyes. He wanted to hold her closely. He wanted things to be as they had been before. And he knew he was so close to breaking down that he forced himself to look at her flanks with the black dress stretched tight because of her posture. At her flanks and at her breasts, and he made himself think of the big brown hands of the college boy, and he thought of them until once more, after many hours,

212

the little doll figures in the back of his mind awakened and began their insensate rhythms, and he could look at her with hate and disgust and rejection.

"Too tight?"

"Uh . . . no, it feels fine. Just right."

She worked the tape around his ankle and under the arch of his foot, changing the spool from hand to hand. When she was satisfied she bent forward and nipped the edge of the tape between her teeth and ripped it across, pressed the loose end down neatly.

"There!"

"I certainly appreciate this."

"Stand on it and see how it feels." She offered her hand as she stood up. He took it and stood up and stepped tentatively, and then confidently. "That's swell! Hell, I could walk miles."

"I think you better stay off it as much as you can. Sit down and I'll call you when dinner's ready. Another drink?"

"A light one."

She went back out with basin and towel and tape. He realized that neither of them had used the other's name, nor had they used any of the almost automatic words of affection and endearment. He had the sudden fear that he would forget to be on guard for a moment and call her darling, or honey—and she would take that as a gesture of appeasement.

At six o'clock she came for him. "Do you want to lean on me?"

He knew that it wasn't necessary and for one astonishing moment was tempted to say yes just to have an opportunity to touch her. "I can manage."

And he made himself walk without the suggestion of a limp. She had set the dining area table with bright grass mats, the gay, crude-looking dishes that had been imported from Guatemala.

"Looks very festive," he said as he sat down.

"Does it? I don't know. I like hot colors with a cold meal." She served the salad and they began to eat in silence, in awkward silence.

"Madge okay?"

"Fine. Lew expects to get up next week. She was glad to have the kids."

"Get back about noon?"

"A little earlier. I . . . went out again."

"I thought you had. I saw your bag on the bed. And I saw you made up my bed. I was going to do that."

"Did you notice the movies in the paper? Is there anything good?"

"I didn't notice."

The silence settled over them again. Once he glanced at her at the same moment she looked up at him. They both looked down again hurriedly. There were small hot biscuits, and she served hot coffee in squatty orange cups.

As she stirred her coffee he felt the silence between them stretching itself thin, stretching into a vibrating tension.

"Have you decided what you want to do, Fletcher?"

"I haven't been able to think clearly. I guess it's a good idea to have the kids away. I think we can be calm about this. I want to be fair. Divorce seems to be a better answer than separation, don't you think?"

She looked up sharply. "If it's going to be that way, I'd rather have it be final."

"You can have the house. I can liquidate enough to pay off what we owe on it, so you'll have it free and clear."

She lifted her coffee and sipped, set the cup down. "I don't think I want to stay here, Fletcher. I'll go out to my sister. I'm perfectly aware that you can take the children away from me if you want to. I'd rather you didn't. I think if we could have some plan where you could have them for summers . . ."

"You seem damn calm about it!"

"I'm not going to get into any shouting contest with you, Fletcher. And I'm not going to let us pile more . . . unpleasant words on top of the unforgettable things we've already said to each other. You've heard the complete truth. You're in possession of all the facts. You have a decision to make. I'll abide by it. But let's not do any more yammering. I don't think I could stand it."

"It would be better if you stayed right here in this house."

214

She lit a cigarette with great care. "I couldn't live in this house after last night."

"You mean Sunday night, don't you?"

"I mean last night. You brought her here to my house, to our bedroom. I can't forget that, Fletcher. Ever. No matter what happens."

He stared at her. "Brought her here? Laura?"

"Don't look so stupid and vacant. Her lipstick was on the sheet. I found it when I changed the bed. And I saw you today as you two were leaving . . . for a picnic, I imagine. On such a lovely day."

"Lipstick! I don't see how . . . Oh!"

She showed her teeth as she smiled. "Memory forcing its way through alcoholic fumes, Fletcher?"

He stared at her. "I've got no reason to lie to you. I'd like to be able to say that it happened right here in this house. I'd enjoy saying that, I think."

Jane looked steadily at him. "Didn't it?"

"No. I got stinking drunk. I took a cab to her house, late, and made such a rumpus the neighbors called the cops. She lied to them to protect me. She drove me back here and got me into the house. Believe me, I was well past the point where I was either willing or able. She got me undressed and dumped me into bed and I grabbed at her and she fell onto me and I guess that's where the lipstick came from. Actually she did me a favor. I couldn't have found my way home alone. She was pretty good at it. Said her father used to tie one on every so often, so she had practice."

"So today you took her out in the country and showed her how grateful you can be. Is that it?"

He looked at Jane and looked through her into a place he had found that day. And again he was watching the world through that slit, looking at the world out of a blackness. "You mentioned last night," he said. "I told you about last night. Anything else is my business. You've got no claim. Remember. You gave away any chance you might have had to do any kind of checking or ask any kind of questions."

Yet, even as he spoke to her in that low tone, showing no anger, he was aware that she was, perhaps, the only person in the world to whom he could talk about this thing that had happened to him, this gesture of rebellion that had turned out to be a strange poison.

"What's the matter?" she asked. "What's the matter, Fletcher?"

"Skip it, goddamn it!" he yelled. "Drop it, can't you?"

She looked at him for long seconds and then got up very quickly, shoving her chair back. She half ran and he heard the soft closing of the bedroom door. He lit a cigarette and sat there for a long time, looking at the empty cups, the gay colors of the dishes.

A memory came back, vivid, clear. He could not understand why that memory should come back at this time. Summer camp, and the boy named Will who was taming a baby red squirrel. Small red squirrel with bright quick eyes, sitting on the palm of his hand, stuffing the food into its mouth with both tiny paws. And the squirrel had nipped Will, bringing blood. To punish it they tied it in the cabin, using a length of fishline. Then they went loftily out, Will saying, "That'll teach him," and the squirrel chittering anxiously at them as they left. They had walked around the ball field and come back, hurrying to release the squirrel from its punishment. But it had evidently slipped while crossing a rafter and the knot in the line had slipped. In the short time of death its bright coat had dulled. With Will holding it they had walked out into the sunlight, and then Will, snuffling, had turned suddenly and hit Fletcher full in the mouth with his knobby fist. They had fought for a long time, crying as they fought. But it hadn't made friends of them, like the camp director said it would. Instead Fletcher had felt a strange guilt each time he found himself near Will. And he guessed that Will felt the same, because for what was left of the summer they avoided each other. And he hadn't thought of Will for a long time.

He poured more coffee and drank it slowly. He carried the dishes over to the sink, scraped the scraps into the disposal, stacked the dishes in the dishwasher. He decided not to turn it on. She might want more in there, and he didn't know how much soap to use.

He looked at the paper for a time, then went and tapped on the bedroom door.

"Jane? You okay?"

"You can come in," she said.

He went in. The room was darkened. She lay on her bed in her black dress with a washcloth folded across her forehead.

"Headache?"

"It's getting better now, thanks."

"Want aspirin?"

"I got up a little while ago and took some. They're working now, I guess."

He sat on the edge of her bed and she moved her legs over a little to give him room. He felt, in some odd way, as though they were the jaded, exhausted survivors of some catastrophe, brought together in a new loneliness. And he felt as though they could talk about the catastrophe calmly.

"I've been thinking, Jane. I think we ought to act as normal as we can and wait until the kids get off to camp. Then I'll talk to John Barnlee and find out what the state laws are. That make sense to you?"

"I guess so. I'm . . . sorry I asked questions. It's none of my business."

"That's all right. I'm sorry I shouted."

"I was just trying to . . . hurt myself by making you talk about her."

"I know. It's a funny thing. I keep wanting you to talk about that kid at the lake."

"I hated him. I guess I didn't make that clear to you. I wanted to kill him for . . . ruining everything for me."

"It takes two," he said coldly.

"I know. I found that out today. When I came back here and found that lipstick stain I called him up, still hating him. I met him today, in the woods near the camp."

He turned to look hard at the half-seen paleness of her face. He felt neither shock nor anger. Just a sickness. "You did it again?"

"I wanted to. I wanted to do anything to get even with you. I told him I had the name and I might as well have the game. There certainly hadn't been any pleasure in it. I

217

... wasn't any good. He sensed right away that I was forcing myself. And he wouldn't do it."

"I don't believe that."

"It doesn't make much difference whether you believe it or not, does it? I wish he'd done it. Then I could keep on hating him. I could have kept on thinking that he was all bastard. But he isn't. And that was a terrible thing to find out."

"What do you mean?"

"It means that I've had to face something. I was building up a little dream for myself. Every time I remembered the lake, it was more like rape. Poor innocent little drunken Janey, taken advantage of, in a classic manner. But today I found out it wasn't like that."

"What are you saying?"

"That first I have to be honest with myself. I know I fought at the last possible moment. Fought as hard as I could. But that was pure ... animal fear. I led him on. All day. So I can't blame him. There was a rotten spot in me. Something that wanted another man, and wanted to know what another man would be like."

He sat still for a long time. He twisted his hand and a knuckle cracked loudly in the silence.

"Wasn't I enough?"

"Yes. It isn't that. It's ... wondering, I guess. And the days going, and the years going, and the kids getting big, getting ready to go away. It's fighting your waistline and watching what's happening to the skin under your eyes, and thinking of being young again, and maybe trying to find out how to be young again with a young person, like he is. And I guess he sensed that, and he was right. I don't hate him. You know, I don't even hate myself any more. I feel a sort of ... far-away pity for myself. A woman growing older. A silly damn-fool woman, as if I were ... somebody else I was watching. . . ." She stopped, turned restlessly on the bed, turned half away from him. He thought she was through speaking. She said, slowly, as though it was something painfully learned, "A person like me ... maybe thinking of getting old is harder. Somehow. Because, except for my body maybe there isn't ... too much to me. I like being quick and strong and good at things."

218

For a moment the urge was strong in him to lie down beside her, to gather her close against him, hold her tight so that the years could not get her, could not get either of them.

Each of them, he knew, had come to a new dark place. She to a place of self-understanding, and bleakness. He to a place of evil spasm, to a golden body that was like a drug.

"Please go," she said. "I'm going to cry. It's going to be messy. I don't want you sitting there listening."

He shut the door soundlessly behind him. For a time he roamed through the house, ignoring the dulled pain in his ankle. He thought of Laura, alone in the big, old-fashioned house. Her sleep, too, would be like a death. Used body slack on the big bed, like one of those dolls they used to put on beds, with boneless legs which could be tied into absurd knots.

Together they had entered a strange land. Yet the new land had not been as strange to her as to him. They had walked a dark path where fleshy flowers grew tall and still around them, petals open to show the membranous depths. She had said he would come back to her. Said it with deadly confidence. The taste of wild honey, unforgettable.

To get her out of his mind as he prepared for bed, he tried to summon up fury at the thought of Jane riding out to meet her juvenile lover. It didn't work. He thought of Jane and felt only a protective sadness. Lost wife—something of gold seen from far away—seen, perhaps, through a cleverly concealed slit, where he could crouch in the naked darkness and watch—and not care.

Chapter Eighteen

On Wednesday morning they breakfasted together like strangers who, resenting being seated together in a crowded restaurant, overdo the small polite formalities.

"The paper says there may be thundershowers this evening, or they may hold off until tomorrow," he said.

"I can't remember a July that started like this one has."

"When do you get the kids?"

"I thought I'd drive up tomorrow. Get there after lunch and have a swim and bring them back. Then they'll be here for Friday, the Fourth, and we planned to drive them to camp Saturday. They're all packed."

"I suppose we ought to both go when we take them."

"I think it would be best."

"You haven't said anything to them?"

She looked at him with a touch of anger in her eyes. "Of *course* not! When it comes time to tell them, we both better do it, together."

"A hard thing to do."

"It's better now than it would have been three or four years ago. They're old enough to understand better."

"This wouldn't have happened three or four years ago."

"I was thinking that too, Fletcher."

"A different crowd then than we travel with now. Fewer drinks. More fun, somehow."

"I know."

"If people were only smart enough to get out before it all blows up in their faces . . ."

"I was thinking that. You better hurry. You'll be late."

"Will you be needing the car?"

"I'd like to have it, if it won't inconvenience you."

"Not at all. You set now?"

He backed the car out and she hurried across the yard and got in. As he turned toward the city she said, "I forgot to ask you. How does your ankle feel?"

"Better. That soaking helped, I think."

"Try to stay off it today as much as you can."

As they neared the plant she said, "Do you think you'll want to come home for dinner?"

"Probably better if I eat in town."

"Whatever you want. But I'd like to know for sure."

"I'll eat in town then. I can get a bus to town, and then a taxi home later. You have any special plans?"

"This afternoon I have to help Midge at the booth at the hospital. Because of the other night, I think I better show up."

He stopped the car and unconsciously turned toward her to kiss her, and caught himself in time, but not in time to keep her from seeing his slip.

"Well . . . I'll see you then."

"Thanks for the car."

"Perfectly all right."

After he had crossed the street he looked back and saw her just turning the corner. He went on into the office. Miss Trevin was in and gave him a quick glad smile. "Oh, I'm so glad you're better, Mr. Wyant."

"Thank you."

"I've got that first report done. Shall I bring it in?"

"In a few minutes, please."

He hung up his hat and sat down behind his desk and went to work on two morning's mail. There was a new tastelessness about his work, but he forced himself to plough along, forced himself to keep going. He checked the report and initialed it for distribution. He dictated answers to some of his mail, told Miss Trevin how to answer the others. She could compose letters indistinguishable in style and phrasing from his. At ten thirty Stanley Forman's secretary called to ask if Mr. Wyant could step up to Mr. Forman's office at once.

It gave him a sudden, sagging feeling in the middle. Forman's call was usually not so peremptory. Mr. Fedder was due for his appointment. He told Miss Trevin to ask Fedder to wait if he arrived before he was back.

Stanley Forman stood at the window, his back to the room. "Close the door and sit down, Fletch."

Fletcher sat down wondering if it was a good sign to be called Fletch rather than Wyant.

"Didn't haul you away from something?"

"Nothing important, Stanley."

Forman let the silence grow and swell. He turned slowly from the window and walked over and sat behind his desk. He picked up a paperweight and shook it and set it down, and they both watched the swirling snow fall on the tiny figure of Santa.

"Self-torture to look at snow during weather like this, isn't it?" Stanley asked.

"Yes, it is."

"Fletch, I'm going to be frank."

"I wish you would."

"What is the greatest industrial shortage in America?"

Fletcher frowned at him. "I don't know. A few of the rare metals . . ."

"Nuts. Rewrite the specs. Use substitutes. Redesign the product if you have to. Our critical shortage is in executive talent, Fletch. That's why there are men in this country who, if they put themselves on the market, could demand and get up to a half million a year. And they aren't young men, either. Organized labor is always bleating that no man is worth that much. If it costs that much to replace, the item *is* worth that much. The market price determines the value. Cut-rate executives mean poor management, dwindling profits, eventual bankruptcy."

"I see what you mean, Stanley. But . . ."

"Why the shortage? Why aren't there more men who can take hold? First, you have to have an unusual combination of talents. You have to have a man who never uses emotional reasoning, on himself, and yet can sway others with emotional reasoning to do something that he knows is coldly practical. He has to be big enough to delegate authority, and yet retain the responsibility. He has to be fast on detail work, and yet see the broad picture at all times. He needs creative imagination. And he has to drive himself endlessly, courting ulcers, heart failure and acute nervous exhaustion. Now, there are more men with these talents than there are men working at it. Know why?"

"I guess not."

"Because society rewards our good tough able executive with a ninety-something per cent tax bracket. He's a target for the half-baked witticisms of smart aleck columnists. And when government can't think of what to do next, it sits on our man's chest for a while. So our man decides the hell with it. So he buys an orange grove. Or a cattle ranch. And he runs it well, because he can't run anything poorly, and he sleeps well nights and every time he thinks of the brethren still sweating it out he laughs himself crazy. The ones who stay in industry do so because they love it better than anything in the world. It's meat and drink for them. A disease, maybe. I've got it. I could sell out and retire. And go crazy watching the mess somebody else would make of this place."

"Why are you telling me all this, Stanley?"

"Because I want you to tell me exactly what the hell is wrong with you. You were coming along. Learning, all the time, how to use more of your capacity. You're young. I've been basing my planning on what you *would* be in a few years. This isn't crap, Wyant. You're fading like a bonus rookie and it disappoints the hell out of me and I want to know why."

"I've had . . . a little personal trouble this past week."

"Past week, hell. Since March is what I'm talking about. What is it? Wife trouble? Physical examination give you bad news?"

"I don't know whether I can explain it or not, Stanley. I get these fits of . . . I suppose you could say despondency. A funny feeling. Like I was missing out on something, and I don't even know what it is."

Stanley looked at him with disgust. "For Christ' sake, are you having a delayed adolescence or something? You want to write poetry in the moonlight?"

"I guess it does sound a little silly."

"Silly is a fine word. And while you moon around, Fletch, you're not giving the firm enough return on your salary dollar. That Corban punk you brought in here is

223

fine for exactly what you intended for him. He's an oily little bastard. At his operating peak he's about forty per cent the executive you are—assuming you're in form. But you're operating at about twenty-five per cent of capacity, so right now he looks better to me than you do. My loyalty, Fletch, is to the outfit. I can't afford deadwood. And don't think I can't chase your ass out the front door in about nine minutes flat."

Fletcher felt the quick anger, and then he let it slowly fade away. If Forman wanted it that way, he could have it that way. He sat and did not answer.

"Okay, Fletch. Corban gets your job."

Fletcher looked at his hand, closed it slowly into a fist. He thought of Ellis' forced joviality, the cold shrewd small eyes. This time he let the anger come up and fill his throat and roar in his ears.

"All right, Mister Forman. See exactly what the hell that gets you. I can tell you what will happen. You'll be too busy to keep a checkrein on him and keep his nose in his own business by force if necessary. So he'll start reaching around with his boy scout knife. He'll work on the rest of the outfit. You'll have cliques and plots and so much dirty conniving that the unity—that team feeling that we've developed—will fall apart at the seams." He stood up in his anger. "If you got the sense God gave little red ants you'll put somebody else in my slot, and if they aren't smart enough to handle Corban, you'll boot Corban out along with me. I got him in here, and I can handle him, but you let him run loose and you might as well stick a time bomb under the office. He'd trap this firm into a million dollar loss if he thought he could get a bigger sign on his door. So don't give me this big time executive crap and in the next breath tell me you can pull that kind of a boner. I got Corban in here so I could milk him, and keep my foot on the back of his neck. You can . . ."

He stopped suddenly, stared hard at Stanley. Stanley was leaning back in his chair, looking extremely pleased.

"Just what in the hell are you grinning at?"

"That's the first sign of life I've seen in months, Fletch. You say you can keep him under control. Splendid! He gets your job then."

"Make sense, for Christ' sake!"

"And I'm creating a new title for you, Fletch. Executive vice-president. We've gotten along without one of those animals for quite a few years. It's been cleared with the board, including a pay boost that ought to make you happy. Wipe the goofy look off your face and sit down. We've got provisional approval from the SEC for a new stock issue. It will be your baby to work out the details. We're absorbing Correy Heater Corporation in Birmingham. They tried to move into air conditioning and flubbed out. You would have been working on this whole thing with me if you hadn't been in a fog. I'm going to have to spend a lot of time down there. There's an executive staff and about half of them are creeps I've got to weed out and replace. While I'm commuting, you're it. This drifting and dreaming you've been doing can really hurt us now, if you keep it up. I'm gambling on shocking you the hell out of it. You're going to find out that you'll have to be a son of a bitch around here. *The* son of a bitch. Slack up on the reins and it'll run away with you. And if it does, word will get around. And when I tie the can to you, you'll have to go work for the government. Industry won't hire you as a timekeeper."

The realization of what was happening to him was like a small warm flame that started in his middle and spread out to the tips of his fingers. He felt nine feet tall, and perfectly capable of walking through brick walls. In his mind the entire new range of responsibilities was being sorted out, dropped into numbered slots. Production, Engineering, Design, Sales, Purchasing, Personnel, Accounting, Maintenance. Each function was tied to a man, and each man was well known to him, and he knew precisely how to get the ultimate effort from each man. He could work them as a unity, and apply all the combined and specialized skills of that functioning unit to the big problems as they appeared.

"How far can I go?" he asked.

"That's the question I wanted to hear, Fletch. You know as well as I do what has to have Board approval. On anything under that top policy level, it is entirely up to you as to whether you make the decision or refer it to me."

Fletcher nodded. "Good enough."

Stanley stood up and stuck out his hand. "Congratulations, Fletch. And luck. You'll need the luck."

Fletcher started to walk out in a daze. There were a million new things to start thinking about. Stanley said, "Hey, don't you want to know when the change is effective?"

Fletcher turned and stared at him. "Hell, I've already started."

"Move yourself into that office right across the hall. I'll leave you the pleasure of telling Corban. And I think that Evans might be a good man to move into Corban's shoes. He seems to be ..."

Fletcher grinned suddenly. "I'll consider that a suggestion, Stanley."

The news traveled fast through the office grapevine. They came into his office singly and in twos and threes to congratulate him. He was inwardly amused at the change in their attitude. Harry Bailey was the only one who seemed to have any resentment. They were all slightly more affable than usual, and a bit speculative, a bit uncertain. After they had all been in, he called Miss Trevin in and asked her to close the door.

"Marcia, I'm going to have to depend on you a great deal."

"It's so exciting, Mr. Wyant!"

"Mr. Corban will be moving in here. I'm going to have to depend on you to be his right arm, Marcia."

She looked as though he had slapped her. "But I thought ..."

"I know. And believe me, I'd like nothing better. We work well together. But you see, we can't take both the key people out of this office. It would be poor planning."

"But ... maybe Mr. Corban would rather have somebody else."

"Marcia, for more reasons than one, and I believe you know what I mean, I am not going to give Mr. Corban any choice. Please understand that I am not asking you to be ... an informant. I don't believe in that sort of thing. I merely think that your obvious loyalty to me will act as a deterrent should Mr. Corban wish to . . . extend himself."

"I . . . guess I understand."

"I'm going to have to have a secretary. I thought you might have a suggestion."

She pursed her lips. "There's one girl in the pool you might like. She's green, but she's very quick and smart. Miss Schmidt."

"I'll give her a try, then. You talk to her and . . . explain all my bad habits, and the way I like things done."

"Yes, Mr. Wyant."

"Thank you very much, Miss Trevin."

She opened the door and started out and then turned back. "Sir, did you call Mrs. Wyant from some other office to tell her the news? I thought you might have forgotten in the excitement and all."

He felt his new confidence slowly leaking away. "She's not home right now," he lied. "Besides, I think I'd rather tell her in person."

Miss Trevin blushed. "I see. Of course, Mr. Wyant."

He found he had no time, however, to think of Jane. The press of new work, new problems, pushed her far enough back in his mind so that she was just a small focal point of despair of which he was barely aware. He had a sandwich and milk shake at his desk for lunch. He spent most of the afternoon going over current planning with Stanley Forman, sorting and filing all manner of facts in his retentive mind. At seven o'clock he rode into town with Stanley and they had dinner at the Downtown Club and then went back to the plant to go over the stock issue and transfer plan in detail. Stanley was flying to Birmingham early in the morning. Fletcher had to be ready, in the morning, to take over the problems of the top management slot. On some points they argued with great heat. On most matters they were in agreement.

At last Stanley stood up, stretched, and began to roll down his shirt sleeves. "Lord! Quarter after ten. How did Jane react to the news, Fletch?"

"She was pleased," he lied.

Stanley gave him a keen look. "You're going to be

knocking yourself out regularly, Fletch. A woman like Jane can make the difference between keeping your head above water, or being sunk without a trace."

"I know."

"One of the reasons I picked you is because you've got yourself a good girl. She knows the score. A lot of men never get around the course in par on account of the nagging, tormenting bitch they've got at home."

"Let's drop it, shall we?"

"Sore point, eh?"

"Listen. *My* sore point. *My* home life. *My* wife. Aside and apart from the Forman Furnace Corporation."

"Nuts! You don't compartment your life, Fletch. You don't work in an emotional vacuum. Each part is equal to the whole. Whatever it is, straighten it out."

"Can't we drop this?"

"Straighten it out, believe me, or this job will sink you. I'll give you a lift home. Nightcap on the way?"

"Good suggestion."

At eleven o'clock Stanley dropped him off in front of the house, refused to come in for another nightcap. He watched the tail lights of the big grey Cadillac go back down Coffeepot Road. There was a light on in the big living room. There was an almost continual glow of heat lightning in the east. The door was unlocked and Jane was on the couch asleep, the lamp shining in her eyes, a book on the floor beside the couch. Her head was tilted awkwardly to one side, and she breathed through her open mouth. She was dressed in grey corduroy shorts and a matching halter, and her hair was tied with a piece of blue yarn.

Fletcher walked quietly over to her and stood looking down at her, with that feeling of guilt that comes from studying the face of anyone asleep. In her relaxation he could see that the past week had left its marks. Dark hollows under her eyes, and a deepening of the brackets around her mouth. He looked at the long lovely brown legs, at the slow rise and fall of the flat, tanned diaphragm as she breathed in her sleep, at the warm breasts pouching the grey corduroy of the halter. In the bright lamplight he could see the white hairs that were usually invisible in her blonde thatch. There was a faint dew of perspiration on her upper lip and on her temple.

He wanted to kneel beside the couch and take her in his arms. And, without willing it, he looked at her body again and began to picture how it must have been with her and the tough-muscled kid. It was torment to think of it. He wanted a knife with which he could cut the imaginings out of his mind the way you cut a rotten spot from an apple. The evil images writhed in his mind, twisting and turning into grotesque depravities of which he knew she was incapable, and yet he could not halt them. It was a sickness in him, and it blinded him.

Slowly he became aware of a change in her breathing. She looked up at him. "Hello. Is it late?" Her voice was rusty with sleep. She looked at her watch. "Little after eleven. I must have slept almost two hours." She sat up and yawned and scrubbed her head vigorously with her knuckles. "Just had a crazy dream. I was running and running to catch one of those old-fashioned open streetcars. I've never even seen one in the flesh. I was running right down the tracks. And they were all pointing at me from the streetcar and yelling and I didn't know why. And then I looked down at myself and I had black gloves that came all the way up to my shoulders and black stockings that came halfway up my thighs and I didn't have another stitch on. I stopped running and I had my big red purse and I knew I had a bed sheet in it. God knows why. I took the bed sheet out and it was all embroidered with great big staring eyes, but I was going to put it on anyway. But I didn't have time because the streetcar was coming back with all the people on it. I couldn't get off the track because there were walls. So I was running again, and it was coming fast behind me. And I woke up. Sounds Freudian as anything, doesn't it?"

"Sounds weird enough."

"Funny in a dream you can be so terrified of being naked. Say, your eyes look terribly tired."

He pinched the bridge of his nose, squeezed his eyes shut. "It was a bear of a day. I left the office about quarter after ten tonight."

"Isn't that awfully late?"

He looked at her, at her slightly puzzled frown, and wished there was some way he could keep from telling her, some way that she would never have to know. "Stanley made some changes. We're taking over a new plant. I'm going to be in charge of the Minidoka Plant. Ellis takes my job. I'm executive vice-president."

He saw her face light up, saw her eyes go pleased and wide. "Darling! How perfectly wonderful!" And he knew that the news was big enough to have made her forget, for just a moment, that their lives had changed.

His own vivid disappointment made him say quietly, "It could have been perfectly wonderful."

She looked down at her hands, flexed her fingers. "Congratulations, anyway," she said quietly.

"Thanks. It . . . it will mean a lot of work until I get my feet under me. I'm grateful for that, at least."

"Did you have dinner yet?"

"I ate in town with Stanley. He's flying to Birmingham in the morning," He yawned.

"You look tired, darl . . . Fletcher."

"I am. All this coming on top of . . . all the other thing."

"I know what you mean." She gave him a quick shy glance and looked away. "All this trouble, and the heat too. I keep feeling as if I was moving around inside of a big funny glass thing that makes everything look too big or too little, all swarmy like when you think you're going to faint. Even voices sound funny."

"Like in cars," he said, "when you're falling asleep."

"Yes. Oh, yes," she said softly.

"Will you want the car again tomorrow, to get the kids?"

"If you don't mind. Yes."

"It's perfectly okay. I can get along."

He unknotted his necktie and pulled it off. She said, "I saw Martha today. She came over here just before lunch. Crying. She said she'd been living in hell since Sunday. I'd thought I'd never forgive her. It seemed like such a betrayal. But it was really her perfectly filthy temper that did it, and the drinks and Hud making a fool of himself. I couldn't stay mad at her, she was so miserable. So we

230

both cried some, and I told her I was even halfway glad it had come out, and even now I don't know whether I was only saying it to make her feel better."

He slowly unbuttoned his shirt to the waist, his back to her. "You're glad it happened."

"I don't know. I don't know. It would be living a lie. Maybe that's good. I just don't know."

"But it did come out, and I can't stop thinking about it."

"Am I supposed to enjoy thinking about that Corban person?"

"We're going to start going around and around in a minute, and I'm just too damned tired. And there's nothing new we can say to each other."

"We're both too tired. Good night, Fletcher."

"Good night."

"I'll keep the clock. I'll wake you at the right time."

"Thanks."

He heard her cross the room behind him, pause in the doorway. "I'm happy you got the promotion, Fletcher."

"Thanks."

The bedroom door closed softly. He took his shirt off, picked up his suit coat and tie. He went over to turn off the light and saw that she had left her book on the floor. He picked it up and glanced at the title. *Sexual Aspects of Modern Marriage.*

It was a book they had bought fifteen years ago and never read. At the time it had been a household joke. They had agreed that the man was silly not to have interviewed them, the real experts, before writing his silly book. Now there was something vastly pathetic about Jane, alone in the house, trying to read that book in the hope that it would contain some formula which could be applied to their problem. Some mystic phrase which, once applied, would fix everything. He tossed it onto the couch and turned out the lamp. He undressed slowly and sat on the made-up studio couch and waited until she was out of the bathroom.

He sensed that there was, in both of them, a strong desire for things to be as they had been before. And children wish for the moon. And adultery is a high wall, impossible to scale, impossible to ignore.

Jane went into the bedroom they had once shared in a remote, improbable life, and closed the door behind her. She turned out the light and undressed and sat nude on the side of her bed. She lit a cigarette, found the ash tray and put it close beside her.

There had been other promotions. She could remember every one of them. The first one had been, perhaps, the best. Five dollars more a week. A desk nearer the windows. Judge had been on the way then. Two months on the way. A winter night so cold that the snow creaked when you walked, and your breath was a plume. A gallon of wine for a dollar nine the sign had said and he had brought home a whole, improbable gallon. Tart red wine to go with the spaghetti she made. Candles on the kitchen table in the two-room apartment, and the table too wide between them, so he had brought his chair around so they sat side by side. Low music on the little ivory kitchen radio. Where had that gone? And the plates for the spaghetti. Afterward he had said he would make a lamp out of the gallon jug, to commemorate the occasion, but he never had, because he wasn't good at that kind of thing.

They had too much of the red wine and the kitchen was suddenly stuffy, and they had dressed warmly and quickly and gone out to walk the late streets, snow creaking underfoot, his arm warm and good around her waist, and after a time she could walk right again, and the giggles were over. She remembered a street where the elms were big and street lights made fat shadows, and he kissed her in each shadow and they marveled at their rare good fortune, marveled that they were the happiest, luckiest, most in love people anywhere south of the Yukon.

Then going home slowly, knowing that this would be one of the best times, knowing that they would be warmth entangled in the big bed. Leaving the dishes, and then the shade up so that they could see the snow coming down again, slanting across the yellow globe of the street light, undressing in the chill room, shaking with the cold, finding each other under the great mound of blankets. . . .

"Oh, Jane, dear! I see by the paper that Fletcher has been made vice-president. How fortunate, darling! I'm so happy for both of you."

"Yes, we're very pleased."

"Jud, your daddy has been put in charge of the plant."

"Hey! Hey, Dink! You hear that, Dink?"

All this could have been . . . the very best. Better even than the first promotion. Better than anything that had ever gone before. And destroyed so utterly. By a silly woman at a camp, a vain silly woman who . . .

She hit her thigh with her clenched fist. It made a small splatting sound in the silence of the room. All gone. All gone. Every bit gone. She wanted to destroy. Smash her entire world. Leave nothing, not even memory.

Her head was bent and a tear fell, like a small hot drop of wax, onto her breast, startling her. She hadn't been aware that she was crying again. There seemed no end of tears. Another fell, hotly, turning cool as it traced its way down her flesh.

No end to tears. She remembered what her father used to do when she was little, and tears would not stop. Cry into a bottle. Save your tears. And as soon as you tried to cry into the bottle, the tears would go away. No bottle. She leaned forward a bit, so that the next tear that fell from her underlid fell onto the roundness of her thigh. It made a small sound. She held the red coal of the cigarette where she thought the next one would fall. Cry a tear to quench the small red coal. And that would stop them. The next tear missed, and the next, and then one struck the cigarette. The red glow hissed and faded and went out. She sat, holding it, and the tears still fell, touching her thighs with tiny spots of warmth. Touching the unused body.

In a lost year as Fletcher slept, she had turned her head to watch the slant of snow outside the window. And cried then, too. But it had been in a different manner.

Chapter Nineteen

On Thursday the city knew the heat wave was going to break. The sun came up with a sullen look and the sky had a poisonous coppery shade. People stopped and listened, thinking they could hear the welcome thunder. The heat remained intolerable, and the humidity climbed one last incredible notch. From time to time small winds slid down the slopes in the valley of the city, spinning up dust devils, herding papers down the blazing gutters, flipping the tired parched leaves. And then the small winds would die again, leaving the city torrid and still.

Because of the heat many firms closed a day early for the Fourth, and cars moved in slow double lines out of the city, into the hills, toward the lakes.

HEAT BREAK DUE, the Herald headlined. Overdue, the people muttered. It was a brave man indeed who said to his neighbor, "Hot enough for you?" Tempers were frayed and thin from the long brutal days and the sick still heat of the nights. Slum kids splashed in the industrial scum of the Glass River.

Fletcher Wyant moved doggedly into his first day as acting head of Forman. Miss Schmidt turned out to be a stringy girl with tiny yellow teeth and a faintly adenoidal look. She was unrelentingly efficient. Fletcher went out of his way to swing Harry Bailey into line. The new problems flooded in on him. Again he had a sandwich at his desk.

Ellis Corban arrived back at the offices at two o'clock. Fletcher had alerted reception to tip him off and give Corban the message that he wanted to see him at once. Fletcher as yet hadn't changed offices.

Ellis came in, wearing his smile. Fletcher glanced at him and knew that Ellis hadn't heard yet.

"Shut the door, please."

"Sure, Fletch. God what a day out there! Hell of a thing coming down out of the air into heat like this." He slouched in the chair beside Fletcher's desk.

"How did you make out?" Fletcher asked.

"It's this way, old man. I tried to get you to report progress over the phone and ask some advice, but you weren't in the office. That was Tuesday. I talked to Stanley. So actually, you see, since Stanley got in the middle of all of it, I think it would make a little more sense if I gave him the detailed report. Actually, Fletch, for your information, we've got nothing to worry about."

"Good of you to tell me."

"Oh, hell. Don't take that attitude, Fletch. You agreed that this was my baby, and I battled it out right down the line. You understand that."

"Yes, I understand, Ellis."

"Good! That's what I wanted to hear." He stood up. "I better contact Stanley right away so we can get this thing set up."

"Sit down, Ellis."

"Don't you think I ought to . . ."

"Sit down!"

"You're in a bad mood today, Fletch."

Fletcher turned and reached down on the floor behind him and picked up the cardboard carton Miss Schmidt had found for him. He opened his top desk drawer and began to take out his personal belongings and put them in the carton. He was aware that Ellis had begun to watch him, tense and wondering.

"What's this all about, Fletch? Changing desks?"

Fletcher let the silence grow. He found a half pack of stale cigarettes and threw them in the wastebasket. "Ellis, Stanley is promoting you to treasurer."

He sat and watched Ellis' face. He saw the look of triumph, of cold-eyed satisfaction, before Ellis brought it under control. "My God, Fletch, I wouldn't have this happen for the world!"

"Have what happen?"

"Just because I happened to jump the gun there in the meeting Monday. What in hell is Stanley thinking about?

235

I'm going to go to him and object to this, Fletch. After all, you brought me in here. I can't let this happen."

"I don't know what you think you're talking about, Ellis."

He watched the sudden puzzlement, then the faint look of consternation, as quickly concealed as his previous look of triumph. "Say! Are you getting a promotion? That's the best news I . . ."

"Oh, shut up, for God's sake!"

"I was only . . ."

"You haven't got any secrets, Ellis. You're a sharpie. Forman knows that and I know it."

"I definitely resent that!"

"I have no interest in whether you resent it or not. Stanley is in Birmingham. We're taking over another firm. I'm in charge here."

"In charge of . . . everything?" Ellis licked his lips.

"Does that seem incomprehensible to you? You're getting this slot I'm vacating only because I promised Stanley I could keep you in line. If that hurts your feelings, you can march right the hell out the front door."

"Just what do you mean? In line?"

"Don't be dense. This is what I mean. You are going to confine your activities, all of them, Ellis, to the responsibilities of this office. You were delighted when you thought for a minute that you'd knifed your way into my job and I was out in the cold. You were crying crocodile tears. That's something I won't forget. You're in here because we hired your brains, and they're good brains. But we're very wary of your ambitions, Ellis. And a certain streak of unscrupulousness. I repeat, I'm in charge here. You can have the job. The first time you stick your nose into some other department, you're out. I'll handle my job and yours until I can find another man. Is that quite clear?"

"You don't have to talk to me like that."

"I'm talking to you just like that and you'll take it, won't you, because it's a nice boost, a nice promotion. Say yes or no. Will you take the job?"

"Yes," Ellis said in a low tone.

"Will you keep yourself in line?"

"Yes."

Fletcher put some more items in the carton. Some you had to bully, some you could kid along. He waited until he knew his timing was right, and then smiled broadly and stuck his hand out. "Congratulations, Ellis. I know you'll do a hell of a job here."

Ellis took his hand a bit weakly. "Well . . . thanks, Fletch."

"While I'm sorting this stuff, give me your report."

"Oh! Sure. I found out that K.C.I. were negotiating for an advance payment, and they were reluctant to have us in on it because they thought it would weaken their case. I was able to show them that it would strengthen their case rather than weaken it, and Tuesday afternoon we had a conference with the contracting officer, a Colonel Fine. He got on the phone to the Pentagon and . . ."

Tuesday afternoon, Fletcher thought, while the silken egocentric body lay on the maroon wool in the dusty stillness of the barn. Tuesday afternoon, while that body, lost and blind in its own sensations, accepted him not as an individual, but merely as Man, as an organism capable of a function that was desirable and necessary to the satin body. And he knew, suddenly, that Ellis would find out. She would tell him, because it was necessary to her to tell him. And Ellis would never make the slightest objection because, in the distortion of his own ambition, he would relate that to his sudden elevation in the company, and in his own twisted way would, even while he pretended to her that she had broken his heart, be grateful to her. All things in the life of Ellis Corban had importance only in the way they related, or could be related, to his ambitions and his progress. And the pitiful knowledge, which Ellis would never realize, was that the very extent of his ambition was a self-limiting factor and that he had, very probably, reached the highest point he would ever reach. They would use him until he could no longer be controlled, and then discard him with the same calculation that any machine tool was scrapped once it became obsolescent. In a sense it was another facet of what Stanley had tried to tell him. If your marriage was right, other things being equal, you would succeed. And each part of your life was somehow equal to the whole.

After Ellis had left to turn over the routines of his job to Evans, Fletcher changed offices and continued to slog his way through the unfamiliar aspects of the job. And, as he labored, it became increasingly and bitterly obvious to him that he was going to fold up under the pressure. Not today, not next week, not next month. But fold, inevitably, because his motivations were no longer clean cut. Triumph was something you carried home in your two hands so that it could be properly admired. The job was within his reach with full utilization of all his resources, and he had not truly realized before how much of his basic strength was dependent on Jane, on her admiration, approval and her love.

He quit at five. He left the desk piled high and quit, knowing he should stay on, knowing that it would make the following Monday increasingly difficult. He walked out with the clerks, sensing remotely their feeling of holiday at the long weekend ahead.

He walked woodenly toward the parking lot and then looked at the empty slot and remembered Jane had taken the car to go get the kids. He turned and walked toward the heart of the city, a mile and a half away. There was no longer sunshine. The sun had disappeared in a bright haze. The wind came oftener, stirring the oven heat of the city. Thunder boomed far away.

The knowledge of his inevitable defeat in the job was clear and bitter in his mind. It was the first time in his life that anything had been too big for him.

He walked into town and up the long slope toward the Downtown Club. He stood silent and remote at the bar, with the noisy after-work drinkers around him, and he drank slowly and methodically, realizing how neatly he had been trapped. He couldn't go backward into the job he could handle. He drank for a long time and discouraged those who wanted to congratulate him on the new job. The liquor seemed to be having little effect on him. He ate dutifully, and drank some more and walked out into the dusk that had come earlier on this night. After he had walked two aimless blocks the first fat drops splatted into the dust. They came faster, harder. Lightning broke the sky and thunder banged across the city, echoed off the hills. The hard rain soaked him as he walked slowly. People, huddled in doorways, stared curiously at him. The rain came in sheets, wind driven, and bounced high in the street, making a silver fringe to the grey curtain of dusk and rain. Cars crept, and running water spread outward from the curbs, and debris blocked the corner sewers.

The thunder was almost constant, and the city power flickered, went off. Each dip in a street became a lake. Water streamed into the Glass River and slowly the level began to rise. He walked and felt the good coldness of the rain trickling down his body under his sodden clothing. He had cashed a check and he had nearly a hundred dollars in his billfold. The city lights came back on, suddenly, just as he was passing a bus terminal. Sell me a ticket to anywhere. Give me forty dollars' worth of distance, please.

He stood for a moment, looking in through the wide pane of glass. A fat tired woman with two children sat waiting, surrounded by bundles. To go would be an escape. An escape from Laura, from the pattern of little silver hooks she had imbedded in his flesh. An escape from Jane, who had taken away all that was good.

But they always found you.

He walked on. The rain slowed for a time and he could hear the distant thunder above the diminished roar of water. Then it came on again, twisted and whipped by the wind. The wind flapped his soaked trouser legs. He walked slowly with his shoulders hunched, hands shoved deep in his jacket pockets, looking ahead at the sidewalk a dozen feet in front of his slow footsteps.

Laura would answer any phone. Answer his call. Make some excuse. Pick him up and they would drive out to a cabin somewhere. Drive out and sink again into the little death that was a temporary end of all memory. Shining body of flax and wine. Open the inner doors and let the blackness come out, the black things, the dark knowledge.

He stopped at a corner and looked around, realizing, suddenly that ancient habit patterns had guided his steps back to a familiar area of small frame houses on quiet streets. This was the neighborhood in which he had grown up. Jane had lived down there, a block and a half further. They had walked these same streets long ago, walked back from the winter movies, her hand in his coat pocket, warm in his. Walked with a slow singing, and walked as slightly different people—as though the mannerisms of those on the screen had rubbed off on them for a bit.

Gable and Ginger, walking home. Oh, we'd rather walk, of course. The chauffeur will bring the car along later. Where shall we go, my darling? The Bahamas? It's quite pleasant there this time of year.

He walked slowly by the house where he had been born. It looked small, shabby. He wondered how his room looked. He saw a young girl and a child on the couch in the living room, turning the pages of a magazine.

He remembered the strange feeling of coming back from honeymoon with his bride, taking Jane up to his room that night, taking her into that bed where he had spent the long restless times thinking of her.

He walked on, slowly, remembering how he had been unaware of her for many years. She'd been a kid on the next street, a slat-thin blonde kid, scabbed knees, wild, loud. A considerable local reputation as the only girl in the area who could put a respectable curve on a hard ball and chin herself twenty times.

He felt himself grinning as he remembered the heap he had in high school and how she hung around all one Saturday while he was working on it, imploring him to teach her how to drive. Damn gadfly. But he'd given in and she'd learned with spectacular quickness, and then she was a sort of a mascot. A mascot until one day in his last year of high school he'd looked at her and suddenly became aware of what she would be, of what she could be.

There was a walk they used to take that last June he was in high school. A good walk because his friends were not likely to see him with her, and that was good because she was too young. A high-school sophomore, for God's sake, and he was at a period when he yearned for worldly women. He followed that walk they used to take. The rain had stopped. The air smelled washed and clean and his clothing had begun to dry.

Past her house, and he didn't want to look at it. Up Collins Street to the park. Through the park and by the tennis courts and up the long wide curving path to the small hill where there were picnic tables. The hill made his ankle hurt again, and he walked more slowly, favoring it.

He came to the tables and stopped there. Rain dripped from the elm leaves overhead. Up on the drive a few cars were parked. Dark and silent. He sat on one of the tables, his feet on the attached bench, and wondered if it was the same table. He took out his cigarettes. The rain had gotten to them and he threw away several, dug back into the pack and found a dry one, lit it.

A hell of a long time ago. Nineteen years. Damn near twenty. Fletcher Wyant sitting on a table in the warm June night with Jane Tibault beside him. Dream talk. Things to do with a life.

And her flat declaration. "Whatever you do, I'm going to be part of it."

It had shocked him, because it had sounded so fierce and so determined. So he had gagged it. "This is so sudden, Janey."

"Not so sudden."

"Well, people drift apart. I'm going away."

"You'll be back. Why don't you kiss me, anyhow? You never have. You act like I was a little kid. I'm not that little."

There, sitting on the table, he had kissed her, and at first it had been a bit awkward, as she had somehow gotten her nose in the way, but then it was all right. Very all right. And it stopped him thinking about her as a little kid. And it kept him thinking about her after he was away at school. Her kiss had been as fierce and determined as what she had said.

He sat and smoked and he felt his hand tremble each time he lifted the cigarette to his lips. How do you make yourself forget something that happened? A little thing. A little foolish thing. A moment of weakness with a husky college kid. It didn't mean anything. It doesn't mean enough to wipe all this out. All the memories. All the damn wonderful years.

He dropped the cigarette and shut his fists hard and

lowered his chin onto his chest and fought against himself with all his strength. What is it, after all? A physical thing. Think of the history of different cultures. Think of the goddamn Eskimos. What the hell makes it so wrong? What makes it so rotten and unforgivable? Think of what I've done. Jesus! Those two overseas. That Chicago tramp. And now Laura, with her sick mind. Can it be right for me, and wrong for Jane?

Me, I'm a big boy now. The locker room talk gets onto women. Sure, I always hint how I have my innings on the business trips. Something shameful about fidelity. Yet fidelity is what I want. For both of us. Once it's gone, it's gone.

I can't live with her, thinking of what she's done. And I can't imagine not living with her.

He hit his balled fists together, heard the small choking sound in his own throat. His eyes filled and stung.

Because it was all impossible. It was impossible, he knew, to force himself to accept any standards of morality except those ground into him by his environment. Through no process of logic could he make himself discount or ignore the fact that someone else had used her body, that some other maleness had made her, forever, secondhand.

He remembered how he had tortured himself, long ago, thinking that on their wedding night he would discover she was not a virgin, and wondering who it was who could have had her. And he had thought of all the lies she might tell to conceal the fact that she had been . . . used. But she had been a virgin bride. Almost too emphatically a virgin bride, so that it had all been most difficult, and very shocking, and quite terrible for her. So bad that it had been a long time before things had gotten right for her, and had it not been for his patience, they might never have been right.

Was it possible, he wondered, to just go on. A nice pleasant formal little life together, and when it became unbearable, there was always Laura and a little trip with her into a fascinating darkness. Oddly how, with Laura, or with any of the others, it did not matter that others used them. It mattered only with Jane. It mattered only with

Wife. Church, Home, Wife, Mother. Anything they could make verses about for greeting cards, and you ran into a whole series of emotional blocks.

Thunder banged loudly, startling him. A bright flash of lightning turned the picnic area a vivid green-white and thunder cracked quickly after it, and again the rain came down, torrents of it, barrelsful, tipped over from the treetops.

The world was a vast place, full of death and atomics—mud ball swinging around a dying sun, and yet, he thought, I, as Jehovah junior grade, sit in judgment on my wife, and I cannot help it. Let him who is without guilt cast the first stone. I have guilt and she has guilt and I cannot forget hers.

Years, perhaps, will dull it. But I cannot forget it.

He walked slowly home through the rain. The rain stopped before he had covered half the distance. It was much cooler. He shivered in the soaked clothes.

As he walked he tried a new way of rationalizing. Marriage, he told himself, is a breeding pact. A mating for the purpose of having children. A legal and spiritual device which is designed to give the children of that marriage emotional security.

And so, he reasoned, sex without procreation is a barren thing. A thing of no importance. An amusement. A device. Perhaps, a disease. It involves only the body, and not the soul. Jane, in that larger view, is guiltless. She succumbed only to a variant of decadence.

Nor did that reasoning work for him.

He went to the back door of the house. Jane heard him and came quickly and opened the inner door and stared at him. "I was worried about you," she said. "You're soaked!"

"I was walking," he said casually, but his teeth chattered.

"Walking in the rain on that ankle? Really, Fletch! Here, I'll spread papers. Get your things off. I'll bring your robe and you take a hot shower."

She hurried off. He emptied his pockets of their soaked contents onto the shelf in the back hallway. She came back with a big towel and his robe and slippers. She said,

"Leave your things right there. I'll take care of them." She turned away quickly. He stripped and rubbed himself dry and belted the robe. The shivering was not as violent now. He went into the kitchen, found a fresh pack of cigarettes, lit one over the gas stove.

Jane came in from the hallway. "I hung your things in the utility room. I think they'll dry there. That suit might shrink some, but the dry cleaners ought to be able to stretch it. You go take your shower."

"I'm feeling warmer now. The kids okay?"

"Sound asleep."

"They have a good time?"

"They seemed to. You better make yourself a stiff drink."

"Good idea." He started for the liquor cupboard, then said, "How about hot coffee laced with brandy? Too much trouble?"

"Of course not. Sit down. It won't take long. I'll use Instant."

He sat at the table and she brought him an ash tray. He realized that she had not looked directly at him, except fleetingly.

"The job go all right today?"

"Fair. I had words with Ellis. I think he'll stay in line."

"It must be odd to be telling him off when you . . ."

"When I what?"

"Never mind. I was thinking out loud. Did you stay late at the office?"

"I left at five."

She gave him a quick oblique look. "Oh."

"There was a lot to do, but I didn't feel like it," he said, a shade too harshly.

She brought him the coffee and the brandy bottle. "Here, you better fix your own."

"You having some?"

"I wouldn't mind. Yes, I guess I will."

By the time the coffee was cool enough to sip, she had brought her own cup and she sat across from him. He sneezed suddenly.

"I'll lay out the antihistamine."

"It never seems to help me."

"You can't tell how bad the cold might have been if you didn't take them, you know."

"I suppose."

She sipped her coffee. "Why were you walking?"

"No special reason."

"Where did you go?"

"I walked through the old neighborhood. Haven't been over there in years. God, it looked small and shabby. The houses were all smaller."

"I know."

"You been over there lately?"

"I drove through there the other day."

They were silent for a long time. He finished his coffee. "Want more?" she asked.

"No thanks. I can't sleep if I have two cups."

"Funny how we both went over there."

"Is, isn't it. I walked up Collins and through the park up to the picnic tables. Sat on one of the tables for a while."

"The . . . same one?"

"I don't know. They've moved them around, and they looked sort of new. Maybe the old ones gave out on them."

The house was cool for the first time since the heat wave had started. Jane wore a pale blue cardigan and a grey flannel skirt. She glanced at him and frowned and reached over suddenly and put the back of her hand against his forehead. Her eyes widened a bit and she took her hand away quickly. "I'm . . . sorry, I thought you looked flushed. You . . . don't feel hot."

"I was wondering over there tonight how it would be if we could jump in our time machine and start it all over again."

"Maybe someday people can do that. Or maybe they do it now on some other planet. I couldn't go back that far. I'd just go back . . . a little way."

He had the strange feeling that they were like a pair of doctors called in on consultation, and now stood over the corpse making learned comment about what had been the exact cause of death.

She looked at him suddenly and her eyes were wide and wet. "Fletch. I . . ."

He stood up. "I better get to bed before this cold gets ahold of me. 'Night, Jane."

"Good night. I put an extra blanket in there."

"Thanks." And later, long after he would normally have been asleep he lay awake, thinking of how precarious even the most orderly life could be. Luck was all on your side, and one bright day it kicks everything out from under you.

Chapter Twenty

Minidoka awoke on the Fourth of July to a perfect summer day. Hot in the sun. Cool and perfect in the shade. Rain had washed the city, and everything sparkled. All the lowering mists of the heat wave were gone. The distant hills were so clear that it looked as if every leaf showed. Mud had been washed into the Glass River and it hurried busily along, the current boiling where it went by the piers of the bridges.

At the Randalora Club the golf course was crowded, and the pool was jammed. Everything had the high gay flavor of holiday. The girls looked prettier. The young men bounced high off the board in clean dives. Children raced in circles and whooped at each other. The big parking lot at the club was jammed with cars.

The Wyants arose quite late, even the kids. They had breakfast on the terrace and the feeling of strain was there, but the gloriousness of the day seemed almost to counterbalance some of it.

After the late breakfast the children began to promote the idea of going to the club early. "We're going anyway for the fireworks and so why don't we just go on out there, can't we, please couldn't we?"

There was a quick family conference and it was decided that it would be wise to go to the club for the whole day. They drove through the city and the streets looked oddly deserted, the unused parking meters standing like fence posts. Fletcher let them all off at the door and then parked the car and walked back to the club. Jane was talking to a young couple named Graves when he got back. She smiled quickly at him and said, "I shooed the kids off to put on

247

their suits. Bill Graves says they need me for a doubles game. Is that all right with you, darling?"

"Go right ahead."

"Sure you don't want to play, Mr. Wyant?"

"I don't want to inflict my brand of tennis on you. I'll just wander around with a tall cold drink."

Jane kept her racket and tennis clothes in her locker in the women's dressing room. She hurried off with Bill and Nancy Graves. Fletcher walked over and found an empty deck chair and sat and watched the turmoil in the pool for a while. He saw his kids come yelping out and hurl themselves in. Dink's swimming was improving fast this summer. Judge was better too, but he'd never been in Dink's class in co-ordination and athletic ability. Just as Fletch wasn't in Jane's class.

The young daughters of Fletcher's friends posed on the high board and took graceful dives into the teeming pool. He watched for a long time and then wandered over to the tennis courts.

All the players were good and they were in a long volley as he approached. Both Jane and her partner had dropped well back. The man on the other side rushed the net and Jane tried to slam one by him but he caught it and hit a slanting shot toward the sideline. Jane went over for it at a full run and got her bat on it and lobbed it back high so that the man at the net had to race back for the far corner. As he was going back Jane charged the net, moving fast, and the man's return came where she had anticipated it and she put it away.

"Lovely, Janey!" Bill Graves yelled. "Lovely!"

Fletcher heard Jane's warm clear laugh when she thanked him, and it gave him a quick hard thrust of jealousy. Jane went striding back to serve. She double-faulted, then aced them, and another long volley started. Fletcher sat on the grass and watched her, watched the good long warm brown legs, the innate grace of her. Damn it, she looked about twenty-one. That's what the kid had seen. That aliveness and that quickness and that grace. And wanted it. Couldn't blame the kid. Couldn't blame any man for wanting it.

He recognized Hud's voice. "We speaking today, Mr. Veep? Congratulations and all that jolly old rot."

Fletcher squinted up at him. "Hello, Hud. Thanks. We're speaking."

"Our wives are. Good thing, too. Martha wasn't fit to live with until she got it straightened out."

Hud sat down beside him. "Your lady is a bear on the court, my friend. Aside from that, a good lady to keep around the house, I imagine."

"No advice, Hud. Please."

"Observations, not advice. And yet another comment before I cease and desist. Had my lady's generous amount of mouth clobbered your hearth and home, I should have personally taken it upon myself to cave in her posterior with one of our set of antique andirons."

"Let's skip it."

"Just one more little thing, ducks. Females do not follow me down the street exactly, but with all my rough-hewn charm, I've had my moments. I warn all my friends. Lock up your wives, boys, because Huddleston can't trust himself. During the years of our long and happy association, I have angled many a pass at your missus. Some of them have been quite carefully thought out. Most of them took place in what you might call ideal environments. A man of my inclinations hears a lot of polite refusals. It's a percentage deal at best. And yon blondie had given me nothing but a fat no each time. Fat enough, indeed, to completely discourage a less hardy and persistent soul. It is a fact I think you should know."

Fletcher waited several long seconds. He knew how it was meant. He fought his anger and finally turned and said, "Okay. Thanks, Hud."

"Want me to depart?"

"Stick around, you lecherous, unprincipled old bastard."

"Now I know you love me again. What's the score?"

"Jane and Bill Graves have taken four straight games."

They watched the match. Jane and Bill lost the fifth game and the sixth and then came back and took two straight to end the set, six two. Jane came over. She was

249

flushed and breathing hard. Fletcher saw her recognize Hud, and saw the sudden shyness. He had a sudden realization of what it meant to her in terms of self-respect to know that Martha and Hud knew about it, and probably Ellis and Laura, and quite probably Midge and Harry. It was something they wouldn't forget, and it was something that would inevitably be known in more or less exaggerated versions throughout their set, and it was something to have to live with.

Jane stretched out on the grass, face down. "I'm fair pooped, gentlemen," she said. "Either old age or dissipation."

Bill Graves sat cross-legged. "Lady, you weren't sagging as bad as I was. Nancy wants to take you on alone."

"Give me a five-minute break first."

Hud got up. "I think I hear somebody rattling my dish. Strive on, silly athletes. See you anon and about."

Jane gave Fletcher a quick, inquisitive glance and then looked away. After a time she got up and cut the air with her bat. "Okay, Nance."

During the set with Nancy, when Jane was leading, three games to one, Fletcher wandered back toward the pool. He signed for a rum Collins at the pool bar, and carried it over and watched the golfers holing out on the eighteenth green for a while. He sat on the stone steps that led up to the terrace. He saw a girl in white walking toward him. No one in the world except Laura Corban walked that way. He stood up as she came up to him, unsmiling. "You haven't phoned," she said.

"No, I haven't."

She sat down on the steps and he sat on one above her. "By the way, congratulations, my dear."

"Thanks."

"It doesn't make you nervous to have me sitting here talking to you?"

He looked down at the curve of her throat, at the dusky separation of her breasts where the round neckline of the white dress fell away from her. The memory of her was in his hands and on his lips and he felt his throat thicken. "It doesn't make me nervous."

"Such tremendous enthusiasm, Fletcher! Don't strain yourself."

"Why are you in such a filthy mood?"

"Ellis, I guess. He's unbearable after any promotion. This is the worst one yet. He keeps looking in mirrors and twitching his mustache. He's even harder than ever for me to bear . . . after our red barn."

"Is he?"

"Like the sleeping princess, Fletcher. And the kiss awakened her. Princess isn't too apt, is it? Sleeping what?"

"Houri? Odalesque? Daemon?"

"Those will do. But now she's awake, and she is waiting."

"What if she waits in vain?"

Laura looked sharply up at him and for a moment her mouth was quite ugly before it smoothed out. "I hardly think so."

"Maybe it was enough."

"I know you. You're not going to go Christer on me, Fletcher. I'm not too rich for your blood. Only it might make it interesting for you to fight a little. To try to wiggle off the hook, maybe. We're both hooked, you know."

"Hud said you were going to explode in my face."

She looked at him calmly. "How shrewd of Hud."

"I have the funny feeling that it will improve my immortal soul to have none of you, Laura."

"How do you go about taking the cure?"

"Maybe sometimes you go at it the same way those flagellantes work. Punish yourself."

"Oh, dear. Cold showers and lots of exercise?"

"Pure bitch."

She stood up slowly and arched her back just a bit. "Of course! And exactly what you want. What do you industrialists say? Machined for the job?"

"And doesn't that make me an interchangeable part?"

She turned a bit white. "That's a little too shrewd too. Think about it. Wait too long and you might find yourself obsolescent." She walked away from him, swinging her round hips just a bit more than necessary, turning back when she was twenty feet away to give him one small quick evil confident smile. His hands were sweaty and he took out his handkerchief and dried them.

He saw Jane and Nancy heading for the locker rooms. Jane seemed to be just a little too engrossed in conversation, and he wondered if she had seen Laura sitting with him. Jane glanced his way and her smile was a little too gay. When she was out of sight he wandered over to the pool again and Jane found him there after she had showered and changed. "Let's round up the kids and get a sandwich," she said. "It will be a long time until dinner."

They sat at one of the picnic tables out in the small grove. Midge and Harry Van Wirt moved in and ate with them. Ellis Corban stopped by to chat, and Jane congratulated him gravely and with beautiful sincerity. The kids were told how long they had to wait before going back into the pool.

Fletcher stopped drinking during the long afternoon. He wandered around, feeling strangely apart from the laughing holiday people. Jane got into a bridge game on the terrace and for a time he sat near her, watching her play of the hands until he realized that he was making her nervous.

As the day began to fade, as the children grew noisier, as the drunks began to laugh louder at their own wit, Fletcher felt the slow increase within him of morose depression. It was depression without anger, without resentment. A vast grey dullness inside of him. Yet he made himself smile at the right moments and say the right things.

The traditional Fourth of July buffet dinner was served. The long buffet was set up in the main lounge. People were eating in the dining room, on the big porch, on the terrace, out by the pool, over in the grove. Talk and lights and laughter, as the day faded. By the time the Wyant family had finished eating, people were already going out with blankets and car robes to pick vantage spots on the long slope of the eighteenth fairway where they would get a good view of the fireworks. The children had raced through their meal and they were itching to be off. To keep them busy, Fletcher gave Judge the car keys and sent them to get the robe out of the back end of the car.

They were back before Jane had finished her coffee. They went out and it was grey dusk. It was not yet dark enough to begin, and down on the flats the fireworks scaffolding had been erected, the wood pale yellow and raw in the dusk. Men moved about down there on mysterious errands. The children picked a spot and Judge spread the robe with much advice from Dink. Jane and Fletcher sat down side by side, the children in front of them.

Slowly it grew darker while the children complained about were they never going to start, for gosh sakes? "When do they start, Dad?"

He saw the Corbans come and find a place a little way down the slope from them. He was barely able to make them out in the gathering darkness, and he saw that Ellis was spreading a blanket, and he wondered if it was the same one, if it held the odor of musty hay, of barn dampness.

Jane had turned a bit, hugging her knees, and her arm touched his, and he felt her move quickly away from the contact.

There was rhythmic clapping which stopped suddenly as a high wild red rocket whooshed high, and banged and dropped a wide silver spray. There was a long slow Aah! of pleasure, and sudden applause.

There were more rockets and Fletcher ceased watching them, watched instead the reflected glow on upturned faces. He felt himself a stranger in this place, among all the people he had known most of his life. A stranger sitting with the small family of some person named Fletcher Wyant. He moved back a bit and turned almost furtively to see the explosive reflections against Jane's face, as though by looking at her he would see an answer to this feeling of apartness. Her lips were parted. There was a small moist highlight on her underlip. He could see the sheen of her eyes.

And she was a stranger beside him. A living, breathing creature of tissue and muscle and nerves and bone. A creature taut in its firm brown skin, with the tendons cleverly sheated, muscles awaiting the messages of the clever little white threads of the nerves. Bride of a stranger. Person forever unknowable. And maybe that was it. You knew so little of yourself. And so any other person was but a deeper mystery. This stranger beside him had been born in pain, and had conceived, and would die and rot and be forgotten. Even as he.

He felt that he was close to an answer, close to something rare and good. He closed his hand hard on her arm, felt rather than heard her small gasp of surprise. She turned toward him with eyes he did not know. A rounded wetness of membrane. Eyes of a stranger and they were aware of him.

The children were oblivious. He stood up and tugged her arm and she rose silently and obediently. She had been looking at the fireworks and they had blinded her. He guided her between the groups of people, took her across the wide yard to the pool, still holding her arm tightly.

On the apron of the pool, near the slim steel of the diving platform, he turned her, roughly, released her. There was no one near them.

"I've got to have help," he said thickly.

"Help?" Her voice was faint.

"I don't know if I can do it. I got to have help to try to do it. It's like . . . being tied up. Knowing how thick the ropes are. You are filth. I've got to stop thinking that. I can't keep on thinking that."

She made no sound. He saw that she had started to cry. She had her arms folded across her stomach and she was bent forward slightly from the waist, standing there in an ugly, stricken way.

"I've got to stop judging you," he said, with no inflection on any word. "I'm not fit to judge. There were two of them overseas. And that one in Chicago. And Laura. And I still want Laura, but not in any way I've ever wanted you."

She made a small sound. Rocket light was against her face. She had bent further forward. He took her shoulders roughly, straightened her up, backing her against one of the steel uprights.

"Did you hear what I said? Four of them since I married you."

"Oh yes. I heard you. I heard you."

254

"How does it make you feel? What does it do to you?"

"Stop, Fletcher. Please stop. Oh, please."

He held her shoulders and pulled her forward and banged her back against the upright. "How does it make you feel?"

"Dirty. For . . . for both of us. Dirty, Fletcher. But . . . but I want us to . . . keep anything we can."

"In spite of it?"

"In spite of it." She had stopped crying. Her chin was high but her voice was dead. "I'm . . . not proud any more. I can crawl. I want you back."

He let go of her. She stood, leaning against the upright. There was a silver waterfall at the foot of the fairway. It made her face silver, and her dress, and made his shadow black across her.

"There's only one way, only one thing I can do, Jane," he said, and the words sounded slurred. "Never again anyone but you. Only on that basis. And . . . you see I can't promise that, even."

"Do you want to try to promise?"

He turned and looked at the dark pool. A rocket burst and he saw the reflection in the still surface of the pool.

"I guess I do," he said quietly.

"Let's have all we can," she said.

"It could be everything, the way it was before, if I wasn't such a . . . a very little person on the inside, Jane."

She moved shyly, her hands touching his coat, sliding up, her fingers suddenly chill against the back of his neck, pulling him forward, down.

He took her wrists and pulled her hands away from him, thrust them down at her sides. He said, "It doesn't go that way." He had the feeling that he was explaining something very difficult. "It isn't a fade-out with soft music. We can't do it that way. I can't do it that way. I've got to do it my way, and all I want is help, but I don't know exactly what kind of help."

She made no sound. He walked away from her and walked to the middle of the lawn. He turned and looked back. It was hard to see her in the shadows of the diving platform. He waited and after a little while he could see her. She was walking toward him. She was walking very slowly in her light dress, and now they were setting the bombs off. The ones you could feel in your belly.